Praisegod Barbon

Holy Altar and Sacrifice

Explained in some familiar dialogues on the Mass and what may appertain to it

Praisegod Barbon

Holy Altar and Sacrifice
Explained in some familiar dialogues on the Mass and what may appertain to it

ISBN/EAN: 9783337392352

Printed in Europe, USA, Canada, Australia, Japan

Cover: Foto ©Andreas Hilbeck / pixelio.de

More available books at **www.hansebooks.com**

✠

HOLY ALTAR

AND

Sacrifice Explained:

In some familiar

Dialogues on the MASS,

AND

What may appertain to it:

For the more easy INFORMATION and INSTRUCTION of those who desire to hear MASS well, and to assist at that great SACRIFICE, according to the SPIRIT and INTENTION of the CHURCH.

By P. B. O. S. F.

LONDON:

Printed in the Year MDCCLXVIII.

ADVERTISEMENT.

THERE is juſt re-publiſhed Mr. *Go-ther*'s Four METHODS of HEARING MASS, in the ſame Letter and Size as this, ſo as to be bound together, for the Conveniency of thoſe who chuſe to have thoſe *Methods* and theſe *Explications* of the *Maſs* in one Book.

PREFACE.

THE following Dialogues contain a short Abridgment of a learned Work, stiled, *A Liturgical Discourse on the Mass*, by *F. A. Mason*, an *English* Friar, published in 1670; a Work wherein appeared the great Piety and Erudition of the Author, who was induced, a few Years afterwards, to make an Abridgment of it, which he printed in the Year 1675. :Both these having been long since out of Print, and not easily to be met with, a worthy Gentleman was very desirous to have another Abridgment made, in order to render it of a lesser Price, and thereby more easily to be come at by devout but poorer People.

This Abridgment I undertook at the Request of the 'foresaid Gentleman, a Person in an eminent Station, and for whom I have the greatest Deference, after having carefully collated the two printed Editions together. *F. Mason* published his Books by Way of Ques-

tion

PREFACE.

tion and Anfwer, I chofe to do it by
Way of Dialogue, or Converfation,
which, in fome Meafure, takes off the
Drynefs of a continued uninterrupted
Explanation, as well as the dull Forma-
lity of a Catechifm, good for Children
and young People. Dialogues have fomething of Spirit in them, and while read,
make the Reader a Party, as it were, in
the Converfation, which gives a Liveli-
nefs to the Whole.

How far and how well I have executed
my Defign, muft be left to the Decifion
of others. I have endeavoured to be as
brief as I could, yet not to omit any
material Part, or to leave out any Thing
proper to be taken Notice of or explained. The Style is plain and familiar,
moft fuitable to Dialogues, or a free and
eafy Converfation. It is to be hoped
it may be ufeful to devout Catholics,
thofe who defire to underftand that Service of the Church they fo often are prefent at, efpecially on Days of Obligation. The Whole is entirely fubmitted
to the Cenfure and Judgment of my Su-
periors, and to that of our Holy Mother
the Catholic Church, by

P. B. O. S. F.

HOLY ALTAR

AND

SACRIFICE Explained.

PART I.

DIALOGUE I.

Theotime. **I** Hope, *Theophilus*, I do not intrude upon, or interrupt any neceſſary Employments by paying you a Morning Viſit, not only to aſk you how you do, as a Friend, but to have a little ſerious Converſation with you, if at Lei-ſure, and it may not be too troubleſome.

Theophilus. That, I aſſure you, *Theotime*, it will not be; am truly glad to ſee you; nor could you come at a more ſeaſonable

B   Time:

Time: I am at full Leisure, expect no Company who may interrupt us, and am ready to hear what you have to say.

Theot. You are very obliging, and without any further Introduction, will tell you the Occasion of my Visit. I have been at Chapel this Morning and heard Mass. Staying there a little while after it was finished, a Thought came into my Mind that it would be a great Help to me, in order to hear Mass and assist at it with greater Attention, if I was thoroughly instructed in the Signification of the Name, or Word *Mass:* The Nature and End of this great *Sacrifice:* The Meaning of the many and various Ceremonies used in the Celebration of it; as also the best and most proper Method of hearing it according to the Spirit and Intention of the Church. To satisfy me in these Particulars I do not know any one more capable than yourself, and am well acquainted with your good Nature, and Willingness to assist your Neighbour in Matters of this Concern. This the Occasion: This the End of my Visit to you at present.

Theoph. A laudable Desire: and with great Pleasure I will endeavour to satisfy it. Propose therefore with the greatest Freedom what Questions you please. I am ready, and hope to give satisfactory Answers to them.

Theot.

Theot. The firft Thing I would gladly be informed of is, what the Word *Mafs* fignifies, and why that Name is appropriated to this public Service of the Church.

Of the Word Mafs.

Theoph. MANY are the Derivations of this Word, as may be feen in the various Writers on the Offices of the Church. That which feems to me moft pertinent to our prefent Purpofe, and to be the moft natural Signification of it is, that *Miffa*, or *Tranfmiffa*, from whence the Word Mafs, is a Miffion, or Tranfmitting the Sacrifice, together with the Prayers of the People, by the Miniftry of the Prieft, to Heaven. The *Greeks* call it *Liturgia*, or *Liturgy*, which properly fignifies Miniftry, and by Way of Excellence, is appropriated to the Holy Sacrifice of the Mafs. Hence *Liturgy* and *Mafs* fignify one and the fame Thing. What the *Greeks* call *Liturgy*, the *Latins* call *Mafs*, which is the great Sacrifice of the New Law, fucceeding to all legal Sacrifices of the *Mofaick* Inftitute, and comprehends all the Differences of them in one pure, holy, and unbloody Oblation.

Theot. You have given me a very fatisfactory Account what the Word fignifies; be pleafed to proceed, and tell me what I am to underftand by *Mafs:* What it is in itfelf.

Theoph. BY the Mafs we are to understand a Sacrifice of the Evangelical or New Law instituted by Christ at
his last Supper; consisting in an Oblation
of Christ's Body and Blood, under the Species of Bread and Wine, for a perpetual
Memorial of his Passion. Here, please to
observe, that from the Creation of the
World, in all the different Periods of it,
God would be, and always was, honoured
and worshipped by offering up Sacrifices to
him. This, the Religion of the antient
Patriarch, before and after *Noah's* Flood;
this, the Religion of the Jews; and this,
the Religion of Christians in all Parts of
the World. This Sacrifice of the New
Law was instituted by Jesus Christ at his
last Supper. As he, and he only, could
institute Sacraments; so he, and he only,
could institute this Sacrifice, and wherein
he exercised the Functions of his Priestly
Order, according to that of *Melchifadeck*,
as a standing and perpetual Memorial of
his Death and Passion, commanding his
Apostles and their Successors to do the same,
saying, *Do this in Remembrance of me*; St.
Luke, c. xxii. that is, as St. *Paul* expresses
it, *To shew the Death of our Lord until he
comes*. 1 *Cor.* c. xi.

From this Definition of what the *Mafs* is,
I may reasonably presume, *Theotime*, you

are

are willing to be told what are the Fruits or Effects of the Holy *Mass*.

Theot. As this will be very useful and instructive, I shall with Pleasure attend to what you say on this Head.

Of the Fruits and Effects of the Mass.

Theoph. MANY are the spiritual Graces and Benefits which the devout Christian gains by seriously attending to, and assisting at this Holy Sacrifice. *First*, By the Sacrifice of the *Mass* the Fruits of Christ's bloody Sacrifice of himself on the Altar of his Cross, are applied to our Souls. This Sacrifice of the *Mass* being the same with that on the Cross, differing only in the Manner. On the Cross Christ offered himself in a bloody Manner, shedding every Drop of his sacred Blood, as a Sacrifice of Redemption for all Mankind. In the *Mass* he offers himself by the Ministry of the Priest in an unbloody Manner. Hence the *Mass* is called by the holy Fathers an incruental, or unbloody Sacrifice: For, as the Council of *Trent* declares, *Sess.* xxii. 6. 2. It is one and the same Host and the same Offerer, now by the Ministry of the Priest, who offered himself on the Cross, differing only in the Manner of Offering, the Fruits of which unbloody Oblation are here most plentifully received. *Secondly*, The *Mass* is *Latreutical*, that is,

B 3   a Hoa Holocauft or Oblation offered to God in Acknowledgement of his fupreme Majefty and Dominion over us; worfhipping him herein with divine Worfhip, due to him alone, and not to any Creature, how excellent and perfect foever. *Thirdly*, It is a *Euchariftick* Sacrifice of Praife and Thankfgiving for, as well as a Commemoration of the ineftimable Benefit of Chrift's Paffion, and of Praife and Thankfgiving for all the Bleffings we have received, fpiritual and temporal. *Fourthly*, It is an *Impretatory* Sacrifice, by which we may obtain whatever we afk, if we afk as we ought, according to what our Saviour fays; *Afk and you fhall receive. John* c. 16. For the Father will not deny what we afk in his Son's Name, much lefs when we afk by his Son, who is here offered to him. With him he has given us all Things. With him he will refufe us nothing. *Fifthly*, It is a *Propitiatory* Sacrifice, by which we may obtain Pardon of our Sins, our daily Failings and Offences againft God, by the Merits of Chrift's Paffion, here renewed and offered up for us.

Theot. What you have faid highly pleafes, and has given me full Satisfaction. When I go home I will commit it to writing for a conftant Memorandum to help my Memory, that remembering the Nature and End of this great Sacrifice, I may be the better able devoutly to affift at it. But I
fhall

shall be further obliged to you, if you will now explain to me the Meaning of the many and various Ceremonies which are used at *Mass.*

Theoph. Willingly, but as you talk of committing to Paper what I have said, it may not be so proper to proceed further at present, lest you should forget something. We will therefore, if you please, defer further discoursing on these Points till I see you again, and which may be as soon as you conveniently can come to me.

Theot. I am content, and will wait upon you after to-morrow, about this Time, if that may be agreeable.

Theoph. I shall be at Liberty to receive you, and your Visits will, at all Times be agreeable, especially on such an Account as this.

Theot. Many Thanks, adieu, Sir.

Theoph. Farewell till I see you again.

DIALOGUE II.

On the Ceremonies of the Mass, *&c.*

Theotime. YOU see, *Theophilus,* I use the Liberty you indulged me with, and am come to pay you a second Visit, but cannot say this will be the last.

 Theoph-

Theophilus. I would not have it. Let us now begin our Converfation from where we left off, and fpeak fomething of the Ceremonies ufed at *Mafs.*

Theot. A brief Explication of them will be very agreeable, and equally inftructive to me; but firft, what do you fay of Ceremonies in general.

Of Ceremonies in general.

Theoph. CEremonies are certain Religious outward Signs or Actions made Ufe of to teftify the internal Adoration and Worfhip we pay to God. They are alfo called *Rites,* as approved by the Tradition, Cuftom, and Injunction of the Church, in the Adminiftration of facred Things, and therefore require a Religious Obfervance; their End being the Honour of God, and to put us in Mind of our Duty to him, by a devout Obfervance of them in his holy, efpecially publick, Service. Hence they were always practifed by all Nations, in all Ages, in their Acts of publick Worfhip of the Deity they adored; either by Heathens, in the Worfhip of their falfe Gods; or by Jews and Chriftians, adoring the one true living God: Nor can there be any outward Worfhip of God, or Affociation of Men in Religion, without certain Ceremonies, Rites and Forms of ferving God. I may
further

further say, these external Signs, expressive of the Honour and Homage we pay to the Divine Majesty, are as perfectly consonant to the Law of Nature and to Reason, as they are to Religion, and are strengthened by the Sanction of our Blessed Saviour's Practice, that of the Apostles, and of the Universal Church, ever since their Time.

Theot. I see they are daily practised, and would gladly hear a Reason given for them.

Theoph. I will give you a very good one from the Council of *Trent*: *Sess.* 22. 6. 9. saying, " The Church uses these Rites and " Ceremonies from the Nature of Man, " which cannot be raised to the Contem- " plation of divine Things, but by some " exteriour Helps and Assistance." The Council also declares the principal End of the Ceremonies used in Mass to be for the greater Majesty of this august Sacrifice, and that the Minds of the Faithful may be moved by those visible Signs to a more easy and devout Contemplation of those high and sacred Mysteries contained in this Sacrifice.

Theot. This Reason is solid and just : I would now willingly be informed of the different Nature or Degrees of Adoration, or Worship, as these Acts are exhibited by different Postures or Gestures of the Body, in Time of divine Service.

B 5 *Theoph.*

Theoph. In compliance with your Defire, pleafe to obferve that Adoration or Worfhip is to be diftinguifhed as *Internal* and *External.* Internal confifts in a Mental Confeffion and Acknowledgement of his fupreme Dominion, which we make to God from a fubmiffive and reverential Affection towards him. External Adoration is the outward declaring thefe Sentiments by exteriour Signs or Actions, as fo many Indications of the Affections of the Heart. This Adoration or Worfhip may be confidered either, 1ft. as Divine, 2d. Religious, 3d. as Civil Worfhip, according to the Object of it. The Worfhip we pay to God is Divine, due to him alone, and to be given to no Creature, how excellent foever. By Religious Worfhip is to be underftood a Refpect and Veneration paid to the Bleffed Virgin *Mary*, to Angels and Saints, as alfo to holy Things, which Veneration is ultimately referred to God, in Regard of the Relation they bear to him, or his holy Service ; and though it is oftentimes paid by the Ufe of the fame exteriour Signs or Actions, as bowing, kneeling, &c. yet by no Means is fignified or intended giving to them the fame, that is Divine Honour, which is due to God. Civil Worfhip is no more than Refpect and Reverence, which are given to others on Account of their fuperior Dignity, Quality, Excellency or Office, and has no Relation either to

Di

Divine or Religious Worſhip. It is only an outward Reſpect to the Dignity or Office of Men, or to the Perſons of Men, on Account of their Office or Dignity.

Theot. All this I perfectly underſtand, am pleaſed with the juſt Diſtinction you make between Divine, Religious, and CivilWorſhip. The Non-attendance to which, either through Ignorance or Prejudice, is the Cauſe of that unjuſt and falſe Charge of Idolatry urged againſt Catholics by their Adverſaries. But, tell me now, if you pleaſe, the Signification of thoſe different Poſtures or Geſtures of the Body, which I obſerve are uſed; Proſtration, Genuflexion, Kneeling, Bowing down, Standing, joining the Hands, and lifting up the Eyes to Heaven, all which have ſome Signification or Meaning, I preſume.

Theoph. You are right, and the Meaning of them is this: They are expreſſive of the Humility, Reverence, and Attention with which we ought to aſſiſt at Maſs, and in all our Prayers and Exerciſes of Devotion, Proſtration, or caſting the whole Body to the Ground, is to denote the profoundeſt Reverence and Reſpect. It was antiently very frequently uſed, eſpecially in the Eaſt, and is now in the Church by the Miniſters of the Altar on *Good-Friday,* on the Eves of *Eaſter* and *Whitſuntide,* and privately by many devout Perſons, deſiring thereby to expreſs a total Submiſſion to
God

God, with an Acknowledgement of their own Nothing, and a Confidence in his Goodnefs and Mercy. *Kneeling* is alfo a Pofture fignifying the fame, and very proper to be ufed in Prayer, efpecially at Mafs, when we are to attend to the Myfteries there reprefented. To ftand up, is ordained by the Church at fome Parts of the Mafs, as at the *Gofpel* and *Creed*, to fhew our Attention to what is there read, and our firm Affent to all the Articles of the Creed. Inclining, or bowing the Head is another Token of Reverence and Refpect, and is many Times ufed by the Prieft at Mafs. And by bowing to the Altar and holy Things, we fhew the Refpect we bear to them. The joining our Hands in Prayer is a very fit Pofture for Suppliants, as in Prayer we make Supplication to God for Mercy, and prefent our Petitions for his Grace and Benefits, fpiritual and temporal. By lifting up our Eyes to Heaven we profefs that our only Hope is in God, and fhews the Intention of the Mind, and Affection of the Heart. Holy *David* often mentions it in his Pfalms, and we frequently meet with it in the Gofpels, in the Actions of our Saviour there recorded. This, I believe will be fufficient at prefent, for I would not load your Memory with too many Things at one Time.

Theot. As Bufinefs requires I fhould be at home about this Time, I will take my

Leave

Leave of you, but shall lay hold of the first leisure Occasion to wait upon you again.

Teoph. With all my Heart. Not to detain you from your Business. Adieu.

D I A L O G U E   III.

Of the Church, Altar, Candles, &c.

Toeophilus. I Suppose, *Theotime*, this Visit is on the same Account as was the last, when I had the Pleasure to see you here.

Theotime. You are no Ways mistaken in your Conjecture. It is to pursue our Conversation that I now come to you.

Theoph. I agree to it readily. What have you now to propose to me?

Theot. A great many Things, I assure you, and which I hope your Good-nature and Friendship will patiently hear, and as kindly satisfy me in. Our Discourse last Time was of Ceremonies in General, but before you begin to explain the particular ones of the Mass, would be glad to hear something of the Word *Church*, what it means; of the *Altar* and *Candles* thereon; their meaning, and why used. You see,

Sir,

Sir, I am cutting out much Work for you.

Theoph. Very well; your Desire shall be complied with. The Word *Church* signifies a Congregation, or Meeting of the Faithful, to celebrate and partake of the Divine Mysteries. To your present Question I answer; we understand by it some particular Edifice, built and set apart for this Purpose, being blessed and consecrated with many Ceremonies. Hence these Material Churches are called Houses of God, Houses of Prayer, and Temples of the Living God, wherein the great Eucharistick Sacrifice is daily offered up to him, that is, Masses are daily said therein. They succeed, in the New Law, to the Temple of *Solomon*, built under the Old, or Jewish Law. No sooner was Peace restored to the Church, on the Empire becoming Christian, by the Conversion of *Constantine* the Great, but by his Command and Encouragement the Christians began every where to build Churches, and that with great Magnificence and Grandeur. The same was done in succeeding Times, in all Nations, by devout Princes and holy Persons. In regard of which Religious Edifices, no Nation surpassed ours in the Stateliness and Magnificence of them. Witness the noble and venerable Remains of many, demolished at the Reformation, and our still remaining

Ca-

Cathedrals of *Canterbury, York, Win-chester, &c.*

Theot. They are truly noble Buildings; I have feen thofe you mention, and beheld them with Admiration. To me there is fomething peculiar in thofe antient *Gothick* Structures, which feem wanting in our modern new-built Churches : I mean that reverential Awe and Dread, as I may fay, we perceive ourfelves ftruck with the Moment we enter thofe Venerable Edifices, which puts us in Mind where we are, in the Houfe of God. On this Account, I fuppofe, it will be granted, that great Reverence and Refpect is due to Churches dedicated to his Service.

Theoph. Doubtlefs there is. If it would be a Crime to commit any Indecency, or to behave irreverently in a King's Palace, or in his Bed Chamber, it muft be much more criminal to profane the Houfe of God ; the Palace of the King of Kings. Hence they are highly to be condemned who fhew little, or no Reverence to Churches, or who behave themfelves fcandaloufly and irreverently, or commit any Indecency in thefe holy and confecrated Temples of the Lord of Hofts.

Theot. I wifh every one would ferioufly confider this ; we fhould then fee Chriftians behave themfelves in a different Manner from what too many do. But from the Church let us ftep up to the Altar ; and tell

me

me why Altars are placed in Churches, and what the Altars reprefent?

Theoph. They are placed to offer up the Sacrifice of the Mafs on them. As an Altar fuppofes a Sacrifice, a Sacrifice imports an Altar to offer it on. Thefe Altars are made of Stone, and have a particular Form of Confecration. They have five Croffes on them, one in the Middle, and one in each Corner, to fignify that the Catholic Church extended to the four Quarters of the World, is united in the Crofs of Chrift; they are raifed higher than the Pavement of the Church, for the Conveniency of the Prieft who fays *Mafs*, and that the People, by more-eafily feeing him, may the more devoutly attend. They are made of Stone purfuant to the Decree of Pope *Sil-vefter*, carefully obferved ever fince his Time. In Times of Perfecution Portable Altars are allowed, that is, leffer Stones confecrated for the holy Sacrifice of the *Mafs*, which may be carried up and down, and ufed in Places not confecrated, as Exigences may require.

The Altar may be faid to reprefent the Crib of *Bethlehem*, wherein our Saviour was laid after his Birth; more fitly Mount *Calvary*, whereon the Crofs was placed, cr the great Stone placed before the Entrance of the Monument, wherein the facred Body of Jefus was laid, when taken down from the Crofs. On this Account we

ought

ought highly to reverence the Altar, not for its material Subſtance or Ornaments, but for the Reference it has to the Euchariſt, that is, the true Body and Blood of Chriſt. As *David* adored towards the holy Temple, and as he adored God's Footſtool, by which the Jews underſtood the Ark. If this was done to the Ark and Temple, why may it not be done before the holy Altar in Churches? ſince all the Reverence we pay to it is referred to God, in whoſe Reſpect, alone, it is due ?

Theot. Your Inference is very juſt. But why is a Crucifix placed upon the Altar, and why Candles lighted in Time of *Maſs?*

Theoph. I ſee you are reſolved nothing ſhall paſs your Obſervation, and to ſatisfy you. The Crucifix, that is, an Image of Jeſus Chriſt on the Croſs, is placed upon the Altar, to put us in Mind of Chriſt's Death, and Paſſion, whereof the Maſs is a daily Commemoration, and for which, according to St. *Paul*, Chriſt has left it in his Church. It alſo correſponds to the Altar, which repreſents Mount *Calvary*, as the Crucifix does the Croſs of Chriſt, and him faſtened to it. The View of it may ſerve to ſtir up in our Souls Sentiments of Compaſſion for the bitter Sufferings of our dear Redeemer; true Sorrow and Contrition for our Sins, the Cauſe of his Sufferings; Thankſgiving for the ineſtimable Be-

Benefit of our Redemption: Admiration at this wonderful Effect of divine Goodness, that the Son of God should become Man, and die upon the Cross for our Sins. Hope, which nothing can more confirm than this, beholding Christ dying to make Attonement for our Sins. Lastly, to omit what other Sentiments every one's Devotion may suggest, Charity, or fervent Love of God, who has so loved us. Thus Catholics entering the Church, beholding the Crucifix, and signing themselves with the Sign of the Cross, may stir up in themselves pious Affections, and find copious and excellent Matter for a devout Reflection during *Mass.*

As for Candles, they are placed on the Altar for the Splendour of the august Sacrifice, especially on solemn Festivals, when greater Numbers are lighted. But they are principally put on the Altar and lighted to signify the glorious Light of the Gospel, by which the World has been illuminated with the Knowledge of the one true God, and Jesus Christ, whom he has sent, and for this Reason, at High Mass, two particular Candles, or Tapers, are placed one on each Side of the Book, where the Deacon sings the Gospel. They are also lighted to put us in Mind that, we be careful to adorn our holy Faith, or the Gospel of Jesus Christ, we profess to believe, with the Light of Good-works in holy

holy exemplary Lives and Converfations; that we may fo let our Light fhine before Men, that they may fee our Good-works, and glorify our Father who is in Heaven. St. *Matt.* chap. v. This I believe may fuffice, as to this Point. Have you, *Theotime,* any Thing farther to fay?

Theot. If Time preffes no more upon you, than it does upon me, at prefent, I fhall be glad to hear a Word or two of the Altar-cloths, and other Linen belonging to it.

Theoph. My Anfwer to this will be brief, and it will be enough to tell you; the Altar is covered with Linen Cloths out of Decorum and Decency to the facred Myfteries, as alfo in Cafe of Accident, by any Effufion out of the Chalice, the Altar-cloths may be more eafily wafhed, and for which Reafon the Church prohibits Woollen Cloth, or Silk to be ufed. The Altar-cloth likewife reprefents the *Syndon,* or Linen Cloths wherein the Body of our Saviour was wrapped when laid in his Sepulchre. Befides thefe large Altar Cloths, there is a fmaller Piece of very fine Linen laid over them in the Middle, which is called a *Corporal,* whereon the holy Hoft and Chalice are placed; and as the Corporal does immediately touch the facred Body of Chrift, it is confecrated or bleffed by the Bifhop, or thofe who have Authority to do it, and is not to be touched but by thofe
who

who are in Holy Orders, as divers Popes and Councils have ordained. The Chalice is a Gold or Silver Cup, wherein the Wine is put that is to be confecrated, conformable to what our Bleffed Saviour did, when he took the Cup, or Chalice, and bleffing the Wine in it, gave it to his Difciples. Over the Chalice is the Paten, which is confecrated with the Chalice, as the facred Body of Chrift is, after Confecration, laid upon it. There is likewife another fmall Piece of Linen called, a Purificatory, its Ufe being to wipe the Prieft's Fingers, and to cleanfe and dry up the Chalice after he has taken the Lotions. It is always to be clean and neat, and having a near Connexion with the Blood of our Saviour, is not to be touched or wafhed, but as the Corporals. This may be faid to reprefent the Napkin wrapped about our Saviour's Head, when in the Grave. You may obferve another Piece of Linen, not bleffed, pinned at the Epiftle Side of the Altar, for the Prieft to dry his Fingers after he has wafhed them, when he fays the Pfalm, *Lavabo.* Add to thefe the Veil and the Pall; the former is a Square Piece of Silk, which covers all the Chalice. The latter is a little Piece of Pafteboard, covered with fine Linen, and is put over the Top of the Chalice, to prevent any Duft or Flies falling into it. Then the Veil is taken off. Both one and the other

may

may be said to represent the covering the dead Body of Jesus, when laid in his Sepulchre.

Theot. I am much obliged to you for these kind Informations and Instructions. At present I will take my Leave of you, but with an Intent to pay you another Visit soon.

Theoph. You will always be welcome to your humble servant.

D I A L O G U E IV.

Of Priests and their Vestments.

Theotime. GOING Yesterday into the Sacristy, or Vestry, a little before Mass began, I saw the Priest put on several Vestments, and beheld many others of various Colours. The Reason for one, and Meaning of them both, shall, with your good Leave, be the Subject of our Entertainment this Morning.

Theoph. I readily agree to it; as for the Priest being clad with several Vestments, you have, doubtless, read in the Old Testament, that God himself commanded *Moses* to make various Kinds of Garments for *Aaron* and the other inferiour Priests and Levites, as the *Ephod, Rationale, Tunick,*

Li-

Linen Garments, Girdle and *Mitre.* Those for the High Priest were to be exceeding Rich and Magnificent. If this was done in the Old Law for the greater Splendour of those legal Sacrifices, wherein all those Things were but Types and Figures, with how much more Reason ought the Priests of the New Law to have Vestments or Garments suitable to their Function and Ministry, in offering up the true and real Sacrifice ordained by Jesus Christ himself.

Theot. I grant the Reasonableness of this, but why so many Vestments, and of different Colours ?

Theoph. To express, or represent the different Seasons or Solemnities the Church observes during the Course of her Ecclesiastical Year. The Colours are five. 1. White. 2. Red. 3. Green. 4. Purple. 5. Black. White is used on all the Feasts of our Blessed Lord, Blessed Lady, Bishops, Confessors, Confessors not Bishops, Abbots, Virgins, and holy Women not Martyrs, on the Feasts of Dedication of Churches, within the Octaves of Festivals, when the Mass is said of the Octave, on all *Sundays* from *Easter* inclusive to *Pentecost* exclusive, on *Trinity-Sunday*, and till the Octave of *Corpus Christi.*

Red is used on the Vigil of *Pentecost*, and during the Octave, *Trinity-Sunday* excepted. On the Feasts of the Holy Cross,

of

of Apostles and Martyrs, and Votive Masses of the Holy Ghost.

Green is used on all *Sundays* from *Trinity-Sunday* till *Advent*, and on the *Sundays* after the Octave of the *Epiphany*, when Mass is said of the *Sunday*: But on *Sundays* within any Octave, the Colour is of the respective Octave. Green is also used on all *Ferias*, or Week-days, unless within Octaves or *Sundays*, from *Septuagesima* till *Thursday* in *Holy Week*, and during *Advent*.

Purple is used on all *Sundays* in *Advent*, and on all *Sundays* from *Septuagesima* till *Palm-Sunday*, inclusive, as also on all *Ferias* during those Times; and on all *Vigils* and Fasting Days, when the Mass is of them.

Black is used on *Good-Friday*, *All Souls Day*, and when Mass is said for the Dead.

Theot. Hitherto you have perfectly satisfied me, tell me now how many are the particular Vestments the Priest is clad with, how they are called, and the Signification of them?

Theoph. Speaking of those which are common to all Priests when they celebrate Mass. There are six. 1. The Amice. 2. Albe. 3. Girdle. 4. Maniple. 5. Stole. 6. Chasuble, which is usually called the Vestment, as being the Chief and Principal, and is also stiled the Priests' Vestment, because none but Priests use it. The *Amice* is a Piece of Linen Cloth with two Strings. The Priest puts it over his Shoulders, on which Account St. *Bonaventure,* with the *Greeks* calls it *Humerale,* a Covering for the Shoulders, and is tied by the two Strings round the Middle of the Priest's Body. Its Name, *Amice,* is from the *Latin* Word *A-mictus,* or covered. Being clean and white signifies, according to *Rabanus,* the Purity and Cleanness of Heart with which the Priest ought to go to the Holy Altar, and represents the Linen with which the Jews blindfolded our Saviour, saying in Derision; *Prophecy unto us, O Christ, who it is that struck thee.* St. *Luke,* c. xxii.

The *Albe* is a long white Linen Garment, representing the white Robe which, by *Herod*'s Command was put upon our Saviour, in Mockery and Derision. It is called *Albe* from *Alba,* which in *Latin* signifies White, or Whiteness. Frequent mention is made in the Old Testament of white Linen Garments made for, and used by the Jewish Priests. The Use of the *Albe* in the Christian Church, is as antient as the Apostles Times. St. *Jerome* affirms that St. *James* used Linen Vestments when he celebrated Mass. The Whiteness of the *Albe* signifies Continency and Chastity, and is as a Memento, to put the Priest in Mind of the unspotted Purity of Life and Manners he ought to be adorned with.

The

The *Girdle*, wove or made of Linen Thread, is to tie the *Albe* about the Priest's Body that it may hang with proper Decency, and represents the Cords with which our B. Lord was bound, when seized on by the Jews ; and may not unfitly signify the Cords of Love and Duty with which all, especially Priests, ought to be close bound to the Service of God.

The *Maniple*, which the Priest puts on his left Arm, represents likewise the Cords or binding of our B. Lord. The Priest before he puts it on, kisses the Cross which is in the Middle of it, as offering himself to attend our Saviour in his Passion, with a Will and Desire to suffer with him.

The *Stole*, from the *Latin* Word *Stola*, is an Ornament of Dignity and Power, and as such it is taken in the sacred Text, where it is said, that when *Pharaoh* would honour *Joseph*, he put on him a Stole; and *Mordecheus* was cloathed with a Stole for his greater Honour. The Priest, when he exercises his Functions, puts on a Stole, as representing his Dignity, Quality, and the Power of binding and loosing he has received from Christ. It also signifies the Cord, wherewith the Jews dragged our B. Saviour to his Crucifixion.

The *Chasuble* is the last Vestment the Priest uses, and is put over all the rest, hanging down before and behind. It represents the scarlet or purple Robe put upon

C

our

our Saviour by the Soldiers, in Scorn and Derision. Before, it has a Pillar, reprefenting the Pillar to which Chrift was tied, during his Flagellation. Behind, it has a Crofs, which fignifies the Crofs our B. Lord carried to Mount *Calvary*. This Veftment is appropriated to Priefts alone, and is by them ufed only when they fay Mafs. The Amice, the Albe and Maniple, being made ufe of by Sub-deacons and Deacons. Thefe Veftments, which the Minifters of the Altar are vefted with, when they go to celebrate and offer up the adorable Sacrifice, are defervedly very rich, on great Solemnities, but at all Times ought to be whole, clean and decent. The Prieft thus vefted, and going to Mafs, reprefents the Perfon of Jefus Chrift, going to his facred Paffion. The Confideration of which ought to fill both Prieft and People with Sentiments of the profoundeft Refpect and Veneration towards the facred Myfteries which one is to celebrate, and the other attend to. I fhall finifh what I have faid on this Subject, with what an antient Writer, *Ivo Carnot.* fays; " Thefe " Veftments are not Virtues, but Marks, " or Signs of Virtues, whereby thofe who " ufe them, and thofe who behold them, " may be admonifhed what to defire, and " what to avoid, and to whom all their " Actions ought to be directed." To the fame Purpofe, with regard to Priefts, is the
Ad-

Admonition of Pope *Innocent*; " Let the
" Priest be careful that he does not bear
" the Sign without what is signified by it ;
" that he carry not the Vestment without
" Virtue, left he be like a Sepulchre, all
" fine without, and nothing but Filth and
" Uncleanness within."

Theot. What you have said is extremely
entertaining and instructive ; will you add
a Word or two concerning the Priestly
Function, and of the Respect due to Priests;
for certainly, as they are Ministers of God,
and Mediators between him and the People, a proper Respect and Reverence is due
to them from those, in whose Regard they
are thus consecrated Ministers of God.

Theoph. You say very right : Their Function being to offer up Sacrifices, as all Ages
and Laws declare. There were Priests set
apart in the Law of Nature, as well as in
the Mosaick Institute, whose peculiar Business it was to offer Sacrifices for themselves
and others. In the New Law, Priests are
ordained to offer up the great Sacrifice of
the Mass : For this they are consecrated,
and in their Ordination, the Bishop says to
them : *Receive Power of offering Sacrifice in
the Church for the Living and Dead.* Consequently to this, there is most certainly a due
Reverence to be paid to them : As, first, on
Account of their Dignity, being God's
Vicars on Earth, his Ministers to instruct,
direct, and feed his People, as so many

 Sheep

Sheep committed to their Care. Hence, St.
Austine says ; " There is no greater Dignity
" under Heaven, than that of God's Priests,
" confecrated to deliver the heavenly Sacra-
" ments to us." Secondly, For their Utility,
and the Benefits we receive by them in their
preaching, inftructing, and adminiftering
the Holy Sacraments. Thirdly, As they
are Mediators between God and us, their
Bufinefs being to pray and intercede in behalf of the People, according to what God
faid to *Mofes* and *Aaron*, fpeaking of the
Priefts : " They fhall invocate my Name
" upon the Children of *Ifrael*; and I, the
" Lord, will blefs them." Laftly, In
refpect of the Power given to them by
God, to bind and loofe on Earth ; to forgive Sins in the Sacrament of Penance, and
to confecrate the facred Body and Blood of
Chrift, in the Holy Euchariſt.   Let me add
the Words of St. *Chryfoftome* ; " What can
" be faid but that all Power of heavenly
" Things is granted to them by God ; for
" he fays: *Whofe Sins you retain, they are re-*
" *tained :* St. John xx. What Power can be
" greater than this ? The Father gave all
" Power to the Son, and I fee this Power
" given to Priefts by God the Son." St.
Bernard admires it, faying ; " O excellent
" and honourable Power of Priefts, to which
" nothing in Heaven, nothing on Earth,
" can be compared." Hence the Admonition of St. *Francis*, to reverence and honour

Priefts ;

Priests ; becaufe, fays he, "they adminifter "the moft holy Body and Blood of Chrift, "which they alone confecrate, receive, and give to others."

Here let me add ; how earneftly it is to be wifhed for by every one, that all thofe who are called to this high and facred Dignity, would endeavour to adorn their fublime Character by fuitable, holy, regular, and exemplary Lives ; to inftruct and incite others to Piety and Holinefs of Life, by Example, as well as by Preaching ; that the facred Function may not be brought into Contempt, and made a Ridicule on account of difedifying and irregular Behaviour. May God, of his Mercy, remove this Evil from the Sanctuary; that the Prieft's Lips may preferve Knowledge, not only for the People, but alfo practical Knowledge for themfelves, by a ftrict Adherence to the Duties of their Station, and to walk worthy of the facred and holy Calling, to which they are called.

Theot. To this I heartily fay *Amen.* I will now take my Leave of you, with many Thanks for the Trouble you have taken. A little Bufinefs calls me into the Country for fome Days, at my Return will fee you again, when I fhall beg the Favour of you, that we may carry on our Converfation further on this Subject.

Theoph. I fhall expect your Vifit, and it will give me a Pleafure. I wifh you a good

 Jour-

Journey, fuccefs in your Bufinefs, and a fafe Return.

DIALOGUE V.

On the MASS.

Theophilus. WElcome, *Theotime.* I hope I fee you well after your Journey, and that your Bufinefs has fucceeded to your Defires.

Theotime. Thank God I am very well, and have Reafon to be pleafed at the Succefs I have met with in my Affairs. But, if you have Leifure and Inclination, I would willingly now enter upon what was the Subject of our laft Converfation.

Theoph. I am at Leifure, very willing to gratify your Defire, and to give you any further Inftruction relative to what we then talked of.

Theot. I fhould be glad to have a fhort and practical Explication of every Part of the Holy Mafs. from the Beginning to the End, as alfo of all the Ceremonies ufed by the Prieft therein, and how they are to be attended to by the People. You have already fpoke of Ceremonies in General.

An

An Explication now of thefe in particular,
will be as agreeable as inftructive to me.

Theot. I will endeavour to comply with
your Defire, as far as I am able, and will
begin with the Prieft's going to the Altar.
Here, previous to that, I recommend to
your Obfervation and Attention the Prieft,
cloathed in his facred Veftments, and going
to the Altar, where we are to confider him
in the Perfon of Chrift, reprefenting Jefus
Chrift going to Mount *Calvary*, and to offer up the fame facrifice of his Paffion,
which was then offered for Mankind. Hence
he carries on his exteriour Veftments the
Signs and Trophies of Chrift's victorious
Paffion. Thus vefted, he proceeds to the
Altar, with Intentions of offering up the
Sacrifice for himfelf, and all there prefent,
who here fhould with him offer up their Intention of hearing Mafs for fuch and fuch
Ends as they propofe to themfelves: Going
up to the Altar the Prieft places the Chalice
upon it, and having difpofed the Miffal, or
Book, he comes to the lower Step, and
there reverently bows his Head to the Crucifix, or makes a Genuflection, if the B.
Sacrament is in the Tabernacle; thus expreffing the Humility and reverential Awe,
with which he defires to approach the Altar
of God, and in Confideration of his own
Unworthinefs, to make his humble Confeffion, and to afk the Help of all prefent,
joining himfelf to them, that by mutual

Prayers, he and they may obtain **Pardon** of God, and being united in their Intentions, may, with pure and joined Hearts, offer up this Sacrifice to God.

Theot. This I readily underſtand, and collect from thence how I ought to join with the Prieſt in theſe Acts of Humiliation and Adoration. Proceed, if you pleaſe, to conſider the Firſt Part, or Beginning of the Maſs, and tell me why he begins in the *Name of the Father, and of the Son, and of the Holy Ghoſt,* making upon himſelf the Sign of the Croſs ?

Theoph. In anſwer to your Queſtion, pleaſe to obſerve, that the Church uſes theſe Words and Ceremonies in the Beginning of all her divine Offices, and in this Manner we were baptiſed; from hence likewiſe we may learn, in the Beginning of all our Works firſt to invocate the holy Name of God, begging his Bleſſing on all we do. Hence, it is ſitting that this ſolemn and ſacred Action ſhould begin by this ſolemn Invocation, and thereby the Prieſt makes a public Profeſſion of his Faith. For, as St. *Paul* teaches, without Faith, nothing is pleaſing to God, and in theſe Words are contained the two principal Myſteries of our holy Chriſtian Religion; the Unity and Trinity of God, and the Incarnation and Death of our Saviour.

Theot. Give me a particular Explication of this ?

Theoph,

Theoph. When the Prieft puts his Right-hand to his Forehead, he fays in the *Name*, in the Singular Number, not in the *Names*, the Plural, and thereby fignifies his Belief in one God only, expreffing by this the *Unity* of God, and by the Expreffion of the Three Perfons, *Father, Son, and Holy Ghoft*, declares his Faith in the Bleffed Trinity, and that thefe Three Perfons are all but One and the fame God. In like Manner, by making the Sign of the Crofs, he profeffes to believe the great Myfteries of the Incarnation and Death of our Saviour. When he fays : *In the Name of the Father*, it is an Acknowledgement that God the Father, out of Love to us, *fent his only Son into the World, that the World might be faved by him.* And *of the Son* is a Declaration that God the Son came into the World to redeem it. And *of the Holy Ghoft*, here he confeffes the coming of the Holy Ghoft, as the Completion of the great Work of our Redemption ; and laftly, by making the Sign of the Crofs, the Prieft profeffes to believe the Paffion and Death of our Saviour. As to the Antiphon and Pfalm which follow, in reciting them the Prieft declares his Intention of going to the Altar, to offer this Sacrifice to God, defiring his Protection from his Enemies, fpiritual and corporal, and animating himfelf to draw near to God, with an humble Confidence in his Goodnefs, and referring what he is about to do to hr.

Ho-

Honour, Praife and Glory : For this he ends
the Pfalm with *Gloria Patri, &c.* or,' *Glory
be to the Father, &c.*

Theot. All this is very fatisfactory. Give
me leave now to afk what is the Meaning
of the *Confiteor,* or *Confeſſion* the Prieſt next
makes.

Theoph. You muſt take Notice that this
Confeſſion is not facramental, or that uſed
in the Sacrament of Penance, but is a publick and general Confeſſion, which the
Prieſt makes, as prefcribed by the Church,
whereby he acknowledges his Unworthinefs,
and confeſſes his daily Sins and Imperfections, humbly imploring Pardon for the
fame. Here it is to be noted, that he makes
this Confeſſion to God, who alóne can pardon Sins, and from whom alone he hopes
for Remiſſion of them.

Theot. This I readily agree to, and as a
Catholick do firmly believe, that none but
God can forgive us our Sins. Why then
does the Prieſt confefs to the B. Virgin *Mary,*
to the Angels and Saints ? Is not this putting
them, in fome Meafure, at leaſt, upon a
Level with God, and afking them to pardon
our Sins ?

Theoph. By no Means : Not in the leaſt.
The Prieſt makes his Confeſſion to God, and
to the Saints in a very different Manner.
To God, whom he has offended by Sin,
and of whom alone he afks Pardon, and
hopes to receive it from his Mercy. He

con-

confesses to the Blessed Virgin, to the Angels and Saints, for his greater Humiliation, and to acknowledge his Unworthiness, in Imitation of the Prodigal Son, who said; *Father, I have sinned against Heaven and before thee*, Luke xv. which St. *Augustine* interprets, as if he said; I have offended against the Angels and Saints. This Confession to the Angels and Saints, is to call them as so many Witnesses of our Sorrow and Repentance, and move their Compassion and Charity to join their more powerful Prayers to ours, to pray for us, that we may obtain Pardon. This is plainly declared in the End of the Confiteor, which the Priest concludes with desiring the Blessed Virgin, the Angels and Saints, and all likewise present, to pray to our Lord God for him.

Theot. Why does the Priest say, *Peccavi, I have sinned*, in *Thought, Word*, and *Deed?* Why *through my Fault, three Times*, and strike his Breast?

Theoph. By attending to the Meaning of these Words and Actions, the *Confiteor* will appear to be an excellent Act of Contrition and Devotion for Lay-people as well as Priests, very proper to be used in the Morning, at Night, and at other Times. But, in Answer to your Questions. By the Word *Peccavi, I have sinned*, the Priest confesses himself to be a Sinner, and to express himself more so, he says, I have sinned exceedingly. How powerful, how efficacious to
ob-

obtain Mercy, we may learn from Holy *David* who having committed the grievous Sins of Murder, and Adultery, only said with a true and penitent Heart, *Peccavi, I have sinned to the Lord,* 2 *Kings,* xii. and immediately those Sins were forgiven him. He says in Thought, Word and Deed, accusing himself of many Sins, Failings, and Imperfections, all these different Ways of sinning. Sin, indeed, properly proceeds from the Will, take away the Will, and there is no Sin; yet this Will finds Matter of Sin in our Thoughts, Words, and Actions. Hence, we daily offend in all these different Ways, as the Apostle, St. *James,* testifies, saying, *In many Things we all offend.* St. *James,* iii. The Priest, therefore, and every one may truly say; I have sinned in Thought, Word, and Deed, through my Fault, this he repeats three Times, expressing thereby the vehement Sorrow of his Mind; to the last he adds, *through my most grievous Fault.* We may also say, that this Repetition is expressive of the three different Ways mentioned, whereby we sin. While the Priest says the Confiteor, you may observe he stands at a Distance from the Altar, bows himself down, as unworthy to look up to Heaven, holding his Hands joined before his Breast. He then strikes himself three Times, as he says *through my Fault,* &c. tacitly saying, Lord be merciful to me a Sinner, imitating therein

the

the penitent Publican in the Gospel, who stood afar off, not daring to lift up his Eyes to Heaven, but knocking his Breast said, *God, be merciful to me a Sinner.* St. *Luke,* xviii. This knocking, or striking the Breast, is a very expressive Sign of Humility, and of Grief and Sorrow, for having offended so good a God, our heavenly Father; which St. *Augustine* thus declares; *What is it to knock or strike the Breast, but to declare what lies hid in the Breast, and by an evident Stroke to chastise the hidden Sin: Or, to chastise our Flesh, because we have offended God.* Serm. 8. de verb Dei. St. *Cyprian* says: *We strike our Breast, as declaring the Sins inclosed inwardly in our Hearts.* Lib. de Orat. Dom. Pope Nicholas I. *in striking the Breast, we signify that we strike ourselves, and confess ourselves to be worthy of Stripes or Punishments.* ad Bulg. c. 54.

Theot. I am highly pleased with what you say; but must ask, as relative to this Part of the Mass, what follows after the *Confiteor?*

Theoph. The Priest having finished the *Confiteor,* the Clerk, or who serves at Mass, prays for him that God may forgive him his Sins, that he may worthily celebrate the holy Sacrifice, and by it come to everlasting Life. In this all present should join their Desires, and to which the Priest says *Amen.* Then the Clerk says the Confiteor in his own Name and of all the Assistants;

which

which finished, the Priest prays for him and them; and making the Sign of the Crofs, pronounces the general Abfolution. By making the Sign of the Crofs on himfelf, he fignifies that he gives the Abfolution by Virtue of Chrift's facred Crofs and Paffion; but here you are to obferve, that this Abfolution is not facramental as that given in the Sacrament of Penance: It is only facerdotal or deprecatory, and by way of Prayer or Impetration, which may be the more available as given by the Prieft, who, according to St. *Paul,* is the Minifter of Chrift, and a Difpenfer of the Myfteries of God, and therefore all Perfons ought to bow their Heads, and with great Humility receive it, figning themfelves with the Sign of the Crofs, as the Prieft does when he gives it. After which he fays fome ejaculatory Prayers, reciting fome Verfes of the Pfalms, expreffing his Confidence in God's Mercy and Goodnefs, with which he prefumes to go to the Altar. After this he fays, *Dominus Vobifcum. Our Lord be with you;* to which the Clerk anfwers, *Et cum Spiritu tuo. And with thy Spirit.* Then the Prieft fays, *Oremus. Let us pray;* as if he would fay; as the Lord is with us, and we hope has fhewn his Mercy and Goodnefs in the Pardon of our Sins, let us join in Prayer, with Confidence and Belief, that whatever we afk, we fhall obtain, by Virtue of this Sacrifice.

Theot.

Theot. Give me Leave to interrupt you. I take Notice that *Dominus Vobiscum*, and *Oremus*, frequently occur in the Mass, tell me, *Theophilus*, why it is used so often?

Theoph. This Salutation, as it may be called, is used by the Priest in all the divine Offices of the Church, and in all his sacerdotal Functions. In the *Mass*, frequently, to raise our Attention to the Mysteries thereof; to put us in Mind that he is with us in a more peculiar Manner, as being truly and really present on the Altar. It likewise imports the mutual Wishes of Priest and People, that one may devoutly celebrate, and the other devoutly hear *Mass*, and when the People, or the Clerk for them, answers: *And with thy Spirit*, it is to express the Unity of the Priest and People, joining in holy Prayers and Desires. Hence St. *Chrysostome* says: *Therefore we salute one another in the Holy Mysteries, that being many, we may be made as one.* When the Priest thus salutes us, desiring us to accompany him, we ought to join our Intentions and Desires with him, devoutly answering, *Et cum Spiritu tuo.*

Theot. Why does he say after this, *Oremus, Let us pray?*

Theoph. He says it as correspondent to his *Dominus Vobiscum*, and to signify the End for which he salutes the People, that is, to pray with him and for him. The Priest having thus prepared himself, by an
hum-

humble Confession of his Sins, and begged the Prayers of the People, goes up to the Altar, and devoutly kissing it, with great Humility, in a short devout Prayer, begs of God to make him worthy to enter the Holy of Holies.   Here it may be observed, that the Priest several Times kisses the Altar in Time of Mass, the Signification of which Kiss is variously given by Liturgical Writers.   Some say, this kissing the Altar signifies that Kiss of Peace and Reconciliation which Christ offered to the Jews, by his sacred Passion.   Others, that it represents the Union of Christ with his Church. According to some, it denotes our Reconciliation to God, by the Incarnation of his Son, completed by Christ's sacrificing himself upon the Altar of his Cross.   After this follows the *Introit*, or, the Beginning of the Mass.   An Explication of which, shall, if you please, be the Subject of our next Conference.

Theot. With all my Heart.   Adieu, till I have the Pleasure of seeing you again.

DIALOGUE VI.

On the MASS.

Theophilus. GOOD Morning to you, *Theotime* ; this Visit is earlier than usual, I am glad to see you, but may I ask the Reason of your coming so soon in the Morning?

Theot. I hope my early coming will be no Inconvenience to you, and my great Desire of pursuing our Conversation on the Subject we began with, must plead my Excuse for the Freedom I take.

Theoph. No Apology for that is necessary. I am equally ready and willing to comply with your Desires. I will now, therefore, proceed, and resume our Conference with considering the *Introit*, which, properly speaking, is the Beginning of the Mass, as all which preceded, or went before, was only preparatory to it. It is therefore called the *Introit*, or the Entrance on the great and holy Sacrifice, in saying of which, the Priest signs himself with the Sign of the Cross, thereby making a Profession of his Faith, and to signify, that what he is to do, is to be done in Virtue of Christ's Death and Passion. In the Middle of the *Introit* is said, *Gloria Patri,*
Glory

Glory be to the Father, &c. ?? ?? an Act of
Praise and Thankfgiving ?. ?? ?? ?? Myftery of Chrift's Incarnation. This *Introit*
may likewife be confidered as reprefenting
the earneft Wifhes and Defires of the antient Patriarchs and Prophets, expecting
the coming of the promifed Meffiah, or
holy One of *Ifrael*, and to exprefs this the
more, the Church immediately adds the
Kyrie Eleifon, whofe often Repetition very
fitly reprefents their continual Prayer, fo
freouently mentioned in holy Scripture.

Theot. What means the *Kyrie Eleifon*, and
why fo often repeated?

Theoph. The Words are *Greek*, and fignify, or are the fame as *Lord have Mercy on
us. Chrifte Eleifon,* is *Chrift have Mercy on
us.* The *Greeks* ufe only *Kyrie Eleifon*, but
that very frequently in their Liturgy, in
fome Parts twelve, and in fome fixteen
Times together. In the *Latin* Church, by
a Decree of St. *Gregory* the Great Pope,
it is repeated nine Times, viz. thrice *Kyrie
Eleifon*, then three Times *Chrifte Eleifon*, and
again thrice *Kyrie Eleifon.* This Repetition
has the Sanction of the holy Gofpel, in
the Perfons of the Blind Man, the *Canaan-
ite* Woman, and the poor Lepers, who re-
peatedly cried out, *Lord have Mercy on us,
Son of David have Mercy on us.* By thefe
Kyrie Eleifons, is alfo reprefented the continual Prayers of the Church in Behalf of
her Children, daily crying out for them,
Lord

Lord have Mercy on us. Chrift have Mercy on us ; for without thy Mercy and Godnefs they will be drowned in the Waters of Iniquity, and perifh. In thefe Petitions the Clerk, in the Name of the People, and the People joining with him, and the Prieft, fay the fame devout and efficacious Prayer. *Lord have Mercy on us. Chrift have Mercy on us.* But the Clerk only repeats them aloud, the People foftly to themfelves.

Theot. I am perfectly fatisfied with what you have faid, and, as I obferve the *Gloria in Excelfis* follows, tell me now what it fignifies, and why here faid.

Theoph. It is called the angelical Hymn, or Hymn of the Angels, being a Song which the Angels fung at the Birth of our Saviour, as St. *Luke* in his Gofpel declares, faying, *And fuddenly there was with the Angel a Multitude of the Heavenly Hoft, praifing God and faying, Glory be to God in the Higheft, and on Earth Peace to Men of good Will. Luke,* c. ii. The remaining Part of this Hymn was added by the Church, and the whole contains admirable Acts of Praife, Thankfgiving, Adoration and Supplications. For the Excellency of it, thofe who underftand *Latin,* will do well to fay it with the Prieft. Others may fay it in *Englifh,* as being full of Unction and Devotion. It reprefents to us the Nativity of Jefus Chrift, in Honour of which great

Myf-

Myſtery we ſing or ſay this Hymn of Praiſe and Thankſgiving, and here we may obſerve, how very fitly the Church has ordered it to be ſaid in this Place, for on this Myſtery of the Incarnation and Birth of our Saviour, all the others of his Life, Paſſion, Death, Reſurrection, and Aſcenſion depend; becauſe the Belief of them neceſſarily ſuppoſes the Birth and Coming of the true Meſſiah, and he who believes this, can have no rational Doubt of the Reſt, nor can any Chriſtian ſeriouſly reflect on this Myſtery, the Manner of the Incarnation, the Angels ſinging and rejoicing at Chriſt's Birth, but he muſt find in himſelf ſome interiour Motions of Piety and Devotion.

Theot. You are right, but go on and tell me what the Prieſt does after he has ſaid the *Gloria in Excelſis.*

Theoph He kiſſes the Altar in Token of that Peace which is given to us by Chriſt's Nativity, and in Reverence to the Altar on which Chriſt is to be immolated in this Sacrifice. He then turns to the People, ſaluting them with *Dominus Vobiſcum, the Lord be with you,* inviting them to join with him in the Prayers he is about to ſay for them; for this End he turns to the Miſſal, and bids us attend, ſaying *Oremus,* or, *Let us pray;* come and join with me, that is, with the Church, in whoſe Name the Prayers are made; from hence it follows, that all preſent ſhould

in

in Heart and Affection, with Fervour and
Devotion, join with the Prieſt in ſo holy and
powerful a Sacrifice, offered up by God's
Miniſter in the Name of the Church, which
certainly, is more meritorious and more
pleaſing to God than any private Prayers.

Theot. What are theſe Prayers, and why
are they called *Collects ?*

Theoph. The Prayers are various Petitions and Requeſts made to God, according
to what St. *Paul* adviſes, that firſt of all
Things, *let Supplications, Prayers, Petitions,
and Thankſgivings be made for all Men. Heb.*
c. iii. In theſe Prayers the Church ſometimes makes Supplications to be delivered
from Evils, as in Time of Perſecution, or
other Afflictions. Sometimes ſhe prays for
ſpiritual Bleſſings, and even temporal Benefits, as for ſeaſonable Weather, againſt
Peſtilence, in Time of Famine, or in other
temporal Exigencies. Sometimes ſhe puts
up devout Petitions for particular Favours,
for the Converſion of Sinners, or of thoſe
who go aſtray. At other Times, to return
Thanks for Benefits received, and whoever
conſiders it, will admire the Œconomy of
God's Church, thus to couch in a few
Words, whatever the Faithful may aſk of
God, for though the Prayers are ſhort,
they are full in Subſtance and Devotion,
and as the principal Thing intended here
is to offer Sacrifice to God, it ſuffices that
the Church expreſſes her Intention by theſe
Prayers,

Prayers, in a few Words, in Order to the Application of this, or that Mass, to such or such Ends. So that although the Prayers may be short in Words, yet they virtually extend themselves to the whole Sacrifice of the Mass, having a Correspondence with the Churches Intention, to obtain by Virtue of this Sacrifice, what the Priest or People present do intend by this Mass.

These Prayers are called *Collects*, as being the collected Prayers, Vows, and Desires of all present, which the Priest unites with his, including in his Prayer the Petitions and Desires of all, and are said over them, or for them, collected or assembled together. It may also be said, that they are called *Collects*, as Prayers collected and accommodated by the Church to the different Times, Festivals, and Seasons of the Year. Here you may observe that these Collects end either expressly with these Words: *Through our Lord Jesus Christ, &c.* or with others importing the same. On which Pope *Innocent* the IIId. says: *We end our Collect through the Lord Jesus Christ, for we implore the Father's Help and Succour for the Love of his Son:* For Christ himself has said; *Amen, Amen, I say unto you, if you ask the Father any Thing in my Name, he will give it to you.* St. *John,* c. iv. All we have to do is to join our Intentions, and offer up our Prayers, in Union with the Prayers of the Priest; for, as *Durandus* notes, the

Priest

Priest alone says the Prayer, while those who are present are silent, and pray only in Spirit, thereby to attend and join their Hearts, that they may justly say, *Amen*. You are further to consider, that these Prayers are not private, but publick, and common to all, though performed and presented by the Priest, who makes them in the Church's Name, and therefore those, who are ignorant of the Words, yet, generally knowing the Conclusion, can, if they attend, answer *Amen*, as well as the Learned.

Theot. Thus far I understand you perfectly well. Let us now consider the *Epistle*, *Gradual*, *Tract*, *Prose*, or *Sequence*, and the *Gospel*, what they mean, and why Read.

Theoph. The Holy Scriptures are not improperly said to be an *Epistle*, for the sacred Books of it are as *Epistles*, or missive Letters sent from God, as Testimonies of his sacred Will, to Mankind for their Salvation, by teaching us the Way to Heaven, and how to please and serve his divine Majesty. It may also be said, that they are so called from their being generally taken from the Epistles of St. *Paul*, and other Apostles. The Epistle is always read before the Gospel, that as the Old Testament preceded the New, we may by attentive hearing them, be disposed for hearing the Gospel, and that the Excellency of
the

the Gofpel may be better known. The Myftical Signification of the Epiftles is to put us in Mind of the written Law, which went before that of Grace, or of the Preaching of St. *John Baptift*, before the Preaching of our Saviour, or the Labours of the Apoftles, in converting the *Gentiles*. In which we may confider our Vocation to the Light of Faith, and give Thanks to God, as the Apoftle fays, for fending his Prophets, Apoftles, and their Succeffors, to teach us the Way of Salvation, and for that, with grateful Hearts, at the End of the Epiftle to fay, *Deo Gratias, Thanks be to God.* Which Expreffion St. *Auguftine* did fo highly Efteem as to fay ; " What better " Thing can we bear in Mind, or fpeak " with the Mouth, or exprefs with the " Pen, than *Deo Gratias?* Nothing can " be faid more briefly, nor heard more " joyfully. Nothing underftood greater, " or more profitable than *Deo Gratias,* " thanks be to God, who has enriched us " with the true Faith of Jefus Chrift."

Thect. You fay the *Epiftle* is read for the Inftruction of the People, why then is it read in *Latin*, which every one does not underftand, and not in the Vulgar Tongue?

Theoph. I will give you the Reafon. The Church defires, and would have a perfect Uniformity in her Liturgy, or publick Service, obferved every where, and to avoid
any

any Variations or Interpolations in it: As for the Inſtruction of the People, thoſe who underſtand *Latin* may piouſly attend to the Contents of them; thoſe who do not, and can read, may find them in their own Language, in Books containing the *Epiſtles* and *Goſpels* for the whole Year; and may, as many do, read them to themſelves at Maſs, while the Prieſt reads them at the Altar; and for every one it will be ſufficient, that they know by the *Epiſtle* the Vocation they have had from God to the true Faith and Knowledge of his holy Will. Let us give Thanks for ſo great a Benefit, and purpoſe, by the Aſſiſtance of his Grace, to perſevere in the Obſervance of his holy Law, and to endeavour daily to make a Progreſs from one Degree of Virtue to another, intimated by the Gradual which follows the Epiſtle.

Theot. You muſt now then give me an Explication of the *Gradual,* &c.

Theoph. Willingly. The *Gradual* is, for the moſt Part, one or two Verſes out of the Pſalms, agreeable to the Office of the Day, which are ſaid or ſung by the Choir in ſolemn Maſſes, between the *Epiſtle* and *Goſpel*; and may be properly called as a Reſponſory, or Anſwer to the *Epiſtle*; for generally it has a Correſpondence to the Subject of the *Epiſtle.* According to Authors, who write upon Church Offices, it has various Significations. The moſt eaſy and natural is to signify the Ascent we ought to make, or going up by Degrees from one Virtue to another. It may also put us in Mind of the Gradation to be made from the Doctrine of the Prophets and Apostles to that of Jesus Christ. As a *Responsory*, it signifies that we ought, in Word and Work, to correspond to those Things which are propounded to us in the *Epistle.*

Theot. Pray what means *Alleluja*, inter-mixed with the Gradual?

Theoph. Alleluja is a *Hebrew* Word, sig-nifying Praise, and not only Praise simply, but Praise with Joy and Gladness, more than can be expressed by the Voice. St. Augustine says, *That no Christian is ignorant that Alleluja is a Voice of Praise:* As it is a sacred mystical Word, the Church mili-tant on Earth uses it in Imitation of the Church triumphant in Heaven, where God is praised with Joy and Jubilation and singing *Alleluja*, as we may learn from *Tobias,* ch. 13. and *Apoc.* ch. 19. Hence the *Greeks, Chaldeans, Syriacs,* and *Arabics,* as well as the *Latins,* retain it. St. *Jerome,* and other Interpreters seldom translate it, but leave it as they find it in the *He-brew.* It is used by the Church in the Mass, to manifest the Joy we have in the solemn Mysteries. In *Easter* Time it is re-doubled, for Joy of the glorious Resurrec-tion of Jesus Christ; but from *Septuagesima* to *Easter,* and at some other Times, she

omits

●mits it, and reads what is called the *Tract* in Place of it.

This Tract confifts of certain Verfes of the Pfalms; and is called the *Tract*, for that in folemn Maffes it is fung very leifurely, with protracting the Words and Syllables, and reprefents the Mourning and Sighs which are fuitable to Times of Penance. It may, according to fome, not unaptly fignify the languifhing Defires of devout Souls, earneftly wifhing for and fighing after the Joys of Heaven.

Theot., A Word or two now, if you pleafe, concerning the *Profe* or *Sequence*.

Teoph. The *Sequence* is fometimes added to the *Gradual*, and is a Continuation of the preceding Joy or Praife. The Church ufes three principal ones, to wit, on the Feftivals of *Eafter*, *Whitfuntide*, and *Corpus Chrifti*. The two firft are very antient, and the Third was made by St. *Thomas* of *Aquine*. Befides thefe, there are two others, one in the Mafs of the holy Name of Jefus, *Laudo nomen Salvatoris*; one in the Mafs of the Dolours of our bleffed Lady, *Stabat Mater*. Sometimes in Maffes for the Dead a *Sequence* is added to the *Tract* conformable to it, very expreffive of the Sentiments we may fuppofe the fuffering Souls in Purgatory have, and of what every Chriftian ought to have in regard of Death and the laft Judgment. This may fuffice at prefent.

 The

The *Gospel* and the *Creed* will afford sufficient Matter for our next Converſation.

Theot. I'm content; and with due Thanks
for what I have learned from you, will
wait upon you again in a few Days.

D I A L O G U E VII.

On the M A S S.

Theotime. YOU ſee, *Teophilus*, I am as
good as my Word. I come
to pay you another Viſit, and on the ſame
Account which has made me hitherto ſo
troubleſome to you.

Theoph. Don't think, my Friend, you
are troubleſome; ſit down, and without
any further Preamble, let us reſume our
Diſcourſe, and begin where we, laſt time,
left off. It is the *Goſpel* and *Creed* we are
now to conſider.

Theot. I ſhall attend with Pleaſure, not
doubting but I ſhall receive great Edification and uſeful Inſtructions from what you
ſay on this Head. What means the *Goſpel?*

Theoph. The *Goſpel* is ſome Part of the
holy Scripture, taken from the holy Evan-
geliſts, and in *Latin* is ſtiled *Evangelium,*
which ſignifies *good Tydings.* In *Engliſh* we
call

call it *Gospel*, as God's Spell, that is, God's Word or Letter sent to us from these Evangelists. They are used by the Church according to the different Times and Festivals, and shew the Correspondence of the *Gospel* with the *Prophets*, represented by the *Epistles*; or it may be thus understood, according to St. *Denis:* "After the Reading "of the ancient Law, the New Testament "is read, as declaring that the Old Testament did foretell the Divine Works of "Jesus Christ, but the New Testament accomplishes them, that is, declaring them "to have been done." Lib. Eccl. Hier. c. 3.

Theot. On what Account is the *Gospel* read at Mass?

Theoph. The Church ordains some part of the holy *Gospel* to be daily read at Mass, out of Reverence to Christ's sacred Words, and for our Instruction, to strengthen our Faith, to animate our Hope, and to inflame our Hearts with divine Love; that so we may be the better disposed to celebrate the sacred Passion of Christ in these holy Mysteries. St. *Augustine* tells us, that *among all the Divine Authorities in the holy Text, the Gospel does most excell.* To hear the Gospel is to hear the Voice of Christ, and we ought to bear as much Reverence to it as if we were hearing Christ himself speaking to us; and that such is the Intent of the Church appears from the Ce-

D 3   remonies

remonies with which she orders it to be read.

Thest. Be pleased to tell me those Ceremonies and explain them to me.

Theoph. In the first Place you are to observe, that the *Missal,* or *Mass Book,* is removed from the right Side of the Altar to the left to signify that Jesus Christ came to call not only the Just but Sinners also. The right Side representing the Just, as the left does Sinners. It also signifies the Transition of the Gospel from the Jews who rejected it, to the Gentiles who readily embraced it, according to what we read in the *Acts of the Apostles,* where St. *Paul* said, *To you,* that is, to the Jews, *it behoved us first to speak the Word of God; but because you reject it, behold we turn to the Gentiles,* Acts, ch. 13. Secondly, we may take Notice of the Humility and Devotion with which the Priest prepares himself to read the Gospel. Going to the Middle of the Altar he devoutly prays, that with a clean Heart he may worthily and competently denounce it. When come to the Book, he solemnly pronounces *Dominus Vobiscum, The Lord be with you;* to give us Notice, that he is about to read the Words of Christ, and to move our Attention, as by his Word our Lord is with us, to make us docile and attentive to the glad Tydings of Salvation, brought to us by the *Gospel:* For our further Instruction he names the Evangelist from

whence

whence the *Gospel* is taken, and in naming it signs the Book with the Sign of the Cross, to signify that the great Work of our Redemption was accomplished by the Mystery of the Cross, or sacred Passion of Jesus Christ.

Theot. But, why does the Priest sign himself on the Forehead, Mouth and Breast? What can that signify?

Theoph. This is not done without significant Instruction. He imprints the Sign of the Cross on his Forehead, to shew that he is not ashamed to profess the *Gospel*, and would have all to know that he is a Servant of Jesus Christ, and a Lover of the Cross. He signs his Mouth and Lips, to testify his Readiness, openly to declare and denounce the sacred Truths of the *Gospel*, and then makes the Sign of the Cross on his Breast, as declaratory that what he professes with his Mouth, he sincerely and entirely believes in his Heart. While he reads the Gospel he stands reverently before the Book, with his Hands joined, bowing his Head in the Beginning, and at the End, and at the holy Name of *Jesus*. When he has read the Gospel he kisses the Book, in Reverence to God's Word, and in a short Prayer begs that the Evangelical Word may have a due Effect on his Heart, and prove Seed sown upon good Ground.

Theot. I have another Question to ask relative

lative to the *Gospel*; Why do the People stand up at reading it?

Theoph. They stand at the Gospel out of Reverence to God's holy Word, and to express their Attention to it, for this they answer the *Dominus Vobiscum* with *Et cum Spiritu tuo, and with thy Spirit*; and when the Priest says, *Sequentia Sancti Evangelii, the Sequence of the holy Gospel*, they make a Reverence, by bowing their Heads towards the Altar, and with a grateful Acclamation say, *Gloria tibi Domine, Glory be to thee, O Lord*, signing themselves with the Sign of the Cross, as the Priest does, and for the same Consideration, all which the People may apply to themselves, and are likewise to bow at the holy Name of *Jesus*. The Priest having finished the Gospel, the People say, *Laus tibi Christe, Praise be to thee, O Christ*, giving Thanks to Jesus Christ, for having revealed this his Word to us, and as in the Beginning, so at the End they make the Sign of the Cross, to express their Willingness to perform what has been declared to them. As to reading the *Gospel* with the Priest, what I have said about reading the *Epistle*, is to be applied to the *Gospel*.

Theot. I understand you well: The *Creed* follows the *Gospel*; go on therefore, and explain that to me.

Theoph. The *Creed* is so called from the first Word of it in *Latin, Credo*, which signifies,

nifies, I believe. Hence it is often called the *Belief*. It is also ftiled the *Symbol of Faith*, which we here make publick Profeffion of. *Optatus* calls it, *An univirfal Charaƈter of our Faith*; whereby, as St. *Ambrofe* fays, *We are known to be Catholics*; and St. *Leo* calls it *a brief and perfeƈt Confeffion of our Faith*, which is figned by fo many Sentences of the twelve Apoftles, and is fo divinely compofed, as by it alone all Herefies may be confuted. If you afk me why it is faid in Mafs? I anfwer, to give the Faithful an Opportunity of making a publick Declaration of their Catholick Faith, as expreffed in the ninth Article, *I believe One, Holy, Catholic, and Apoftolic Church.* We may further obferve, that as the *Gofpel* is a *Code*, or Body of Chrift's Law, the *Creed* is a Declaration of our Affent thereto, or our Acceptance of the Doƈtrine of Chrift, delivered in the Gofpel. *Durandus*, a learned Writer on the Church Rubricks, fays, " The Creed aptly " follows the Gofpel, to fhew we receive " the Evangelical Word, or Preaching, " which we manifeft by Effeƈt. The Sym- " bol after the Gofpel, Faith after Preach- " ing, according to what St. *John* fays, " relative to Jefus Chrift: when he had " fpoke thofe Words, *many believed in him.*" St. *John*, c. viii.

Theot. Is kneeling or ftanding the moft

proper Pofture, while the Prieft fays the Creed?

Theoph. You may do either one or the other. as your Devotion inclines you. In my Opinion, ftanding feems to be the moft proper Pofture, as it fhews a Promptitude and Readinefs of Mind, to fupport and maintain the Catholick Faith we profefs, which may be faid myftically to be commended to us by St. *Paul,* faying ; *Stand ye therefore, having your Loins girded in Truth :* that is, ftand conftant in the Faith, in Oppofition to all Herefies, believing with all Integrity of Heart, whatever God, by his Church, propofes to you, and let your Life correfpond thereto by Chriftian and fuitable Practice, walking before God and Man, according to the Doctrine of the Gofpel you have been taught.

Theot. Why does the Prieft kneel at thofe Words : *Homo factus eft ?*

Theoph. Not only the Prieft, as *Gavant* in his Commentaries on the Rubricks fays, but all who are prefent are to kneel at thofe Words, as well as at *Verbum caro factum eft, the Word is made Flefh,* both fignifying the fame Thing, the Incarnation of the Son of God, or Chrift's being made Man for us. The Words being fo full of Majefty and Reverence, expreffing the infinite Condefcenfion of the Deity to our Humanity, juftly requires, whenever mentioned in thefe Words, that every one

fhould

should with the greatest Humility bend their Knees, and all the Powers of their Souls, in a grateful Acknowledgment of so great a Grace and Favour.

Theot. I observe that the Priest, at the End of the Creed signs himself. Why does he do that?

Theoph. As well to arm himself against the Devil, who, by his Suggestions, seeks to make us stagger in our Faith, as also to seal this Faith in his Heart and Mind, and to shew, that for the Profession of this Faith he is ready to die with Jesus Christ on the Cross. This is very fitly done at those Words, *Vitam eternam, Life everlasting,* which by the Cross and Passion of our Saviour, he, and all of us hope to obtain. Lastly, he finishes with saying *Amen,* in his own, and in the Name of all who are present, thereby ratifying and confirming the Profession before made, as if he should say, I do certainly, and without any Doubt or Hesitation, believe all and every Article of this *Creed,* to be most true, most certain, and infallible, since Christ, who is *Amen,* the faithful and true Witness, has revealed and testified it. With the Priest, the People should join themselves, silently and devoutly saying *Amen.*

Theot. By your Servant's delivering to you that Packet, I presume you may have some Business to dispatch; will not therefore detain you from it; shall be glad to
know

know when I may come to you again, to carry on this inſtructive Converſation.

Theoph. In two or three Days I ſhall be at Leiſure, and be glad, as I am at all Times, to ſee *Theotime.*

Theot. You are very obliging, at preſent farewell.

DIALOGUE VIII.

On the MASS.

Theophilus. GOOD Morrow, *Theotime,* I hope I ſee you well; I am ready for you, and at Leiſure to continue our Converſation about the Holy Maſs.

Theot. You are truly kind, and with Pleaſure I ſhall hear you. The *Offertory,* I believe, is the next Part of the Maſs to be conſidered, and therefore, firſt tell me what the *Offertory* means.

Theoph. This is, properly ſpeaking, the firſt Part of the Sacrifice, as all that went before was only preparatory to it, which is the actual Oblation of what is to be offered in this Sacrifice. The Prieſt, before he begins it, ſalutes the People with *Dominus Vobiſcum,* deſiring that the Lord may

be

be with them, and enable them to join with him, the Prieſt, with all the Devotion and Reverence due to ſo great a Sacrifice; turning then to the Altar, he ſays, *Oremus, Let us pray,* admoniſhing all preſent to lay aſide all other Thoughts, and ſeriouſly to attend to the Actions of the Prieſt, during the Celebration of the Holy Myſteries. After this he recites what in the Miſſal is called *Offertorium,* and is generally ſome Sentence out of the Pſalms, and repreſents the Hymn our bleſſed Saviour ſaid before he went to Mount *Olivet,* where he made his firſt Oblation. Then follows the *Oblation,* which is principally intended in the Maſs, and is one of the chiefeſt Actions or Functions of the Prieſthood, according to that of St. *Paul; Every High Prieſt taken from Men, is appointed for Men, in thoſe Things which appertain to God, that he may offer Gifts and Sacrifices for Sin. Heb.* c. v. which in this Place ſignifies the Action of the Prieſt, now beginning to offer Sacrifice to God, wherein he offers Bread and Wine, according to Chriſt's Inſtitution, in Order to the Conſecration of it.

Theot. To whom, and for whom does the Prieſt make this Oblation?

Theoph. In this Place he offers the whole Subſtance and Action of the Maſs to God the Father, for the whole World. For himſelf, that God would be pleaſed to take away his Sins; for all preſent at this Sacrifice

crifice, who more particul..rly partake of it, then for all the Faithful, living and dead, and laſtly, prays that this *Oblation* may be profitable to him and them, to the Health and Comfort of their Souls; and this he does in the Oblation of the Hoſt, and in that of the Chalice.

Theot. I obſerve he makes an Oblation of the Hoſt and of the Chalice ſeparately. Why that?

Theoph. In this the Church follows the Example of our bleſſed Saviour, who firſt took Bread and then Wine; now, though each of them do repreſent the ſame Body and Blood of Chriſt, yet, as the Species are different, and have different Acts of Confecration, ſo they have a different Oblation. Here we are to note, with *Durandus,* although there be two Species, yet not two Sacrifices; for the Unity of the Word of Chriſt makes the Unity of the Sacrifice. Theſe two Oblations, therefore, make but one total Oblation of one Thing, thereby ſignified, namely, Jeſus Chriſt, who gave his Body and Blood under two Species, for the more complete Signification of his Paſſion, where his Blood was ſeparated from his Body. This Action of Oblation may here be conſidered likewiſe as a Repreſentation of that Preparation the Diſciples made for the laſt Supper, as it is a preparatory Diſpoſition to the Act of Confecration, and myſtically repreſents the

Ob-

Oblation which Chrift made of himſelf to
his Father, in the Garden of *Gethſamoni.*

Theot. In this Oblation of the Hoſt and
Chalice, I take Notice the Prieſt uſes ſeveral Ceremonies. Be ſo good as to explain
the Signification of them.

Theoph. Willingly. As this Oblation repreſents myſtically the Oblation which
Chriſt made of himſelf in the Garden, we
may conſider in theſe Ceremonies the various Circumſtances of what our Bleſſed Saviour then and there did. Firſt, after the
Offertory, the Prieſt takes the Veil off the
Chalice, ſignifying thereby Chriſt's going
into the Garden, there beginning plainly
to diſcover his Paſſion to the Diſciples,
which before he had but obſcurely intimated to them. Secondly, by removing
the Chalice and Patten from the Corporal,
is repreſented the Separation of Chriſt from
his Diſciples, in order to diſpoſe himſelf
for his Sufferings, and to make an Oblation thereof to his divine Father. Thirdly,
the Prieſt taking the Hoſt and Patten, denotes Chriſt's ſeparating himſelf from St.
Peter, St. *James,* and St. *John,* whom he
had taken from the other Apoſtles, when
he entered into the Garden.

Theot. Why is the Hoſt, or Bread, here
offered in a round Form, and why is it unleavened Bread?

Theoph. As to the Subſtance of the Sacrament, it is of no Importance what Form

it

it is in, provided it be true Wheaten Bread.
This round Form is not ufed in the Eaftern,
but in the *Latin* Church. The Reafons
affigned for its being round, are, 1ft. To
denote to us that Chrift is *Alpha*, and
Omega, the *Beginning and End* of all created
Things, yet in himfelf, without Beginning
or End, as the round Form reprefents.   2d.
This Form is moft perfect and excellent of
all Forms, and moft proper for the moft excellent of all Sacraments.   You may obferve that the Bread, or Hoft, is made very
thin, by which it may be feen, there is no
Mixture, that it is pure Bread, and of
clean corn.   If it was made thicker, fomething might mingle therein, not capable
of Confecration, and not becoming fo great
and holy a Sacrament.   Here, in this you
may take Notice of the great Care of the
Church, that no Crums or Particles of the
Hoft fhould be fcattered, or let fall on the
Altar or Ground, which might eafily happen in other Forms of Bread; and for the
fame Reafon, the Wine is confecrated in a
fmall Quantity, to prevent any Effufion of
it out of the Chalice.   As for the Hoft being made of unleavened Bread, it is not
abfolutely neceffary, for in the *Greek* Church
they ufe leavened Bread.   Either are fufficient Matter for Confecration.   In the
Weftern Parts they always did ufe *Azyme*,
or unleavened Bread, as Chrift did at his
laft Supper.   According to *Durandus*, the
Church

Church received this Rite from St. *Peter* and St. *Paul*; and, as St. *Epiphanius* affirms, it was always the Cuſtom of the Church.

Theot. Have you any Thing further to add concerning theſe Ceremonies?

Theoph. Yes: The Prieſt having made the Oblation, with the Hoſt and Patten he makes the Sign of the Croſs, to ſignify that the *Oblation* has its Effect from the Croſs and Paſſion of Jeſus Chriſt, which he voluntarily accepted for our Redemption. This done, the Prieſt lays down the Hoſt on the Corporal, repreſenting thereby, our Saviour's proſtrating himſelf with Submiſſion to his heavenly Father's Will, offering his Body to be ſacrificed on the Croſs; in like Manner the Prieſt lays down the Hoſt, as Matter ordained for the Sacrifice of the Maſs. Laſtly, he puts, or hides the Patten under the Corporal, which denotes the Diſciples leaving their divine Maſter to the Power of his Enemies, while they fled away and hid themſelves. A little Part of the Patten remains uncovered, which repreſents our Bleſſed Lady and St. *John* the Evangeliſt, who did not leave Jeſus Chriſt, but continued with him, even to the Croſs. Theſe Ceremonies duly attended to, will greatly help to more our Souls to Devotion, and to a ſerious Attention to the holy Myſteries enſuing.

Theot.

Theot. I agree with you in this, let us now con... ... ...hat is done in the Oblation of the Chali...

Theoph. The Prieſt takes the Chalice, to prepa... ...e Wine f...r the other Oblation by t... ...ſenting our Saviour's accepting the ...ce of his ...ion, when he ſaid ; *No, as I will, but as thou wilt :* St. *Mark*, c. xiv. and ...hen puts Wine and Water into ...he Chalice. This the Church has always done, as delivered to her by Apoſtolical Tradition, and it is held by many that our Bleſſed Saviour did mix Water with his Wine, in the Inſtitution of the Sacrament. The Wine, thus mingled with Water, repreſents likewiſe the Water and Blood which iſſued out of our Saviour's Side, when it was pierced with a Lance. Concerning this Mixture, Pope *Alexander* the Iſt, thus ſays : " In the Sacrifice of the " Maſs, Bread only, and Wine mixed " with Water, is to be offered. In the " Chalice of our Lord, neither Wine alone, " nor Water alone, ought to be offered, " but both mixed ; for we read that both " did flow from Chriſt's Side, in his Paſ- " ſion." Let me add, that this Mixture of Wine and Water, is a Symbol of the Union Chriſtians have with Chriſt in this Sacrament, as the Fruit principally intended in this Sacrifice : It is alſo an Aſſurance that Chriſt is united to us, and we to him, by this Euchariſtick Sacrifice.

Theot.

Theot. I obferve the Prieft bleffes the Water, but not the Wine, and that he puts very little Water into the Chalice. The Reafon of this, if you pleafe.

Theoph. The Reafon is, the Wine reprefents him, who needs no Bleffing, and the Water fignifies the People, who ftand in need of Benediction ; therefore the Prieft bleffes the People, in the Water, for a Difpofition for that Union, which by this Sacrifice they are to have with Chrift. In Maffes for the Dead, this Benediction is not given, becaufe the Souls in Purgatory are in a State of Grace. As to your Queftion, why fo little Water is put into the Chalice ? I anfwer, That what is in the Chalice may be true Wine. The Water incorporated with the Wine fignifies that the Church, or People, are incorporated with him.

Theot. What does the Prieft do after the Oblation of the Chalice ?

Theoph. He fets it down on the Corporal, and then devoutly prays that God would accept of this Sacrifice, that the Holy Ghoft would fanctify thefe Things, ordained for the Sacrifice, and making the Sign of the Crofs fhews that what he afks, he expects from the Virtue of Chrift's holy Crofs and Paffion. In confidering thefe Ceremonies, the principal Thing to be regarded in the Mixture of the Water with Wine, and to our ferious Meditation, is the Union of our Souls with Chrift, which

which it reprefents, and is one of the principal Effects of the Euchariſt, according to
what Chriſt ſays ; *He who eats my Fleſh,
and drinks my Blood, abides in me, and I in
him.* St. *John,* c. vi.   Hence we may conſider further the pious Intention of the
Church, of uniting us to God by this Sacrifice, in perfect Love of him and our Neighbours, and that as Members of Chriſt we
may be united to the Prieſt, during the
whole Courſe of the Maſs.   But here I muſt
put an End to our Converfation at this
Time, as an Appointment to tranfact ſome
Buſineſs, now calls me out.

Theot. I would by no Means hinder you,
I ſhall take another Opportunity to wait
upon you again.   At preſent adieu.

D I A L O G U E IX.

On the M A S S.

Theotime. I Am come, *Theophilus,* to aſk
if you are at Leiſure to fa-
vour me with your Converfation for a little
while, and to reſume your Explication of
the Maſs, which has hitherto given me
very great Satiſfaction.

Theoph.

Theophilus. You find me at your Service, nor can I refuse my Friend so reasonable a Request.

Theot. After the Oblation, the Priest goes to the right End of the Altar, and washes the Tops of his Fingers. Why is this done ?

Theoph. He washes the Tops of his Fingers, that no Dust or Dirt may cleave, and no Particle of the Host, which he has handled, might stick to them, and that with the utmost Cleanliness and Decency he may touch the blessed Sacrament in the Consecration. This washing would be very improper and indecent to be done before the Altar, therefore he does it at the right End. It also signifies the great Purity of Body and Soul with which the Priest ought to celebrate these Holy Mysteries, and the People to assist at them. This Ceremony is derived from Apostolical Tradition, and of which St. *Dennis* gives this Signification ; *Washing is used to the Tops, or extream Parts of the Fingers, before the most holy Sign is observed, as if it were before Christ, beholding our most hidden Thoughts,* &c. Eccl. Hier. c. iii. And St. *Clement* says, · that *it is done to shew the necessary Purity of the Soul, and that this Sacrifice ought to be performed with all Purity of Body and Mind.* Lib. 8. Const. c. ii. After this the Priest continues the Oblation, in Memory of Christ's Passion, Resurrection and Ascension, which are the

great

great and effential Myfteries of our Salvation, and the Subftance of our Juftification;
the Paffion being our Redemption, the Refurrection our Life, and the Afcenfion our
Glory. Hence he prays that this Sacrifice
may be accepted for the Salvation of him
and all Perfons, and for this humbly begs
the Prayers and Interceffions of the Bleffed
Virgin and all the Saints.

Theot. According to the Order of the
Holy Mafs in my Prayer Book, *Orate Fratres* follows next. Explain that to me.

Thesph. The firft Thing here to be confidered, is the Connection of this *Orate
Fratres* with the precedent Prayer. Having
implored the Interceffion of the Saints in
Heaven, that his Oblation may be acceptable to God, the Prieft turns to the People,
to beg their Affiftance to the fame Effect,
and fealing his Defires with a Kifs of the
Altar, he fays; *Orate Fratres. Brethren
pray that mine and your Sacrifice may be acceptable before God the Father Almighty.* He
falutes the People under the Title of Brethren, which is a Title of Unity, Love,
and Friendfhip, and under thefe Apella-
tions, as Children of Chrift and Brethren,
defires them to join their Prayers to his,
according to the Obligation of Chriftian
Charity, and to this he urges them by their
own Intereft. for faying, *mine* and *your Sacrifice,* he puts all prefent in Mind that he
offers the Sacrifice not only for himfelf,
but

but for them likewife; and that they are to offer it with him, as being their Sacrifice as well as his. It being the fame Sacrament, the fame Grace, the fame Fruit and Benefit, which both Prieft and People may receive by it. In this the Prieft may be confidered as our Proctor and Mediator, not unlike to him who brings a lighted Candle into a Room, whereof every one partakes in as full a Manner as he who brings it. He likewife expreffes the End of his Salutation to be jointly to pray with him, that God would receive and accept this Sacrifice for the Good of their Souls, and for what they intend in hearing Mafs. *Alcivinus* calls this *Orate Fratres, the Union of the Prieft's Prayers and Intentions, with the Prayers and Intentions of the People,* that as St. *Paul* fays, *with one Mind, and with one Mouth we may glorify God, and the Father of our Lord Jefus Chrift.* Rom. c. x.

Theot. What is the Anfwer to this?

Theoph. The Clerk, in the Name of the People, anfwers in a pious and fhort Prayer thus: *May our Lord receive this Sacrifice from your Hands, to the Praife and Glory of his holy Name, for our Profit, and for the Good of his holy Church.* This Anfwer perfectly correfponds to the Prieft's Invitation; for here the People pray that the Sacrifice may be acceptable by the Prieft's Miniftry; that it may be to the Glory of God, to their fpiritual and temporal Benefit,

fit, and for all Chriftians throughout the World. To this the Prieft fays *Amen,* and proceeds to fay certain Prayers ordained in the Miffal, onformable in Number and Subftance, to the Collects or Prayers which are faid before the Epiftle.

Theot, I obferve they are read privately; why fo?

Theoph. As they are read privately, or fecretly, they are ftiled in the Miffal *Secreta,* that is, the fecret Prayer, and are prefcribed to be faid fecretly, to intimate to us that the Prieft having invited all to pray, leaves them thus employed, while he in Silence prays for them, fpeaking to God, like *Anne* the Mother of holy *Samuel,* in his Heart, and only moves his Lips, his Voice not being at all heard, and therein reprefents alfo the Prayer of our Bleffed Saviour in the Garden, who retired from his Difciples that he might pray alone. Every one would do well to learn the Anfwer to the *Orate Fratres,* which the Clerk makes in their Name, and to fay it devouly, but filently, in *Latin* or *Englifh.*

Theot. All being thus prepared in Silence, how does the Prieft procced to the next Part of the Mafs, which, as I collect from what has been faid, is the principal Part of it, and requires a particular Explication.

Theoph. You are in the right. The next is the principal Part, or rather the whole

Sub-

Subſtance of the Maſs, or the holy Action contained in the *Canon,* which before he begins, with a loud Voice he recites the *Preface,* which may be called a preparatory Diſpoſition to the great Work of this Sacrifice. Hence the Prieſt endeavours to raiſe his own, and the Hearts of all preſent, gratefully to thank and praiſe God, that they may be better prepared to attend with due Reverence to the great Myſteries following. By ſome the Preface is called the *Angelical Song,* as being full of Angelical Praiſes. The *Greeks* call it a *cherubical* or *ſeraphical* Hymn. As the Maſs is a Repreſentation of the Paſſion of Chriſt, this Hymn, in its myſtical Senſe, may be ſaid to repreſent the Angel comforting our Bleſſed Lord in his Agony.

Theot. But why does the Prieſt, at the End of the Secret Prayers, ſay with a loud Voice, *Per omnia ſæcula ſæculorum.*

Theoph. Having ſaid the *Secreta,* he lays his Hands upon the Altar, to ſignify that he lays aſide all earthly Cogitations, that he may better employ his Mind to the Immolation of this great Sacrifice ; and making a little Pauſe between his Prayer and the Preface, he then raiſes his Voice, and ſays *for Ever and Ever,* or *World without End* ; making it the End of his Prayer, and the Beginning of the Preface. To this the Clerk, in the Name of the People, ſays *Amen,* to denote the Union of all preſent in Devotion,

E

and

and that they join their Vows, Suffrages, and Intentions with the Priest, who then says *Dominus Vobiscum, the Lord be with you,* by which he wishes all present may be so well disposed, that our Lord may vouchsafe to be with them. To this is answered, *Et cum Spiritu tuo, and with thy Spirit.* The People here reciprocally praying for the Priest, that our Lord may be with him, for the better performing this holy Action. He then says, *Sursum Corda, Lift up your Hearts,* admonishing the People to raise up their Hearts and Minds to heavenly Things, particularly to the heavenly and divine Mysteries about to be celebrated. St. *Augustine* says, the *Sursum Corda* is an Aversion from earthly Things, and an Elevation, or raising our Mind to God alone. And in another Place, speaking of this he says, " No " Man who remains ungrateful to the " Giver, is blessed by these Gifts ; we are " therefore, in the sacred Mysteries, bid " to have our Hearts lifted up, he helping " us, that we may be able to do that which " by his Command we are admonished to " do." Lib. de. Vid. In saying *Sursum, Corda,* the Priest lifts up his Hands and Eyes, that the exteriour Man may be conformable to the interiour, by lifting up the Heart with the Hands and Eyes. The Heart is principally required, for, as St. *Cyril* says, In the Mass we must have our Hearts lifted up to God, natural Expressions

ons of. which are the Elevation of the Hands and Eyes. To *Surfum Corda,* the People anſwer, *Habemus ad Dominum, We have our Hearts lifted up to the Lord.* Which St. *Cyprian* thus explicates; " When the " People anſwer *Habemus ad Dominum,* " they declare that they ought not to think " of any other Thing but of our Lord." Every one ought to take Care that here he does not give the Lie to himſelf, when he ſays, *Habemus ad Dominum,* and at the ſame Time have nothing leſs than their Hearts lifted up. After this the Prieſt ſays, *Gratias agamus Domino Deo noſtro. Let us give Thanks to the Lord our God* for all his Mercies and Benefits, particularly for this great Euchariſtick Sacrifice. To this is anſwered, *Dignum et juſtum eſt. It is meet and juſt* ſo to do. *Meet,* becauſe he is our ſovereign Lord. *Juſt,* becauſe we are his People. *Meet* and *Juſt* together, that we his Servants ſhould, together with the Prieſt, give Thanks to God, from whom we have received all Things. *Meet,* in Reſpect of his manifold Benefits. *Juſt,* in Regard of the Debt of Gratitude we owe to him for making us Partakers of the Treaſures of his Mercy in this Sacrifice. I would recommend to every one to conſider theſe Words, and learn to ſay them either in *Latin* or *Engliſh,* it would greatly help their Devotion, as they are full of Energy, and truly affecting.

E 2

Theor.

Theot. What you have been saying gives me the highest Satisfaction, nor do I expect less from what you are now to say concerning the Preface, which next comes under our Consideration, but I beg Leave to observe, the Preface is not always the same, as varying in some Times of the Year.

Theoph. True, there are different *Prefaces*, as to the Words, but are all the same in Substance, and all terminating in the same *Sanctus, Sanctus,* &c. The Difference arises from their being appropriated, some of them to the greater and more solemn Festivals of the Year, as One for *Christmas*, or the Nativity of Christ, which is also used on the Feast of the *Circumcision*, the holy Name *Jesus*, the Purification of the Blessed Virgin, the Feast of *Corpus Christi*, and during the Octave, and on the Feast of the *Transfiguration*. One for the *Epiphany*. One for *Lent*. One for *Passion Time*. One for the *Resurrection*, or *Easter*. One for the *Ascension*. One for *Whitsunday*, and One for *Trinity Sunday*. There is One for the Feasts of the *Blessed Virgin Mary*, One for the *Apostles*, and One for common Festivals and common Days, which is also used in Masses for the Dead. It is not necessary to explain them all, as it will sufficiently answer our present Purpose, to give you a brief Explication of the common, or daily Preface.

The

The Preface, as I have already obferved, is a preparatory Difpofition to the holy Action contained in the Canon. Thofe who underftand *Latin*, would do well to attend to it, as it is full of holy Unction, and affords abundant Matter of Devotion; for thofe who do not underftand *Latin*, or may not have it in *Englifh*, or who perhaps cannot read, a fhort Explication may be of Service to them, nor, I believe, difagreeable to you.

Theot. Not in the leaft. Pray, Sir, go on.

Theoph. The Prieft confirms the Anfwer the People made concerning giving Thanks to God, by telling them it is meet and juft, right and wholfome, to praife God, and to declare that he is our holy Lord, omnipotent Father, and eternal God, from whom all Sanctity comes. In the Preface the Intention of the Church is, that all her Children fhould unite their Hearts and Voices with the Angels and Archangels, and all the Powers of Heaven, in Praifing and adoring God with the profoundeft Humility and Devotion, both interiour and exteriour, efpecially at the End of the *Preface,* which always concludes with *Sanctus, Sanctus, Sanctus, &c.* or, *Holy, Holy, Holy, Lord God of Sabaoth, the Heavens and the Earth are full of thy Glory. Hofanna in the higheft, bleffed is he who comes in the Name of the Lord.*

 Hofanna

Hosanna in the highest. The first Part of this Conclusion of the Preface, *Holy, Holy, Holy, Lord God of Sabaoth,* is called by the *Greeks Trisagion,* on Account of *Sanctus* being repeated three Times, and is the Song or Canticle which the Angels in Heaven continually sing, as we learn from the Prophet *Isaias,* and St. *John* Evangelist, To which is added the Song of the *Hebrew* Multitude, with which they ushered our Blessed Saviour into *Jerusalem,* singing aloud, *Hosanna in the highest, &c.* In thus concluding the Preface, the Priest bows down with great Reverence, and all the People should bow down, or incline their Bodies, devoutly, but silently, saying it with him.

Theot. I observe the Clerk, or Server at Mass, rings a little Bell at this Time; why is this done?

Theoph. It is rung to excite the People to renew and stir up their Attention to the sacred Mysteries, the most solemn Part of which the Priest is entering upon in the Canon of the Mass. As also to let the People know what Part of the Mass the Priest is then at, necessary in large Churches, when full of People, and the Altar at a Distance, or the Priest's Voice but low, and not so well heard by those who are not very near. The ringing of this little Bell may seem to have some Analogy with what God ordained in the Old Law, that there

should

fhould be little Bells in the Hem of the
Prieft's Tunick, to the End that the found
might be heard when he went in and came
out of the Sanctuary, in the Sight of the
Lord; which was to move the People to
due Reverence to the Prieftly Function, and
t. an humble Adoration of God's Majefty
in that holy Place. In like Manner the
Church ufes a little Bell, which here in
England we call *Sanctus Bell*. The Canon
of the Mafs follows next. That, if you
pleafe, fhall be the Subject of our next
Converfation.

Theot. I am content. Adieu for the prefent.

HOLY ALTAR

AND

SACRIFICE Explained.

PART II.

DIALOGUE X.

On the MASS.

The CANON.

Theophilus. I Am glad to see you, *Theo-time*, and can eafily guefs at the Purport of your Vifit this Morning.

Theotime. It is not hard to guefs at my Intention in it after the Converfation we have had. Without any farther Preamble then, pleafe now to explicate the remaining

ing Part of the Holy Mafs, beginning with the Canon.

Theoph. Willingly. Here begins the fecond Part of the Mafs, and requires a ferious Attention. After the Preface the Prieft begins the Canon, which is a *Greek* Word, fignifying a Rule or Order to be obferved in what we are to do, and is applied to this Part of the Mafs, becaufe it is always the fame, and conftantly obferved in all Maffes that are faid. In the Miffal it is called the *Action*, fo named by way of Excellency, as it contains the Confecration and Converfion of the Bread and Wine into the Body and Blood of our Saviour. It is alfo called *Sacrifice*, for in it the Sacrifice of the Mafs is principally accomplifhed. The Name of *Secretum*, is given to it, as being a fecret or private Myftery, belonging only and folely to the Prieft, nor is to be faid by any one but the Prieft, and by him to be faid in fecret, that is, with a low Voice, as the Rubricks of the Miffal prefcribe, and not as fome do, aloud, in direct Contradiction to the Rubricks, and Prefcript of the Church. Here you are to obferve that, although the Mafs is principally ordained as a Reprefentation of Chrift's Paffion, in Memory of which it is inftituted, yet there is in the Canon a Renovation of Chrift's laft Supper. Hence *Durandus,* with Pope *Innocent* I. fay, that in the Canon the Words fignify one Thing,

 and

and the Signs or Ceremonies fignify another; for the Words principally belong to
the Confecration of the Eucharift; but
the Signs chiefly appertain to the Remembrance of Chrift's Paffion. The Words are
in order to the Converfion of the Bread
and Wine, but the Signs or Ceremonies
here before the Elevation, are in Regard of
what happened before his Crucifixion, and
after in Regard of what he fuffered on the
Crofs.

Theot. I beg Pardon for interrupting you;
but before we proceed, tell me why is the
Canon faid in fecret?

Theoph. For the following Reafons: 1ft.
The perpetual Cuftom of the Church
from the Apoftles Times, which may be
fufficient to fatisfy the devout Chriftian.
2d. The Prieft now turns his Mind wholly
to God, with whom alone he is now to
treat for himfelf and all the Faithful, and
that he may do this with greater Fervour
and Devotion, and with greater interiour
Recollection pray for the People, as their
Mediator between God and them, in this
holy and facred Action. *Hugo de Sanĉto
Viĉore,* and *Alcivinus,* give a third Reafon,
for that it is a fecret Myftery, not to be di-
vulged to the common People, left the principal Words in this Sacrifice fhould lofe
their Efteem. So that we may fay, this
fecret Manner of reciting the Canon, is
out of Reverence to the facred Action, and
                                          the

the Words of Confecration. Hereby is alfo
reprefented the Silence of our Bleffed Saviour in his Sufferings; for though he
wrought the great Work of our Redemption, he did it alone, and was filent during
the greateft Part of his Paffion.

Theot. I am fully fatisfied with your Anfwer, and the Reafons given. Proceed to
explain the Canon; but give me Leave to
propofe any Queftion that may occur to
me.

Theoph. Do fo: The more Queftions you
afk, the more Occafion I fhall have to explicate to you every Part of this holy Sacrifice, and to which you will pleafe to
continue your Attention.

In the Beginning of the Canon the Prieft
lifts up his Eyes, opens and joins his Hands,
making humble Supplication to Almighty
God, that he would accept of, and give a
Blefling to his Action, renewing his Oblation, and fpecifying thofe, for whom he is
to offer this Sacrifice; which alfo may reprefent Jefus Chrift freely offering himfelf
to the Jews, in order to his Paffion, and
alfo freely offering himfelf to his heavenly
Father, for the Redemption of Mankind.
The Prieft opens his Hands, and lifts them
up to fhew he is ready for the Performance
of his Function, and then joins them, to
fignify his being bound to do God's Will,
to whom he lifts up his Eyes, expecting
Power and Grace from him to perform
this

this Action right, in hopes of which he lays his Hands upon the Altar, and with humble Confidence and Assurance kisses it.

Theot. Why does the Priest make three Crosses on the Host and Chalice?

Theoph. Knowing that what he is to do principally depends upon the Passion of our Saviour, he makes the Sign of the Cross three Times in Honour of him who is Three in One, by whose Power alone the following Work of Consecration, or Conversion of the Bread and Wine, is to be made; and to declare that the whole Mystery of this Sacrifice is to be wrought by the marvellous Power of the most holy Trinity. St. *James,* St. *Chrysostome,* and St. *Basil,* have the same Ceremonies in their Liturgies. These Crosses, in the mystical Signification of them, represent the threefold Delivery of our blessed Saviour: 1. God the Father delivered his only begotten Son to us by his Incarnation. 2. *Judas* delivered him to the *Jews.* 3. The *Jews* delivered him to *Pontius Pilate* to be crucified. The first was of Grace. God so loved us, as he gave his only begotten Son for us. The second was of Avarice. *Judas* asked what they would give him. The third was of Envy. *Pilate* knew that for Envy they had delivered him. The Priest then proceeds to pray, that this Sacrifice may be acceptable to God, and profitable to his holy Church in general. Praying for the Peace, Union, Protection,

and

and Direction of it.   For its Peace,
that we may ferve God in Peace ; for its
Union, that it may be free from all Schifms,
be protected againft all Herefies, and directed by the Holy Ghoft. Secondly, he
prays for the chief Paftor of the Church,
the Pope, as it has been the Cuftom in
all Ages, that, as *Alcivinus* obferves, *the
Union of Charity and Faith of the Members,
with the vifible Head of the vifible Church,
may be prefented to God.*   Thirdly, for the
Bifhop of the Diocefe or Diftrict, for fo St.
Paul commands us, to remember our Prelates.   Fourthly, for the King, Prince, or
State under whom he lives, that God would
direct them in their Government, that in
Peace and Juftice they may rule their Subjects.   This is the Advice of St. *Paul*, to
pray for all Men, for Kings, and all who
are in Power and Pre-eminence.   Fifthly,
for all the Faithful in general ; for all Ec-
clefiaftical Orders, *Minifters and Preachers*
of God's Word ; for all who labour for the
Converfion of Souls ; and for all who are
in any manner of Neceffity, fpiritual or
temporal.   After this follows the firft *Memento,* called the *Memento* of the Living.

Theot. What means this *Memento ?*

Theot. It means the particular remem-
bring, or filent Mention of thofe particular Perfons or Things for which the Prieft
more efpecially prays : Having prayed in
general, for thofe for whom he ought
always

always to pray, in Silence and Recollection, he specifies mentally those for whom in particular he applies his Mass, or these to whom he may have any particular Obligation; as his Parents, Patrons, or those on whom he may have any particular Dependence; for particular Friends or Benefactors, from whom he may have Help, Charity, or Assistance : He is also to pray for all who are present at Mass. The Church requires this of him as Part of his Function; and God ordained in the Old Law, that the Priest, at the Altar, should pray for the People, and therefore the Priest prays here for all who are present at Mass, and for their Intentions, supposing that their Vows and Intentions are to hear Mass for themselves, and those now mentioned; hence he prays that this Sacrifice may be for the Good of their Souls, and for their spiritual and corporal Safety. The Priest having finished his Memento, opens his Hands and goes on, invocating the blessed Virgin, the holy Apostles, Martyrs, and all the Saints, to help him, by their Prayers, in this sacred Action.

Theot. I shall be glad to know the Reason of here invocating the Saints ?

Theoph. In Answer to this Question, I must observe to you in the first Place, that in all the ancient Liturgies we find this Commemoration and Invocation of the Saints; and herein the Church imitates the
Royal

oyal Prophet, and the *Hebrew* Children in the Furnace, inviting the Angels, Saints, and all Creatures, to praife our Lord; and having, in the Preface, invited the Angels, fo here fhe invites all the Saints to praife God in this wonderful Work of his Love and Goodnefs manifefted to us in the holy Eucharift. Three Things are here to be taken Notice of: 1. The *Communicantes*, or Communion of the Saints. 2. The venerable Memory of the Saints. 3. The Confidence we may have in their Merits and Prayers. We profefs, in our Creed, the Communion of Saints, wherein we profefs to believe, that we have a Communion, not only with the Faithful on Earth, but alfo with the Angels and Saints in Heaven. In the Preface we exprefled our Communion with the Angels; here with the Saints, that they may affift us in the Praifes of God, as here is the fame Object which they contemplate in Heaven; and that they, here with us, may praife our common Lord, that fo the Church Militant, united to the whole Church Triumphant, may worthily receive our great Lord and Mafter, coming to us in this holy Sacrifice. 2. The venerable Memory of the Saints: *Memoriam venerantes.* Of this St. *Auftin* makes mention, faying, " We honour their Memories as Saints of " God.——We offer only to him as both " their God and ours, at which Offering " thofe Conquerors of the World, as Men

" of

" of God, has each one his peculiar Com-
" memoration ;" Lib. de Civit Dei. c. 27.
which, as St. *Chryfoſtome* obſerves, Lib. 22.
c. 10. is to their Honour, and this Honour the Catholic Church has always, and
in all Ages, paid to them, and thereby
endeavours to keep the Memory of the
Saints in the Hearts of the Faithful. The
third Thing to be taken Notice of, is the
Confidence in their Merits and Prayers,
which the Prieſt humbly begs, that, by
their Aſſiſtance, he may obtain Grace from
God rightly and duly to perform this moſt
holy Action. Conformable to this, the
Words of St. *Auſtin* deſerve to be taken
Notice of. " We do not," ſays this holy
Father, " make Mention or Memory of
" the Martyrs at our Lord's Table as of
" others, but rather to the End that they
" may pray for us, and that we may imi-
" tate and follow them." Again, he ſays,
" It were an Injury to the Martyrs to pray
" for them, to whoſe Prayers we ought to
" commend ourſelves." Tract. 4. in Joan.
The myſtical Signification of this Part of
the Maſs, may be a Repreſentation to us
of Chriſt ſitting at the Table with his twelve
Apoſtles, for here the Church names twelve
Apoſtles, joining to them twelve Martyrs,
as to accompany the Prieſt in this holy Sacrifice.

Theot. Pleaſe to go on and explain what
follows, for I am highly ſatisfied with the
Expli-

Explications you have given me hitherto.

Theoph. After this Memory of the Saints the Prieſt returns to his Oblation, humbly begging of God that it may be *bleſſed, adſcribed, ratified, rational,* and *acceptable:* 'That it may be made to us the Body and Blood of his moſt beloved Son our Lord Jeſus Chriſt. He prays here, that by this Oblation we may be *bleſſed* in heavenly Things. 2. That we may be *adſcribed* or numbered among the Elect. 3. That we may be confirmed and eſtabliſhed in all Good. 4. That our Duty may be a *rational* or reaſonable Service, according to St. *Paul.* 5. That by it we may be acceptable to God. St. *Auſtin* thus expounds it. " *Bleſſed,* " by which we may be bleſſed in Heaven. " *Adſcribed,* by which we may be enrolled " in Heaven. *Ratified,* by which we may " be thought to be true Members of the " Church. *Rational,* or different from " all Sacrifices of Beaſts : And *Acceptable,* " that we may be acceptable to God in his " only Son." In this Prayer of Oblation the Church ſpecifies the End, or chief Thing aimed at in this Sacrifice, which is the Converſion of the Bread and Wine into the Body and Blood of Chriſt.

Theot. I muſt here aſk you, why the Prieſt extends his Hands over the Hoſt and Chalice ; and on what Account he makes five Croſſes ?

Theoph.

Theoth. The fpreading of his Hands by the Prieft over the Oblate, is done by way of Submiffion of his Action to the divine Power, acknowledging thereby that he depends wholly thereon, without which no created Power could have any Effect in the Confecration. The Impofition of Hands is likewife a Symbol or Sign of Authority, and therefore in this Oblation the Prieft lays his Hands over the Things offered; and as, according to the Church's Order he lays his Hand over thofe who are baptized or abfolved, fo here he lays his Hands over the Hoft and Chalice, to teftify that this great Work of Confecration is to be done by Vertue of his Ordination, which he received by Impofition of Hands. The Prieft makes five Croffes, to fhew that all his Confidence is in the Merits and Virtue of Chrift's Paffion, reprefented in the Sign of the Crofs, which he makes here five Times. The three firft reprefent God the Father, to whom this Oblation is made: The Son who offers it, and the Holy Ghoft who tranfubftantiates or converts the Bread and Wine: The two following Croffes fignify the Divinity and Humanity of Jefus Chrift under one Subftance, who is to accomplifh the Myftery of the Crofs in this Sacrifice.

Theot. How do you explain what is faid in this Prayer, *That it may be made the Body and Blood of our Lord,* &c.

Theoth.

Theoph. This Prayer may be confidered as a Preamble to the principal Act of this Sacrifice, or the Confecration, in order to which the Prieft makes this Prayer, and which we find to have been ufed in the very early and primitive Times, as appears from the Liturgies of St. *Clement,* St. *Bafil,* St. *John Chryfoftome,* and from all the antient Liturgies of the Church. We will now proceed to confider the great and principal Part of this Sacrifice, the Confecration.

Theot. As you pleafe; but I had rather defer that till I can have the Pleafure to fee you again, as Bufinefs now obliges me to leave you for the prefent.

Theoph. Adieu then; but come again foon.

Theot. Fear not: I will be with you To-morrow Morning.

D I A L O G U E XI.

On the M A S S.

The Confecration.

Theophilus. I Find *Theotime* a Man of his Word. He is punctual to his Time, and I am ready for him.

Theot.

Theot. You are truly obliging, *Theophi-lus.* I must then desire you to continue your Explication of the Holy Mass. In our last Conference, we left off at the *Con-secration,* and there, if you please, we will now begin.

Theoph. By the Consecration we are to under-stand the Action, or Conversion of the Bread and Wine into the Body and Blood of Jesus Christ, made by the Power of God : The Priest performing this Action in the Person of Christ, whose Actions and Signs, or Ce-remonies in his last Supper, are here repre-sented and applied by the Priest, according as our Saviour himself did leave it in his Church ; and such has been the Belief and Practice of the Church in all Times since Christ. If we look back to Antiquity, we shall find St. *Justin Martyr* affirming, that the Eucharist is consecrated by the Power of the Word which we have received from Christ. St. *Gregory* of *Nyssen* says, " This " Bread, as the Apostle faith, is sanctified " by the Word of God and Prayer, by " which Word the Transmutation is made, " to wit, This is my Body." In another Place he says, " The Bread, in the Be- " ginning, is common Bread ; but when " the Mystery is sacrificed, it is called, and " is the Body of Christ, in the same man- " ner the Wine." In Orat. Catech. b. 37. St. *Cyril,* of *Jerusalem,* speaks in the same Strain, and not to trouble you with too

many

many Citations, will only add the Testimony of St. *Ambrose,* or the antient Author of this Work attributed to St. *Ambrose.* " This Bread is Bread before the sacra-" mental Words; but when the Conse-" cration is added, from Bread it is made " Christ's Flesh. Let us prove this: How " can that which is Bread be Christ's Flesh? " By Consecration. With what Words " then is the Consecration made, or with " whose Words? With those of our Lord " Jesus Christ.——When the venerable Sa-" crament is to be consecrated, the Priest " then uses not his own, but Christ's " Words." Lib. 4. de Sac. c. 4.

Theot. I observe that the Priest, immediately before the Consecration, takes the Host in his Hand, and lifting up his Eyes, makes the Sign of the Cross on it: Did Christ do so?

Theoph. We have not, indeed, any Mention of our blessed Saviour doing this, either in the Evangelists or St. *Paul,* in the Account they give of the Institution of the blessed Eucharist; yet, as we learn from the sacred Oracles, that Christ often lifted up his Eyes to Heaven when he wrought his miraculous Cures, so we may piously believe, according to the Tradition of the Church, that here he did lift up his Eyes, in this greatest of his Works. St. *Clement* relates it, and it is found in the Liturgy of St. *Peter,* or that which is attributed to

him

him, and is very ancient; as also in the Liturgies of St. *James* and St. *Basil*. Doubtless Chrift did not make the Sign of the Crofs, but the Prieft being his Vicegerent or Deputy, has juft Reafon to lift up his Eyes to Heaven, from whence only he expects Power and Virtue to do this Action that the Holy Ghoft may affift him in this great Work. He makes the Sign of the Crofs, by Virtue whereof, that is, the Merits and Paffion of Jefus Chrift, he receives a Power to blefs the Hoft, fhewing, by it, the Badge of his Commiffion, and acknowledging that as his Ordination was made with the Sign of the Crofs, fo here he executes it by the fame.

Theot. After the Confecration the Prieft kneels down : Why this ?

Theoph. Having finifhed the Words of Confecration, the Prieft kneels with great Humility and Devotion, to adore Jefus Chrift, there truly and really prefent on the Altar, and under the facramental Species, and to excite all the People to kneel down and adore, humbling themfelves in the Prefence of Jefus Chrift, true God and true Man. If the Jews, when *Mofes* related to them the Ceremonies and Rites of the Pafchal Lamb, bowed themfelves and adored, with much greater Reafon Chriftians adore the true Lamb, Jefus Chrift, really prefent. If when *Mofes* entered the Tabernacle in a cloudy Pillar, wherein an

Angel

Angel fpoke to him, the People adored, furely Chriftians ought to adore Jefus Chrift here on the Altar ; and, if when Fire came down from Heaven and confumed the Holocauft, and the Temple was filled with Glory, the Children of *Ifrael* feeing it fell flat on the Earth, adoring and praifing God. Shall not Chriftians bend their Knees and adore the true King of Glory, the eternal Word of the Father in this great Sacrifice, of which all the former Holocaufts, Victims, and Sacrifices, were but Figures and Shadows. .

Theot. All this I readily allow ; but why does the Prieft elevate, or hold up the Hoft ?

Theoph. He does this to excite all prefent to join him in this proper Act of Humility and Adoration, thereby to profefs their firm Faith and Belief of this facred Myftery, and with exteriour as well as interiour Devotion, to make Acts of Adoration, by humbly bowing down the Body, lifting up the Hands and ftriking the Breaft. Now this Elevation was always ufed in the Church, as is apparent from the antient Liturgies, St. *Bafil*'s, St. *Chryfoftome*'s, and is the Cuftom of the *Ethiopians*, Oriental *Indians*, *Grecians*, &c. and is juftly retained in the Church.

Theot. But, will not fome fay this favours of Idolatry ?

Theoph.

Theoph. Nothing can be more unreason-
able, or more unjuſt, than to charge Catholics with Idolatry on this Account.　If
it was Bread and Wine we adored, or if
the Species of Bread and Wine were the
Object of our Adoration, the Charge would
hold good againſt us, but nothing leſs than
Ignorance, or the higheſt Prejudice, can
ſuppoſe this.　Catholics, believing that in
the bleſſed Sacrament there is really and
truly the Body of Chriſt, both God and
Man. He and He only is the Object of their
Adoration: A divine Object God himſelf
in his Humanity; there can therefore be
nothing of Idolatry in the Action, for in
it we adore Jeſus Chriſt, true God as well
true Man.

Theot. Are there no further Reaſons to
be aſſigned for this Elevation? I would
willingly know, as alſo why a little Bell is
rung at this Time.

Theoph. This Elevation of the holy Hoſt
in its myſtical Signification, may be conſidered as a Circumſtance agreeable to the
Oblation, and a Repreſentation of Chriſt
elevated on the Croſs. The Conſecration
being made, the Oblation is perfected by
this Elevation as a Circumſtance making
it compleat. The ſeraphical Doctor, St.
Bonaventure ſays, that " in the Elevation
" the ſacred Hoſt is ſhewn to God the Fa-
" ther, to obtain the Grace we have loſt
" by our Sins; as if the Prieſt ſhould ſay:
" O

" O heavenly Father, we have finned and
" provoked thy Wrath, but now behold
" the Face of Chrift thy Son, whom we
" prefent to thee, and who has moved thee
" from Anger to Mercy." In Expof. Myf.
Hugo à St. Victor tells, " That when we
" come to Chrift's Words, the Prieft lifts
" up on high both, that is, the holy Hoft
" and Chalice, fignifying this Meat and
" this Drink is more excellent than all
" other, for it is the moft excellent of all
" Sacraments." In Spec. Eccl. c. 9.   *Durandus,* among other Reafons, gives this,
That all prefent may fee, adore, and afk
whatfoever may be profitable for their Souls.
The laft Thing fignified by this Elevation is,
that beholding the fame Chrift who fuffered
fo much for us, we may be moved to be willing to fuffer fomething for him. The little
Bell is rung to make all prefent attentive to
the facred Action, to recollect their Minds,
that they may devoutly proftrate and adore
Jefus Chrift their Saviour, dying on the
Crofs for their Redemption. It is alfo rung
that thofe who in large Churches may be
at a Diftance, and not fee the Prieft's
Actions, or perhaps are otherways diftract-
ed, or intent on their private Prayers, may
know that the Prieft is at the Elevation,
and confequently bow down and adore Jefus Chrift.

F

Thee.

Theot. I see most People, at the Time of the Elevation, knock their Breast. Why this Ceremony?

Theoph. For many Reasons. Knocking the Breast is oftentimes done to express Admiration. God, as the royal Psalmist observes, *Psal.* cx. has made a Memorial of his marvellous Work. He is truly marvellous in all his Works, but in none so much as in this, and we have great Reason here to admire his infinite Goodness and Love in so humbling himself, not only to become Man for us, but also to give himself to be our Food, thus exalting us above the Angels. We may well stand in Admiration, and strike our Breast in considering this incomparable and wonderful Goodness. To knock our Breast is also a natural Sign of Sorrow and Grief. Since then in the Elevation is presented to us the dolorous and affecting Object, Christ suffering on the Cross, no wonder if devout Christians knock their Breasts to testify the Compassion they have for his cruel Sufferings. Many do it with Reflections upon, and with deep Sorrow for their Sins, as the Cause of his cruel Sufferings, and in Acknowledgment of their Unworthiness of so great a Good. We may likewise be said here to imitate the devout Multitude who were present at Christ's Passion, and when they saw the Things which were done, returned knocking their Breasts.

Theot.

Theot. I am perfectly satisfied with what you have said of the Consecration and Elevation of the Hoft: Favour me now with fomething of the Confecration and Elevation of the Chalice. But firft, what do you mean by the Chalice?

Theoph. The Chalice is a Cup wherein is contained the Wine that is to be confecrated. The Evangelifts tell us that Chrift took the Cup into his Hands and having bleffed it, gave it to his Difciples. In the Form of Confecration it is called the Chalice of Chrift's Blood. This is the Chalice which *Paul* calls the Chalice of Benediction, affirming it to be the Communication of the Blood of Chrift, concerning which *Theophylact*, and other antient Fathers fay; that which is in the Chalice is that which flowed from Chrift's Side; and receiving, we communicate, that is, we are united to Chrift. As to the Confecration of the Chalice, the fame may be faid of it, as was before faid of the Confecration of the Bread. The Prieft in the Perfon of Chrift, imitating his Actions and Words, confecrates the Chalice, calling it as Chrift did, the *New Teftament unto Remiffion of Sins.* What has been faid of the Adoration of the holy Hoft, is to be faid of the Adoration of the Chalice, for it is done in the fame Manner, and for the fame Reafons, as being the felf-fame Thing, under different Species, or outward Forms. The like to

be

be faid of this Elevation, and therefore not neceffary to be repeated again.

Theot. Since, as you fay, it is the fame in both, why is the Confecration and Elevation of the Chalice, made feparately and apart from that of the Hoft?

Theoph. The Example of our Saviour, his Command to the Apoftles, *Do this in Remembrance of me,* and the Practice of the Church in all Ages, as plainly appears in all Liturgies, is more than a fufficient Reafon for it; yet, you will pleafe to obferve what St. *Paul* fays, 1 *Cor.* xi. As often as you fhall eat this Bread, and drink this Chalice, you fhall fhew forth the Death of our Lord. This could not be fo well reprefented in one Species as in both; and both together, they more fully reprefent Chrift's Death and Paffion. Further, both Species are requifite to correfpond with the Nature of Chrift's Priefthood, which, as the Pfalmift and St. *Paul* fay, is according to the Order of *Melchifedeck.* In Pfal. 33. Hence St. *Auftine* fays, that he *inftituted a Sacrifice of his Body and Blood, according to the Order of Melchifedeck.* And St. *Cyprian*, " Who " is more a Prieft of the High God than " our Lord Jefus Chrift, who offered Sa- " crifice to God the Father, and offered " the very fame which *Melchifedeck* had of- " fered, that is, Bread and Wine, to wit, " his Body and Blood." Ep. 65.

Theot.

Theot. May it not be here said, that as there are two Species, there are two Sacrifices ?

Theoph. By no Means. The Bread and Wine are different Things, and in a different Manner signify Chrift's Body as our Food, and Chrift's Blood as our Drink, and so make the full Refection of our Souls, both making but one perfect Sacrament, inasmuch as they contain the same one Chrift, God and Man in Flesh and Blood, which are equally contained under the Species of Bread, as under the Species of Wine, for the Body and Blood is equally in the one and in the other, producing the same Effect of Grace and Glory. In like Manner these two Species make but one Sacrifice, as they signify one bloody Sacrifice made by Chrift on the Crofs, in the Effufion of his Blood, and Separation of his Soul from his Body, which is not so exprefsly signified under one only Species ; and the two Confecrations do not multiply the Sacrifice no more than the daily Oblations which the Priefts make in all Places of the World. On this St. *Ambrofe* thus delivers himfelf ; " Do we not offer every " Day ? Surely we do. We offer always " the felf-fame, and not now one Lamb, " and To-morrow another, but always the " fame. Therefore it is one Sacrifice, it is " one Chrift in every Place, here entire, " and there entire in one Body : But this

F 3 " which

" which we do, is done for a Commemo-
" ration of that which was done, for we
" offer not another Sacrifice, as the High
" Priests of the Old Law, but always the
" self-same." In fine, though the Species
be different, the Actions of the Priest
various, and the Confecrations distinct;
yet it is the same Thing offered, and the
same Offerer Jesus Christ, who did offer it
to his Father, and by his Priests, as his
Ministers, continually offers it, and will
do so to the End of the World. So that as
the Mass is an Application of one and the
same Passion, so the Priests by their mini-
sterial Actions, concur to the same Sacrifice which Christ made at his last Supper.

Theot. Has not the Elevation of the
Chalice some particular Signification?

Theoph. Yes: It represents our Saviour
continuing on the Cross, and principally
the Blood and Water, which, by piercing
his Side, flowed from his sacred Body. It
likewise represents the Separation of Christ's
holy Soul from his sacred Body. But, now
I will give a little Respite to your Attention, and defer any further Explication
of these sacred Mysteries, till we meet again.

Theot. Agreed; but you must expect to
see me very soon.

Theoph. Whenever you please, I shall be
glad to see you.

D I A-

DIALOGUE XII.

On the MASS.

Theotime. YOU fee, *Theophilus*, I am come again to trouble you.

Theophilus. Had you ftaid away till I thought you troublefome, I fhould not have the Pleafure I enjoy in your Company, nor have now wifhed you a good Day.

Theotime. Compliments apart; favour me now with an Explication of what follows the Elevation in the Holy Mafs.

Theoph. After the Elevation, the Prieft addreffes himfelf to God in three devout Prayers, and therein imitates our Bleffed Saviour, who offered up this Sacrifice on the Crofs to his Eternal Father, for the Salvation of Mankind, fo here the Prieft immediately makes an Oblation thereof, expreffing the Intentions he has in the offering this holy Sacrifice; continuing, or by Degrees afcending, from the Oblation which formerly he made of Bread and Wine, now to make it of the true Body and Blood of our Saviour. In thefe Prayers he joins the People with him, that all who are prefent may alfo offer, and join with him in Prayer, that the Sacrifice may have the defired Effect, as it is their Oblation as well as his, different only in the Miniftry of the Action, which only and properly belongs to the Prieft.

Theet. I obferve that the Prieft in this Part of the Mafs makes feveral Croffes: Let me know why, and the Meaning of them.

Theoph. The Church ordains the Sign of the Crofs to be often made in the Mafs, efpecially in the Canon, both before and after the Confecration, but differently in their Meaning. The Croffes made before, are in order to the Confecration, by way of Benediction to the Matter, that is, the Bread and Wine. After Confecration they are made as reprefentative, or fignificative, to renew in our Minds Chrift's Paffion. The Croffes before fignify the feveral Paffages of his Paffion, before he was nailed to the Crofs. Thofe after fignify what he fuffered on the Crofs, and are confequently applied thereto in what follows. Here the Prieft makes five Croffes, which fignify the five precious Wounds in his Hands, Feet, and Side. Of thefe the three firft are made over the Hoft and Chalice together; the fourth over the Holy Hoft, and the fifth over the Chalice. Thefe two laft being made feparate, reprefent the Confequence of his bitter Pains, the Separation of his holy Soul from his Body. Now, as to the Antiquity of making thefe Croffes in Time

of

of Mafs, we find the Practice in all the Church Liturgies, and all Expofitors for 800 Years make mention of them.

Theot. Why, after this, does the Prieft bow down, and lay his Hands joined on the Altar?

Theoph. Proceeding in his Prayer of Supplication, he bows down to fhew the Humility of his Heart, and by his joined Hands reprefents the united Defires of the Faithful prefent. Thus inclining, as expecting God's Mercy and Goodnefs, he prays that God would be propitious to him by this Oblation, in an humble Confidence of which he kiffes the Altar, in Token of Reconciliation with God, by Virtue of this Holy Sacrifice.

Theot. You muft now tell me why he makes three more Croffes.

Theoph. To intimate to us, that as Chrift had offered his Body on the Crofs, fo from the Crofs he offered his Blood for our Redemption. The firft Crofs is on the Hoft; the fecond on the Chalice; and the third on the Prieft himfelf, to fignify, that by the Oblation of his Body, and Effufion of his Blood alone, we muft come to receive the aforefaid Effects of celeftial Benediction.

Theot. I take Notice, that from the firft Elevation, till the Communion inclufive, the Prieft holds his Thumb and Forefinger of each Hand joined together. Give me a Reafon for it.

F 5

Theoph.

Theoph. I will give you three Reasons: First, Out of Reverence, not to touch any Thing after touching the sacred Body of Christ. Secondly, It denotes that the Mind and Body of the Priest ought to be united and joined together in the Action of the Sacrifice. Thirdly, A natural Cause, left any Particle of the Host remaining on the Fingers, should fall on the Altar, or on the Ground.

Theot. The next Thing that occurs is the second *Memento*, which you will please to explain to me.

Theoph. This is called the second *Memento*. The first was that wherein the Living were prayed for, and in this the Priest prays for the Dead, according to the antient Custom of the Church in all her Liturgies. In this *Memento* the Priest specifies any particular Person or Persons, for whose Soul he may say Mass, or desires in a particular Manner to recommend to God, as also all the Faithful departed, that they may obtain eternal Peace and Rest in the Fruition of God in Heaven. Here it is to be observed, that in praying for the Dead, the Church only prays for those who being Baptized, made a Profession of the true Faith, and were Members of her Communion, and died in a State of Grace. Concerning which St. *Austine* thus delivers himself:

" When

. " When Sacrifices, either of the Altar
" or of whatsoever Alms are offered for
" the Dead, who have been Baptized, for
" those who are very Good, they are only
" Thanksgivings; for those who are not
" very Evil, or Wicked, they are Propiti-
" ations; for those who are very Wicked,
" or Evil, they are no Helps when they
" are Dead, whatsoever the Living do for
" them : But to whom they are profitable,
" they profit to this, that they may have
" full Remission; or, that their Punish-
" ment may be made more tolerable."
In Enchis. c. xi.

Theot. Why is praying for the Dead af-
signed to this Place in the Mass ?

Theoph. To alledge the Custom of the
Church in all Ages, and in all her Liturgies, might be esteemed Reason sufficient ;
but I will give you another, and very rational Motive, drawn from that Article of
our Creed, *the Communion of Saints*, which
includes not only the Faithful on Earth,
but also the Angels and Saints in Heaven,
and the Souls departed, detained in a Suffering State, as not having satisfied divine
Justice, or attoned for their Sins in this
Life, yet partake of this Communion on
Account of their true Faith, Devotion, and
Piety when living, and accordingly are
more or less capable to share in the Suffrages and Prayers of the Living, and of
this Oblation. Hence the Church having
re-

reprefented the Communion of the Angels and Saints, as alfo of the Faithful prefent and abfent, who, in their feveral Degrees, concur to the Oblation of this Sacrifice, makes a Remembrance of thofe who cannot actively concur, but by the Mercy and Goodnefs of God, are capable to receive proportionably to their State, the Effects of this Sacrifice, and therefore after the Oblation is completed, fhe thus prays for the Dead.

Another Reafon may alfo be affigned; namely, The Mafs being a Reprefentation of Chrift's Paffion, as in each Part of it may be obferved: In this the Church reprefents the Defcent of Chrift into Hell, according to another Article of the Creed, *He defcended into Hell,* that is, into Limbo, to deliver the antient holy Fathers, and others, from the Prifons wherein they were detained, as St. *Irænæus* fays; *Chrift defcended to them, to draw them out and to fave them.* In Signification of which the Church here prays for Releafement of the Souls in Purgatory, by an Application of the Death and Paffion of Jefus Chrift.

Theot. Go on.   What follows next?

Theoph. The Prieft having thus prayed for the Dead, returns to pray for himfelf, and for all prefent, under the Title of Sinners, whereof he efteems himfelf one, and raifing his Voice, he ftrikes his Breaft, faying, *Nobis quoque Peccatoribus;* and to us

Sin-

Sinners. It is, indeed, one of the moſt proper Titles we can give ourſelves; for ſhould the Prieſt, or any preſent, think themſelves otherwiſe, they would not be worthy of this holy Sacrament, according to that of St. *John; if we ſay that we have no Sin, we ſeduce ourſelves, and the Truth is not in us.* St. *John,* c. i. The Prieſt then in his own Perſon confeſſes himſelf ſuch, and preſuming the ſame of all preſent, he implores the Mercy of God for himſelf and them. He raiſes his Voice that all preſent may hear and attend to what ſo much concerns them. He ſtrikes his Breaſt, that he may by this outward Action expreſs the interiour Humility and Sorrow of his Heart, after the Example of the Publican, who knocking his Breaſt ſaid, *God be merciful to me a Sinner.* St. *Luke,* c. xvii. So the Prieſt here, by ſtriking his Breaſt, virtually cries out, Lord be merciful and propitious to us Sinners. After this he proceeds to pray for the greateſt Effect of this Sacrifice, viz. the Participation of, and Society with the Apoſtles, Martyrs, and all the Saints, that God out of his infinite Mercy would pardon our Sins, and admit us into their holy Company. After this the Prieſt makes the Sign of the Croſs ſeveral Times, elevates the Hoſt and Chalice a little, and concludes the Canon of the Maſs with theſe Words, *Per omnia Sæcula Sæculorum, for Ever and Ever. Amen.*

Theot.

Theot. Pray tell me the Meaning of this?

Theoph. The Prieſt makes three Croſſes with the holy Hoſt over the Chalice, to repreſent the three Hours during which Chriſt hung on the Croſs; as alſo to ſignify that all Things are ſanctified, vivified, and bleſſed by the Virtue of the Croſs and Paſſion of Jeſus Chriſt. Theſe three Croſſes may alſo denote, that the Redemption of Mankind was wrought by the joint Co-operation of the Bleſſed Trinity. He then makes two Croſſes between the Chalice and himſelf, thereby ſignifying the Blood and Water which flowed from our Saviour's Side, and then raiſes up, or elevates a little, the Hoſt and Chalice, myſtically repreſent-ing the taking down our Bleſſed Saviour from the Croſs; and places them again on the Corporal, to put us in Mind of the Syndon, or white Linen Cloths, with which his ſacred Body was wrapped and laid in the Grave by St. *Joſeph* of *Arima-thea.* Laſtly, The Prieſt concludes the ſa-cred Action with giving all Honour and Glory to God, and deſires it may be ren-dered to him by Angels and Men, *for Ever and Ever, World without End. Amen.* Having now conſidered the Canon of the Maſs as the principal and eſſential Part of it; at our next Meeting I will explain to you the Remaining Part, beginning with the *Pater Noſter,* but muſt defer that for

the

the prefent, as a little Bufinefs calls me out of Town, and it will be a Week or ten Days before I return.

Theot. I wifh you a good Journey, and hope you will let me know, by a Card, when you are come back.

Theoph. You may depend upon my doing it.

D I A L O G U E XIII.

On the M A S S.

The Pater Nofter, &c.

Theotime. TO anfwer your obliging Meffage, I wait upon you, my dear Friend, and with Pleafure welcome you to Town. If you are at Leifure I fhall be glad to refume our Converfation, now, or any other Time more fuitable to you.

Theoph. As I have no particular Bufinefs on my Hands, we may as well do it now, and begin where we left off laft Time, and fpeak of the *Pater Nofter*, and what follows in the Mafs.

Theot. I take Notice the Prieft fays fomething before the *Pater Nofter*; what is it, and why faid?

Theoph.

Theoph. With this he begins that Part of the Mass, which is of the Communion, whereof all present are invited to be Partakers, if not sacramentally, at least spiritually; for this End he says, *Oremus, Let us pray*, that by devout Prayer we may dispose our Souls worthily to receive it, and as there is no Prayer more excellent than that which Christ has left us, he invites every one to join with him in saying the *Pater Noster*, or the Lord's Prayer, to which he makes a short Preface, saying; *Admonished by wholesome Precepts, and informed by divine Institutions, we presume to say, Pater Noster, &c.* Herein, the Priest with joined Hands and Heart expresses his Humility, intimating that he durst not come to God in such a familiar Way as to call him Father, or to ask any Thing of him under that Notion, unless he had been commanded and ordered to do it. He likewise propounds most efficacious Motives to excite us to this Prayer above all others, from the Author of it, who was Christ himself. Of this divine Prayer St. *Austine* says; *All Christians ought to have the greatest Reverence for this one Lord's Prayer, because it was made by him, who is the supreme Doctor or Master.* St. *Cyprian* thus speaks of it: *What Prayer can be more spiritual than that which is given us by Christ Jesus? And what Prayer can be a truer Prayer before the Father, than that which is from the Son, and*

uttered

*uttered by the Mouth of him who is Truth it-
felf?* Serm. 6. de orat Dom.

Theot. Was the Lord's Prayer always ufed in the Mafs, and why is it fo fhort?

Theoph. We find it in all the Liturgies of the Church, and as for the Brevity of it, why it is fhort, he knows beft who made it. This may be faid of it, that though brief, it is very full and comprehenfive, as containing the Subftance of all that may be fpecified in all other Prayers, and has this great Utility, that every one may eafily learn and retain it in their Memory. In the *Greek* Church all the People fay it with the Prieft; but in the *Latin* Church it is ordained, for greater Decency, and to avoid Confufion of Voices, that the Prieft fhould alone fay it, which he does in a loud Voice, till he comes to the Conclufion, *fed libera nos a malo, but deliver us from all Evil,* which is faid by the Clerk who ferves Mafs, in the Name of all prefent. The Prieft then fays *Amen* filently to himfelf, and profecutes his Prayer, begging to be delivered from all Evils paft, prefent, and to come, that is, to be wholly delivered from the great Evil of Sin, that our paft Sins may not be imputed to us, that our prefent Sins may be forgiven, and that we may be preferved from Sin for the future.

Theot. Why does the Prieft here uncover the *Paten?*

Theoph.

Theoph. For the better underftanding the Myfteries here reprefented, you are to confider, that covering the Paten with the Purificatory fignified the Apoftles hiding themfelves, and the Church in this Part of the Mafs being to reprefent the Refurrection of of Chrift, firft intimates to us that the Apoftles, on Account of what the devout Women faid to them, went to the Monument, and found the Linen Cloths removed and laid afide; this is denoted by the Prieft taking off the Purificatory, or Linen Cloth from the *Paten*. He then takes up the *Paten*, and holding it in his Hand, reprefents the Monument of Chrift, which the Difciples faw without his Body; figning himfelf fhews that all our Hope of Peace is grounded on the Paffion and Crofs of Chrift, in whom we are to feek for Peace, which can never be better found than in the Crofs of Chrift, in Token of which he kiffes the *Paten*, as afking of God Peace, both of Soul and Body; and laftly, in all fubmiffive Manner puts the *Paten* under the Hoft, that armed with the Sign of the Crofs, he may proceed in the Performance of the Holy Myfteries, and to that End uncovers the Chalice, which reprefents the opening of the Graves, and aptly fhews the Refurrection of Chrift.

Theot. This Explication of the Myfteries reprefented by the Ceremonies ufed in Mafs are as entertaining as inftructive, and afford excellent Matter of Devotion, pray go on and tell me why is the Hoft here broken.

Theoph. The Church herein follows Chrift's Inftitution, who, as the Evangelifts inform us, did break the Bread. St. *Luke* expreffes it with the ufual Ceremonies of Confecration; and from this Circumftance the whole Sacrifice had the Name of breaking Bread, not that the Body of Chrift is broken, or one Part of it feparated from another. The Divifion is of the Species, or Accidents which brings no Divifion in Chrift's Body in the venerable Sacrament of the Altar. He is whole and entire in the whole Hoft, and whole in every Part. The fame Body, whole and entire, without Separation or Divifion, remains in all the Hofts over the whole World, and in every Part, or Parcel of every one of the Hofts after Confecration.

Theot. I perceive the Prieft divides it firft into two Parts. Your Reafon for this?

Theoph. This is to fignify the double State of the Predeftinate, to wit, thofe who are in eternal Glory, and thofe who are yet in this Vale of Mifery; or in other Words, the one reprefents the Church triumphant in Heaven, the other, the Church militant on Earth. The firft Part is laid on the Paten, as being now in Reft and Peace.

Theot. Why is this Divifion made over the Chalice?

Theoph.

Theoph. The natural Reason is, left any Particles, which otherwise may happen in breaking the Host, might be scattered abroad; whereas by breaking it over the Chalice, they will easily fall into it. The mystical Reason is to signify that the Gates of Heaven were opened to us by our Saviour's Passion, as the Purchase of his sacred Blood.

Theot. What means the other Division?

Theoph. This signifies the Church militant, represented by that Part of the Host held over the Chalice, which is again divided, whereof one Parts represents those who are in Purgatory, with Hope and Assurance of being joined to the Church triumphant, in Sign whereof the Priest lays it down, joining it to the former Part on the Paten. The third is held over the Chalice while the Priest concludes his Prayer, saying as usual, *for ever and ever,* to which the Clerk answers *Amen.*

Theot. On what Account does the Priest say, *Pax Domini fit semper vobiscum. The Peace of our Lord be always with you.* And make three Crosses over the Chalice with a small Piece of the holy Host:

Theoph. Consequently to the preceding Prayer which was for Peace, which now the Priest declares to the People, and wishes to them saying, *the Peace of our Lord be always with you.* It was always used in the Church, and all Liturgies have it, and is taken

ken from Chrift himfelf who immediately after his Refurrection faluted the Apoftles with *Pax vobis, Peace be to you.* As the Prieft here prays for the People, and declares his good Wifhes to them; they alfo fhew they pray for him in the Anfwer the Clerk makes in their Name, faying; *Et cum Spirtu tuo, and with thy Spirit.*

The three Croffes made over the Chalice, intimate that Chrift's Peace is not to be had but by the Crofs planted in our Hearts, profeffed by our Mouths, and imitated in our Actions.

Theot. Why is this Particle put into the Chalice?

Theoph. To fhew that there is but one Sacrament under both Species, and that Chrift in his Refurrection re-affumed his Body and Blood. It is likewife added by the Church for the better and fuller Reprefentation of the Myfteries in this holy Sacrifice, whence in all her Liturgies it has been obferved, fo that it may be truly faid to come from apoftolical Tradition.

Theot. Let us now, if you pleafe, confider the *Agnus Dei,* and what follows.

Theoph. Willingly. The Prieft having put the Particle of the Hoft into the Chalice, kneels down, and then rifing, lays his joined Hands on the Altar, to fhew, that his whole Intention is conformable to his Words, and in this exteriour Action of fubmiffive inclining his Body, as a poor
Sin-

Sinner, before Jesus Christ, jointly with the People, he asks Mercy of Almighty God, in Token of which he, and all present, knock their Breasts saying, *Agnus Dei, Lamb of God which takeſt away the Sins of the World, have Mercy on us.* Christ is here called the Lamb of God, from those Words of St. *John Baptiſt*; *Behold the Lamb of God, behold him who taketh away the Sins of the World.* St. *John*, c. i. He is called Lamb, becauſe as a Lamb he was offered on the Croſs for the Redemption of the World. He is called Lamb, becauſe of his Innocence, Meekneſs, Patience and Obedience, of which the Lamb is an Emblem, all which he manifeſted in his whole Life, but principally in Paſſion.

Theot. Why is the *Agnus Dei* ſaid three Times, and at the End of the third, *Give to us Peace?*

Theoph, Biſhop *Ivo* will have it in correſpondence to the three Particles of the Hoſt. *Durandus*, to declare that this Lamb, Chriſt Jeſus, was ſent by the Holy Trinity, according to that of the Prophet *Iſaias*; *Send forth, O Lord, the Lamb, the Lord of all the Earth, Iſaias.* c. xvi. Chriſt, who is the Lamb, who takes away the Sins of the World, and rules and governs the whole Church, have Mercy on us. To this may be added, that it is ſaid thrice for a deeper Expreſſion of our Faith, Adoration and Supplication in Thought, Word, and Deed.

Anti-

Antiently, as *Gavant* obſerves, it was thrice
ſaid, *have Mercy on us*; but as divers Per-
ſecutions and Calamities did frequently
happen, it was changed in the third Place
to *Grant us Peace*, and is always now ſo
ſaid, except in Maſſes for the Dead, when,
inſtead of *have Mercy on us*, the Prieſt ſays,
Dona eis Requiem, Give to them Reſt, and
in the third Place, adds Everlaſting, or
everlaſting Reſt.

Here we are to obſerve that the Church
ſuppoſes theſe departed Souls to be in
Peace, as they are freed from all the Miſeries of this World, and no more ſubject
to Sin, yet not in Reſt or Repoſe, as being
in a ſuffering State, wherein they muſt remain till they have fully ſatisfied the divine
Juſtice for their Offences committed in
this World, and for this Reaſon it is ſaid,
Grant them Reſt. This is repeated three
Times, to expreſs our warmeſt Deſire that
they may be freed from their Pains, and
enjoy God in the Beatifick Viſion.

Theot. What follows next ?

Theoph. The Prieſt having finiſhed the
Agnus Dei with *Grant us Peace*, then ſilently prays for that Peace wherein, as in
the two other following Collects, he ſtands
in all Submiſſion and Humility, with
joined Hands on the Altar, inclining his
Body, and devoutly caſting his Eyes on the
holy Sacrament, reflects on the Promiſe
Chriſt made of giving his Peace to his
Apoſ-

Apoſtles, and in them to his Church, in Confidence of which, not truſting to his own Merits, he humbly begs this Peace, by the Faith of the Church, to whom this Peace was promiſed, praying, that Chriſt would vouchſafe to pacify all Troubles, and keep Peace therein, and unite all the Members of it in one and the ſame Faith.

Theot. Why does the Church here particularly pray for Peace?

Theoph. When Chriſt came into the World, Peace at his Nativity was proclaimed by an Angel to the Shepherds of *Bethlehem,* and when he was about to quit this World, he bequeathed his Peace to his Diſciples, and in them to us. After his Reſurrection he more frequently gave this Peace to them. Now, in this Place the Church myſtically repreſents to us what our Saviour did after his Reſurrection, in giving us his Peace, and prays that we may all be made worthy to receive that Peace ſo ſweetly commended and imparted to us.

Theot. As I ſometimes am preſent at High Maſs, I obſerve then, that the Prieſt gives the *Pax,* or Kiſs of Peace, to the Deacon, and he to the Sub-Deacon, who gives it to the other Miniſters; or one of them gives it to the Reſt. Why is this done?

Theoph.

Theoph. The Prieſt having prayed for Peace, gives the *Pax* to the Deacon, but firſt kiſſes the Altar to ſhew, that the Peace he gives comes from Chriſt himſelf, and then in the Perſon of Chriſt gives it to others. Formerly, it uſed to be given to all preſent, and every one devoutly kiſſed what was called the *Pax*, in Token that with the ſame Peace and Charity they were united to each other in Heart and Affection.

Theot. On what Account is it now generally omitted, and never given in private, or low Maſſes?

Theoph. Two Reaſons may be aſſigned, firſt, to hinder Diſtractions and Diſturbance, which at this Time are carefully to be avoided. Secondly, Communion was antiently *Quotidiem*, or Daily, and to which this Ceremony is a Diſpoſition, but this ſo frequent Communion ceaſing, it was omitted, and only obſerved in high, or ſolemn Maſſes, in the Manner I have ſpoken of.

Theot. With many Thanks I will now take my Leave of you, and refer the Reſt till next Time I ſee you.

Theoph. As may be moſt agreeable to you. Come again when you pleaſe, I ſhall be glad of your Company.

G					D I A-

DIALOGUE. XIV.

On the MASS.

The Communion.

Theophilus. GOOD Morrow, *Theotime,* you are very early this Morning; pray fit down.

Theotime. If I miſtake not, the Morning is the moſt leiſure Time with you. 'Hope I am not come too ſoon.

Theoph. Not at all; and, if you pleaſe, I will continue my Explication of the Maſs, beginning where I left off in our Diſcourſe laſt Time.

Theot. As this is the Purport of my Viſit, it will be very agreeable to me, and I ſhall begin our Converſation on this Subject with aſking you, why at the End of the three Prayers following the *Agnus Dei,* the Prieſt kneels down?

Theoph. Becauſe, being immediately to receive the ſacred Body and Blood of Jeſus Chriſt, he firſt kneels with great Humility and Devotion to adore Jeſus Chriſt, truly and really there preſent on the Altar; for, as St. *Auſtine* ſays, *None do eat this Fleſh of Chriſt,*

Chrift, unlefs firft he adores, which plainly
fhews, that in his Time it was the Cuftom
to adore the holy Sacrament.   Then rifing
up, he reverently takes the holy Hoft in
his Hand, and devoutly fays, *I will take
the heavenly Bread, and will call upon the
Name of the Lord.*

Thect. Explicate this to me.

Theoph. Two Things are here to be noted.
Firft, The heavenly Bread.   Secondly, Invocating the Name of the Lord.   Of the
firft, St. *Cyprian* fays,   " We call it
" Bread, becaufe Chrift, to whofe Body
" we come, is our Bread; for Chrift faid,
" I am the Bread of Life which defcended
" from Heaven, heretofore figured by the
" Manna which the *Ifraelites* eat in the
" Defart; but of his own Body Chrift
" fays: Amen, Amen, I fay unto you,
" *Mofes* gave you not Bread from Heaven,
" but my Father giveth the true Bread
" from Heaven.—I am the living Bread
" which came down from Heaven.   It is
" here ftiled the true Bread from Heaven,
" truly celeftial, not only becaufe it comes
" truly from Heaven, but becaufe it is fo
" by Nature and Subftance, and produces
" heavenly Effects, Grace and Life in Je-
" fus Chrift, as alfo bringing us to the
" celeftial Kingdom,   or Life everlaft-
" ing."

As to the fecond Thing, invocating the
Name of the Lord.   Here the Prieft ex-
                cites

cites himself to Devotion, by confidering what it is he takes, and how he is to take it, to wit, by invocating, or by calling on the Name of the Lord. Here we may ob-ferve, that this Invocation of our Lord's Name, or by our Lord's Name, is the beſt Manner of praying, which our Saviour himſelf commends to us, faying; *Amen, Amen, I fay to you, if you ſhall aſk the Father any Thing in my Name, he will give it to you.* St. *John,* c. xvi. Wherein, as St. *Chryfoſtome* obferves, Chriſt ſhews the Virtue and Power of his Name, for being only named, (invocated) he doth wonderful Things with his Father. Hence we may truly fay, that calling upon the Name of Chriſt, is a great Affurance of obtaining what we pray for, and gives a firm Hope and Confidence in the Mercy and Goodneſs of God. Laſtly, in theſe Words, *I will call upon the Name of the Lord*; confequent-ly to the whole Action of the Maſs, the Prieſt offers up the celeſtial Bread to God the Father, and by invocating his Name, begs that this Sacrifice he is now to con-fummate, may be acceptable to his divine Majeſty, which in all fubmiſſive Manner as he has exteriourly adored, fo interiourly in Heart and Affection, he adores and wor-ſhips what he is to receive, and in a few Words ſhews the interiour Devotion of his Soul, and the Defires he has that what

he

he does may be to the Glory of God, his
principal End in this holy Action.

Theot. Tell me now the Meaning of
Domine non sum dignus. Why said thrice
with the Priest's knocking his Breast?

Theoph. Having taken the holy Host, devoutly bowing down with his Eyes fixed
upon it, he says, *Domine non sum, &c. Lord,
I am not worthy thou shouldest enter under my
Roof, but say the Word only and my Soul shall
be healed.* This he repeats three Times, and
at each Times strikes his Breast, to denote
his Humility and the Fervour of his Devotion, with a deep Sense of his Unworthiness to receive this adorable Sacrament, by
Reason of his manifold Sins and Imperfections, but with an humble lively Faith
in the Power and Goodness of God, both
willing and able to cure his Soul, sick by
Sin. They are the Words of the humble
Centurion in the Gospel, on Christ's saying, he would go and heal his sick Servant,
and are here aptly adapted by the Church,
and put into the Priest's Mouth just before
he receives. They are full of Energy and
Force, very expressive of those reverential
Sentiments with which the Priest ought to
be filled at this Time. The holy Precursor
of Jesus; St. *John Baptist*, though sanctified
in his Mother's Womb, did not think himself worthy to loose the Latchet of our Saviour's Shoes. How much more ought we
to think ourselves unworthy to receive his

G 3

ado-

adorable Body and Blood in this holy Sacrament? Bleſſed *Elizabeth*, Mother of the ſame humble Saint, when the Bleſſed Virgin *Mary* viſited her, cried out, *Whence is this to me, that the Mother of my Lord ſhould come to me.* St. *Luke*, c. i. She juſtly admired that Jeſus and his Mother ſhould come to her. With how much more Reaſon may every one ſay; whence is this to me, poor miſerable Creature, that my Lord and my God ſhould come to me in this humble Manner?

Theot. Proceed now, Sir, to ſay ſomething of the Communion, and why does the Prieſt ſign himſelf with the holy Hoſt before he receives it?

Theoph. Saying theſe Words, *the Body of our Lord Jeſus Chriſt keep my Soul to everlaſting Life.* He ſigns himſelf with the Hoſt, in Form of a Croſs, as expecting Chriſt's Benediction, and other Effects of the holy Euchariſt, by the Merits of Chriſt's ſacred Croſs and Paſſion, which the learned Ritualiſt *Durandus*, thus expreſſes; "The Prieſt, ſays "he, being about to take the Body of our "Lord, ſigns himſelf with it before his "Breaſt croſswife, for as before, by ac- "tively making Croſſes as a Miniſter, he "ſanctified the Bread and Wine, and re- "preſented Chriſt's Paſſion. Now, in ſign- "ing himſelf with it, he paſſively aſks to "be ſanctified, as if in Effect he ſhould "ſay, O my Lord, who by thy Croſs and "Paſſion

" Paſſion haſt ſanctified the whole World,
" ſanctify now my Soul by the ſame, and by
" this Benediction make me worthy to re-
" ceive thee, now mercifully coming to me."

Theot. But why does he ſay *to Life ever-laſting?*

Theoph. Becauſe this is the principal Effect of the Bleſſed Euchariſt. Here, therefore, with a lively Faith and a firm Hope, the Prieſt humbly prays that this holy Sacrament of the Body of Chriſt, may keep him from Sin, and preſerve him in the Grace of God, that ſo he may come to Life everlaſting. Having ſaid this, he devoutly receives the Communion.

Theot. Tell me why it is called Communion?

Theoph. By Communion we underſtand the Communication, or Reception of the Body and Blood of our Saviour, which is an eſſential Part of the Sacrifice of the Maſs, and without it there would be no compleat Sacrifice. St. *Denis* frequently calls the receiving the holy Euchariſt, Communion, that is, a Union, by which we are united in Chriſt Jeſus ; for, as St. *Paul* ſays, *Being many, we are all one Body ;* all that partake of one Bread. Of which St. *Cyril* ſays, *If we all eat one Body, we are made all one Body.* St. *Chryſoſtome* ſays, *We are reduced into one Maſs with him, we are made one Body and one Fleſh of Chriſt.*

G 4

Theot.

Theot. Why does the Priest oftentimes communicate alone ?

Theoph. This comes from the Coldnefs and Indevotion of the People. The Church excludes from Communion none who duly prepare themfelves for it ; but wifnes all Chriftians, if not daily, yet frequently to receive facramentally, and where any juft Hindrance occurs, fhe invites and admonifhes them to do it fpiritually, by uniting their Intentions with the Prieft, who as a publick Minifter offers up the Sacrifice, for all of which each one in particular, according to his Devotion, may be a Partaker.

Theot. How does the Prieft take the Chalice ?

Theoph. The Prieft having meditated a little while on the facred Body of Chrift, now received, proceeds to accomplifh the holy Sacrifice, kneels down to adore the Blood of our Lord, and, as deeply fenfible of the Favour, devoutly fays ; *Quid retribuam, &c. What fhall I render to the Lord for all that he has done unto me ?* Here he takes the Chalice and goes on, faying, *I will take the Chalice of Salvation, and will call upon the Name of the Lord. Praifing I will call upon the Lord, and I fhall be fafe from my Enemies.* Pf. cxv. He then figns himfelf with the Chalice, as he did before with the holy Hoft, and fays ; *The Blood of our Lord Jefus Chrift keep my Soul to everlasting Life*; as if he should say, the Blood of our Lord Jesus Christ, the Fountain and Laver of our Sanctification, the Price of our Redemption, shed upon the Cross, preserve my Soul in Security against all my Enemies, and bring me to Life everlasting. Having received the holy Blood, he pauses a little in devout Meditation, and then he takes a little Wine, which the Server at Mass puts into the Chalice.

Theot. On what Account is this done?

Theoph. Such is the Reverence the Church bears to this holy Sacrament, that she ordains this taking of Wine after the Communion of the Chalice, left any Drop of the holy Blood should remain therein, as also to cleanse the Chalice after the holy Species is taken.

Theot. I observe, after this he takes another Ablution, and that with Water and Wine. Why this? -

Theoph. As he took Wine to cleanse the Chalice, he goes to the Corner of the Altar, there to wash the Tops of his Fingers which had touched the Blessed Sacrament, that no Particle of the Host may remain on them, as also, it may justly seem indecent that those Fingers should touch any other Thing before they were washed. It also serves for a thorough and further Purification of the Chalice. This Ceremony, though it is rather for Decency than otherwife, yet may have a myſtical Signification given to it.

Theot. In what Senſe ?

Theoph. As this Sacrifice may be ſaid to have a Mixture of Joy and Sorrow. Joy for the holy Euchariſt, and Sorrow for the Paſſion of our Saviour, therein repreſented. The Wine denotes the Joy and ſpiritual Exultation with which the devout Soul is filled by receiving the Bleſſed Euchariſt. Sorrow for the Paſſion of Jeſus Chriſt, and for Sin, the Cauſe of it. Both theſe Myſteries concur to our Salvation, and the joining Wine and Water in this Action, may denote, that the Affections of the Mind ſhould correſpond to what they ſignify. We are now ccme to the laſt Part of the Maſs, called the *Poſt-communion,* which ſhall be the Subject to be talked of at our next Meeting.

Theot. Agreed. At preſent adieu, *Theophilus.*

Theoph. Adieu, *Theotime.*

PART III.

DIALOGUE XV.

On the MASS.

The Poſt-Communion.

Theotime. **I** Shall make no Excuſe, *Theophilus*, for coming again ſo ſoon. You know my Errand, and the Occaſion of my viſiting you.

Theophilus. Very well. I am ready for you, and we will begin, I ſuppoſe you would have the *Poſt-communion* explained to you.

Theot. You ſuppoſe right. What is the *Poſt-communion?* I obſerve that the Prieſt, after he has communicated, goes to the Corner of the Altar, and ſays a Verſe out of the Pſalms, or ſome Place in the Sripture; is this what you call the *Poſt-communion?*

Theoph. No; this Verſe, which correſponds to the Introit, and the Verſe before the Offertory, is here ſaid by the Prieſt as a Hymn of Praiſe and Thankſgiving after he has communicated. At High Maſs it is often ſung during the Time the Prieſt receives, and communicates the People.

At

At Low Maſſes he ſays it after he has taken the Ablutions, and covered the Chalice, and on this Account is called in the Miſſal *Communion.* This is conformable to the Practice of Chriſt, who, after he had inſtituted the Bleſſed Euchariſt, ſung a Hymn of Praiſe and Thankſgiving. St. *Denis* ſays, " The divine Communion being re-" ceived and given, he, that is the Prieſt, " ends with holy Thankſgiving." *De Eccl. Hier.* ch. iii. From hence we may gather, that all which follows in the Maſs tends to Thanſgiving and Prayer, for the Benefits and Effects of the Holy Maſs, and we may further conſider it as repreſenting the Joy of the Apoſtles ſeeing our Saviour after his Reſurrection. *The Diſciples were glad when they ſaw the Lord.* St. *John,* ch. xx.

Theot. Why is the Book removed, and the Prieſt to ſay this at the Right End of the Altar?

Theoph. The Miſſal is here brought to that Side, to finiſh the Maſs where it was begun. We are further to obſerve, that as before reading the Goſpel, the Miſſal was removed from thence to ſignify the Apoſtles going to preach God's Word to the Gentiles, forſaking the Jews, who obſtinately rejected Chriſt's Law. So now the Miſſal is again brought to the Epiſtle Side, to inform us, that in the End of the World, the Jews ſhall receive the Chriſtian Faith,

and

and be united to the Flock of Chrift. This is further intimated by the Cloks covering the Miffal with the Veil, and which the Prieft takes off to fhew that God, in his good Time will remove the Veil of Obduratenefs from their Hearts, and move them to acknowledge Jefus Chrift his only Son, their Saviour and Redeemer.

Theot. Does not the covering the Chalice with the Veil, after the Prieft's Communion, fignify fomething?

Theoph. Yes: It reprefents the great Stone which was placed before the Door of Chrift's Monument, and fignifies, that whenever we have received Chrift's facred Body in holy Communion, we fhould clofely fhut the Door of our Hearts againft all finful Affections, and unlawful Defires of any Worldly Things.

Theot. Proceed now to explain the *Poft-communion* to me.

Theoph. The *Poft-communion* confifts of certain Ceremonies and Prayers, prefcribed by the Church after Communion, or after the Verfe I have fpoken of, and are ufed to compleat the Sacrifice with Prayer and Thankfgiving, and you may obferve firft, how the Prieft kiffes the Altar, to fignify the interiour Peace of his Soul, and to acknowledge the Goodnefs of God in this holy Sacrifice. Secondly, he turns to the People, and falutes them with *Dominus Vobifcum, the Lord be with you,* admonifh-

ing

ing them to conserve and keep the true Peace of God in their Souls, with all the salutary Effects of the holy Eucharist and Sacrifice of the Mass, and also invites them to join with him in the following Prayers. The Clerk answers in the Name of the People, and they may softly say with him, *Et cum Spiritu tuo; and with thy Spirit,* testifying the same good Wishes to him. The Priest then says, *Oremus, Let us pray,* and goes on to say the Collects or Prayers, which correspond in Number, Form, and Conclusion, with those said before the Epistle, and what has been said of them may be applied to these.

Theot. At the End of these Prayers he says again, *Dominus Vobiscum.* Why repeated again?

Theoph. You may observe, in this Part of the Mass the Priest kisses the Altar, then turns and salutes the People twice, in Token of the double Peace which is given us by Virtue of this holy Sacrifice and Sacrament, that is, Peace of our Minds in this World, and the Peace of Eternity promised in Christ's Ascension, which is mystically signified here, who, according to St. *John,* before he ascended into Heaven, redoubled his heavenly Salutation of *Pax Vobis, Peace be to you;* So here the Priest reiterates his *Dominus Vobiscum, the Lord be with you,* to comfort us, and to assure us that he is with us according to his Promise: *Behold I am*

with

*with you all Days, even to the Consummation,
or End, of the World.* St. *Matt.* c. xxviii.

Theot. Having explained this last Part of
the Holy Mass, tell me how, or in what
Manner it is concluded.

Theoph. There are three different Con-
clusions of the Mass; two when it is said
for the Living, and one in Masses for the
Dead. The First, and most common is,
Ite Missa est, Go, Mass is finished, the Oblation is offered up to appease God's Wrath,
and to obtain his Blessings upon us. *Go,
Mass is accomplished,* depart from the Church
in Peace; remember where you have been,
and labour to reap the Benefit of the great
Sacrifice which has been offered up for you.
The second Conclusion is, *Benedicamus Domino, Let us bless the Lord.* This the Church
uses in all penitential Times, as *Advent,
Lent, Ember*-days and *Vigils,* as also on the
Ferial-days, out of *Easter* Time. As on
those Days she omits the *Gloria in Excelsis,*
it being a Hymn of Joy, so she omits the
Ite Missa est, and in its Place says *Benedicamus Domino, Let us bless the Lord,* as more
consonant to Times of Mourning and Penance.

Theot. But, why does he stand with his
Face to the People when he says *Ite Missa
est,* and with his Back towards them when
he says, *Benedicamus Domino?*

Theoph. The one being a Salutation of
Joy and Peace, the Priest turns to the People,

ple, as denouncing this Joy and Peace to them, or rather giving it to them in Virtue of the holy Sacrifice. The other is an Exhortation, or summoning them to join with him in giving Thanks for these holy Mysteries, left us in the Church. The third Conclusion is, *Requiescant in Pace, May they rest in Peace.* This always is used in Masses for the Dead, and is suitable to the whole Course of the Mass, in which no special Prayer for the Living is said, and the People are incited to pray for the Dead, as the Priest does all along, and consequently standing at the Altar. In the End he salutes not the People, but prays for the Dead, and so passes on, without giving any Benediction, as in all other Masses he does.

Theot. After the *Ite Missa est,* I see the Priest lay his Hands on the Altar, and makes a short Prayer. What is it he then prays for?

Theoph. With this Prayer he finishes the Mass, humbly begging with joined Hands on the Altar, that the Action, or Service he has performed, not out of Presumption, but in Obedience to Christ and the Church, may be pleasing to God. That the holy Sacrifice, notwithstanding his Unworthiness, which he has offered, may be acceptable before the Divine Majesty, as well for himself, as for all those for whom he offered it. This Prayer being

ended

ended, the Prieſt kiſſes the Altar, as in Confidence of this Sacrifice being accepted by God, and then turning to the People, with his right Hand makes the Sign of the Croſs over them, and thus bleſſes them with theſe Words; *Benedicat vos omnipotens Deus, Pater, et Filius, et Spiritus Sanctus, Amen.* The Omnipotent God, Father, Son, and Holy Ghoſt, bleſs you. Amen.

Theot. Was it always the Practice of the Church to give this Benediction at the End of the Maſs?

Theoph. Yes: We find it preſcribed in all the antient Liturgies, with ſome Variation indeed, as to the Form, but in Subſtance the ſame. The *Greek* Prieſts uſe this Form; *Our Lord keep you all in his Grace and Goodneſs perpetually, now, always, and for ever. Amen.* This Form is to be found in the Liturgy of St. *Baſil,* and St. *Chryſoſtome.* The *Latin* Church uſes the Form juſt now mentioned. *Benedicat vos omnipotens Deus, Pater, et Filius, et Spiritus Sanctus. Amen.* Here it is to be noted, that the Church, in all her Sacraments and Benedictions, invokes the Bleſſed Trinity, and that as the Maſs begins with Invocation of the Holy Trinity, ſo it ends with the ſame.

Theot. Tell me why the Prieſt lifts up his Hand, and makes the Sign of the Croſs, when he gives this Benediction?

Theoph.

Theoph. To shew that all Benedictions and Blessings flow from, and are imparted to us, by Virtue of the sacred Cross and Passion of Jesus Christ, our great Redeemer and Mediator. The Priest here blesses the People in the Person of Jesus Christ, and after his Example, who ascending into Heaven, lifted up his Hands and blessed his Disciples. From hence comes the Tradition and Custom of the Church, that the Priest having finished Mass, blesses the People.

Theot. This Benediction is sometimes omitted. Why so?

Theoph. It is omitted in Masses for the Dead, which are concluded with *Requiescant in Pace. May they rest in Peace*; for Mass being said for the Repose of departed Souls, all that is peculiar to the Living is omitted, and the Benediction cannot be imparted to them, as not present. The People indeed answer *Amen*, praying that in the one they may receive the Effects of the Priest's Benediction; and in the other they pray that the Dead may rest in Peace.

Theot. Ought the People to sign themselves with the Sign of the Cross at the Benediction?

Theoph. I observe that it is done frequently, and signing ourselves with the Sign of the Cross is very good at all Times, but here seems to be not so congruous or

pro-

proper. It is better to attend to the Prieft's Benediction and Signing, as an Act of Authority and Power, in the Perfon of God, by his Minifter, and our beft Difpofition to receive it is to bow down humbly, with our Hands joined to receive it. The fame alfo may be obferved when the Benediction of the Bleffed Sacrament is given, as Chrift himfelf then gives us his Bleffing.

Theot. Why, after this, does the Prieft read St. *John's* Gofpel? Is that Part of the Mafs, or belong to it?

Theoph. No: It is no Part of it, and the Cuftom of faying it was brought into the Church in later Times. *Gavant,* in his Commentaries on the Rubricks, of the Miffal fays, that after the Liturgy of St. *Peter,* fomething was read from the Law and the Prophets, probably fome Inftructions to the People before they departed; in Place of which the Reading St. *John's* Gofpel was introduced, and for which this Reafon may be affigned: As the Mafs was began with the Memory of Chrift's Nativity, fo it might end with a Memorial of his Divinity and Humanity joined in one Perfon, that we may always retain the Memory of it, with a *Verbum caro factus eft. The Word was made Flefh.*

Theot. I take Notice that fometimes this Gofpel is not read. On what Account is it omitted?

Theoph.

Theoph. When any Feast falls on a *Sunday*, in *Lent*, or on *Vigils* and *Ember* Days, as the Mass is said of the Feast, and a Commemoration is made of those Days, by a proper Collect or Prayer, so the Gospel for those Days is read at the End of the Mass. Of the Gospel of St. *John*, St. *Austine* affirms, that of all the divine Authorities contained in the sacred Text, " the Gospel is worthily esteemed the most " excellent, and among the Gospels that " of St. *John* has the Pre-eminence, and " of all the Parts of St. *John*'s Gospel, " the Beginning is most sublime; for in it " are contained the highest Mysteries of " our Faith, the Trinity, eternal Genera- " tion of the divine Word, the Creator of " all Things, the Incarnation, and the " wonderful Effects thereof, as Life, " Light, and Grace, which Christ brought " unto us, whereby also we are made the " Sons of God."

Theot. Are there any Ceremonies used in saying this Gospel?

Theoph. The same as are observed in reading the Gospel in Mass. During the saying St. *John*'s Gospel the People stand, and at the Beginning sign themselves with the Sign of the Cross on the Forehead, Mouth, and Breast; all ought likewise devoutly to kneel with the Priest at the Words *Et verbum caro factum est; the Word was made Flesh;* as in the Creed, at these Words,

Et

Et homo factus est ; *and was made Man.*
But in the End, inſtead of *Laus tibi Chriſt* ;
Thanks be to thee, O Chriſt, we here ſay,
Deo Gratias, Thanks be to God, thus con-
cluding the whole Office with due Praiſe
and Thankſgiving.

I have now, *Theotime,* given you a brief
Explication of the Maſs, of all the Ceremonies uſed in it, and of whatever apper-
tains, or belongs to this great and auguſt
Sacrifice of the New Law, I hope to your
Satisfaction. Is there any Thing elſe that
you deſire to be informed of, or that I can
ſerve you in ? If there is, command my
little Aſſiſtance, and I ſhall give it with
Pleaſure.

Theot. As you are ſo very obliging,
I will make uſe of the Liberty you
give me. There are two or three
Things more, relative to what we have
been ſpeaking of. I ſhould be very glad
to have ſome Inſtructions from you concerning the Reſpect due to the holy Sacrifice ;
of frequent hearing Maſs ; of the Intention and Attention with which we ought to
hear it : as likewiſe ſome proper devout
Method of aſſiſting at it. If I have not
already tired you, to carry on our Converſation on theſe Points will greatly add to
the Obligations I lie under to you.

Theoph. I cannot but commend your pious Deſire, and I ſhould be much wanting
to the Friendſhip you have for me, was I

to

to refuse so reasonable a Request. I will therefore endeavour to satisfy you at our next Meeting, which, if you please, may be after To-morrow, when I shall be at Leisure to enjoy your good Company.

Theat. That Time will suit me very well. I will not fail to wait upon you, and am your obliged humble Servant.

Theoph. Your's, Sir, Adieu.

D I A-

DIALOGUE XVI.

On the Respect due to the Holy Mass.

Theophilus. GOOD Morning to you, *Theotime*, you are a Man of your Word; fit down.

Theotime. This I will do very readily, and defire you will now fay fomething of the Refpect due to the Holy Mafs, in which I fear too many are much wanting.

Theoph. I am forry to fay your Apprehenfions are too well grounded. There are too many who go to this folemn Service, and during it behave with fo little Decency and Refpect, as muft give great Scandal and Difedification. Of thefe it may be faid they fee *Mafs* celebrated, but do not hear it, not, at leaft, according to the Intention and Spirit of the Church, and juftly deferve a fevere Animadverfion on a Conduct fo oppofite to what they do, or pretend to believe.

Theot. It will therefore be a Work of Charity to endeavour to reform fuch, by fhewing briefly the Reverence and Refpect due to thefe facred and auguft Myfteries.

Theoph. I am very willing to fecond your pious Defires, and offer fomething on this

Point

Point to the serious Consideration of such,' and not only to them but to all Catho- licks.

It is certain that too great Reverence and Respect cannot be shewn to the Service of Almighty God, particularly in this high and peculiar Part of his Service, this great and tremendous Sacrifice, wherein Jesus Christ offers himself up, by the Hands of the Priest, to his eternal Father in our be- half, where Jesus Christ, God and Man, is truly and really present on the Altar, after Consecration, and in the Tabernacle where the holy Host is reserved. On this Account Churches are truly called Houses of the living God, Temples consecrated to his peculiar Worship. Can this be spoke, or even thought of, and our Minds not be filled with the most reverential Awe and Dread, when we are in his immediate Presence, and assisting at the Sacrifice of the Mass.

Theot. What you say is undoubtedly true, and will be readily acknowledged by every one, was the Question put to them; yet, notwithstanding, a want of Reverence and Respect is too visible in the Conduct of many. You may see them staring and gaz- ing about most Part of the Time of Mass. A Book in their Hand perhaps, but they draw their Eyes off it to look at every one who comes in. If any Acquaintance is

near

near enough, a little Chit Chat follows, as if the Church, a House of Prayer, was an Assembly Room for Conversation. Kneeling is certainly the most proper Posture for Suppliants at the Throne of God : But to kneel may spoil a fine Gentleman's Silk Stockings, or dirty a Lady's Petticoat. Some, indeed, will vouchsafe to kneel, at the Elevation, a little, and with one Knee. Can this be any ways suitable to the great Majesty of God, the Dignity of the sacred Mysteries, and the End for which we go to Church ?

Theoph. You are pretty smart, *Theotime,* upon our fine Ladies and Gentlemen. Such Behaviour, indeed, has nothing in it of that Reverence and Respect due to the Mass ; and it is to be apprehended such People go from Mass with little or no Benefit by hearing it : But there are other Circumstances denoting this Want of Respect to the holy Mysteries ; as the Practice of those who studiously, as I may say, aud purposely come late to Mass, when the Priest has begun, perhaps when he is reading the Epistle, or even after the Gospel. This, when the Practice is frequent, shews an extreme and very culpable Neglect. The same may be said of those who search after the shortest Mass they can find, and are ever grumbling if they are obliged to hear a Gentleman say Prayers gravely and delibe-

H

rately,

rately, and not hurry it over as quick as they would have him.

Theot. But, are there not some Priests too long at Mass, and who tire even the Devout and Serious?

Theoph. This may be the Case sometimes, but, I believe, not very frequent. When it does happen, a little serious Reflection where we are, in whose Presence, and about what, will help to lengthen our Devotion, and take off all Uneasiness.

Theot. I have heard some say, they had rather hear two short Masses, than one long one. What is your Opinion?

Theoph. I widely differ from such. To hear two Masses is certainly a pious good Thing; but if they are so very short that I can never go on, or accompany the Priest, either in my Attention nor with my Prayers, I freely confess, I am neither pleased nor edified: I am rather scandalized to see a Gentleman at the Altar, hurrying over the sacred Action with so much Precipitation as if he grudged every Minute he was employed in it. However, I am no Friend to very tedious long Masses, and think the devout *Thomas a Kempis* gives very good Advice to Priests, when he says, " In ce-
" lebrating, be neither too long nor too
" short, but observe the common Method
" of those with whom you live. You
" ought not to make others uneasy or tire
" them, but to follow the common Rule
" pre-

" prescribed by the Antients ; and rather
" seek the Profit and Utility of others, than
" your own private Devotion and Affec-
" tion." Imit. J. C. l. iv. c. 10.

Theot. I readily subscribe to your Opinion, and believe you will to mine, when
I tell you, I can't well approve of the Custom of some who are in such vast Hurry
to be gone, as they can scarce stay till the
last Benediction is given ; or if they stay the
Reading of St. *John*'s Gospel, the Instant
that is finished, are upon the Wing, and
hasten out of the Church as if they were
afraid it would fall on their Heads.

Theoph. I agree with you, and think such
People's Behaviour to be not a little de-
fective, and their Devotion very cold. They
would not be in a Hurry to run out of the
Presence Chamber of an earthly King, were
they admitted into it : And surely the
Church, the Presence Chamber of the great
King of Heaven and Earth, may invite
them to stay a little in it after they have
had the Honour of an Audience, as I may
say, of his adorable Majesty. I will conclude this Point with a most pathetic Exhortation from St. *Bernardin* of *Sienna*, who,
in one of his Sermons, thus addresses himself to his Hearers : " Let our Entry in-
" to the Church be humble and devout ;
" let our Stay there be silent and quiet,
" acceptable in the Sight of God, which
" may not only edify others, but also en-

H 2

" courage

" courage them ; let us attend, in those
" Places, to the sacred Solemnities with
" intense Affections, and continue in de-
" vout Prayer ; let all vain Things cease,
" much more filthy and prophane ; away
" with all idle Talk and Confabulation.
" Woe, woe to those who are confounded
" with greater Shame before Men than be-
" fore God; who are bold to do many
" Things in the Sight of God, which they
" would be ashamed to do before Men."

Theot. What you have said is very instructive, and much to the Purpose. What
have you to say about frequent hearing
Mass ? Would you have me hear it every
Day ?

Theoph. To hear Mass devoutly every
Day, is doubtless an excellent Practice,
and earnestly to be recommended to all
those whose Circumstances will allow Time,
and they have a Conveniency to do it. To
hear Mass on all *Sundays* and *Holydays* is
strictly obligatory, and not to be dispensed
with but in Case of Sickness, or some other
just and lawful Impediment. Whoever,
without some such just Cause, wilfully
omits to hear Mass on those Days, com-
mits a grievous Sin, by not sanctifying the
Lord's Day, and not observing the Precept
of the Church to hear Mass on those Days.
At other Times it is left to every one's Devotion to hear or not to hear Mass. There
are many working labouring Men, and

Shop-

Shop-keepers, whose Circumstances will not allow them to be present every Day, but such may intentionally hear Mass, by joing their Intention with the Church, and every Day offer up, in their Morning Prayers, the Masses that may be said that Day. This is a good and profitable Devotion, and will make them Partakers of the Benefits of the Holy Sacrifice, though not actually present at it. As for others, who have none of these Impediments, but are entire Masters of their Time, to hear Mass daily is much to be recommended to them. The whole Day is in their own Disposal. They can, and willingly do, spend Hours and Hours together in Diversions and Amusements, oftentimes, at best trifling, if not worse. Such ought not to think much, or grudge to give some little Part of the Day in Attendance on the public Worship of God, as well as to their private Devotions.

Theot. Have you no Motives to induce Catholics to a daily or frequent hearing Mass?

Theoph. Yes. Their own spiritual Interest in the Profit they may thereby reap to their own Souls; and the Example of the Saints. Their own temporal, as well as spiritual Interest, is here concerned: The more devoutly we serve God, and the more we attend to his Service, the more we may expect his Blessing upon us, and to prosper in all our lawful Undertakings, according to what our blessed Saviour says, *Seek first the Kingdom of God, and all other Things shall be added to you,* St. Luke c. xii. As to our spiritual Interest, and what regards our Souls, it is certain our best and greatest Interest, is to take Care of them; for, *What will it avail a Man to gain the whole World, and lose his own Soul?* St. Matt. xvi. We are daily exposed to a thousand Dangers of losing them. What can preserve us but the Grace of God? And by what Means can we more efficaciously obtain this Grace, than by the Merits of Jesus Christ applied to us in this holy Sacrifice, the endless Source of all spiritual Graces and Blessings, and a sovereign Remedy for all our Evils. If we consider the Examples of the Saints and holy Persons of all Ages, how diligent and fervent were they in this holy Exercise! never letting a Day pass without hearing one, two, or three Masses. They never thought their Time better spent than when they were in the Church, adoring and worshipping God in these holy Mysteries. This we may learn from the Lives of St. *Anselm,* St. *Thomas of Aquine,* St. *Bonaventure,* St. *Lewis,* St. *Elzear,* and many others. Let us imitate their Piety; let us imitate their Devotion in this Point, that we may share in their Graces here, and their Glory hereafter.

Theot. I acknowledge the Justness and Reasonableness of what you say; but pray tell

tell me whether it is neceſſary to have an Intention to hear Maſs when I go to Church?

Theoph. Certainly. Man being a rational Creature muſt perform all his Actions rationally, that is, with Reaſon and Prudence, propoſing ſome good and laudable End in what he does, whereby he is induc'd ſo conſider the proper Means to obtain that End. The firſt Thing therefore required is, Intention, from whence all human Actions generally have their Worth and Value, or the contrary.

Theot. I have heard there are three Sorts of Intentions; actual, virtual, and habitual. Explain them, and tell me which of them I ought to have.

Theoph. Actual Intention is when, by an Application of the Mind, we actually intend ſuch or ſuch an End of our Actions. Virtual Intention, is when we do ſuch or ſuch Actions, conſequently to, or in Virof, ſuch a precedent actual Intention. Habitual, is when we are accuſtomed to ſuch or ſuch Actions, which imply ſuch Intentions, though we do not, at that Time, reflect upon them. To apply this to our preſent Purpoſe: When I go to hear Maſs for ſuch or ſuch an End, for the Remiſſion of my Sins, to obtain Grace, or the like, then my Intention is Actual. When I go to Church, by Virtue of my precedent Intention, it has a Virtual Influence on what I do, and is a Virtual Intention. An Ex-

H 4

ample

ample of the third, or Habitual Intention, may be of one who is accustomed to give Alms, yet in giving it does not actually reflect on the Motives why he gives it, nevertheless would not give it but for the Love of God, and from a Motive of Charity.

Theot. Would you counsel me always to have an Actual Intention when I go to hear Mass?

Theoph. I would not have you go to hear Mass, without considering why, wherefore, or to what End you go; or meerly out of Custom, and to do as you see others do. I recommend therefore, to make an Actual Intention to hear Mass for such or such Ends as you may propose to yourself, and so prepare yourself to assist at the holy Sacrifice. This you may do either before you go from your House, when you are in the Church, or at the Beginning of the Mass. An Intention, thus made Virtually, accompanies the whole Action; and though we may have many Distractions, Coldness, or Want of Fervour, not wilfully entertained or given Way to, yet we then hear Mass as we ought. From hence it follows, that such a Virtual Intention is sufficient.

Theot. I am satisfied with what you say about Intention: Tell me what is Attention, and whether requisite at Mass?

Theoph. Doubtless it is; and you'll please to observe, that Intention refers to the End proposed.

propofed. Attention regards the Action
we are to do for that End; fo that we may
fay, Attention is but a continual-Effect of
our Intentions. That Attention to what
we are doing in all our Actions of Importance is neceffary, will be acknowledged
by all who would act prudently, and defire
to fucceed in what they are doing. Hence
the old faying; *Age quod agis. Mind what
you are about.* If this holds good in temporal Actions, it can't be lefs neceffary in
fpiritual ones, as Prayer and hearing Mafs.
It is the Advice of the Wife Man; *Before
Prayer prepare thy Soul*, to wit, with good
Intentions and Defires; *and he not as one
who tempteth God.* Eccl. c. xviii. He tempts
God, who at his Prayers, and when he
hears Mafs, attends not to what he fays,
or what he is about, but wilfully lets his
Mind and his Thoughts be rambling here
and there on other Things.

Theot. You fay well, neverthelefs I find
Diftractions will come into my Mind in
'Time of Mafs; and I am fometimes very
uneafy and dejected on this Account.

Theoph. In anfwer to this, you muft
know, *Theotime*, there are two Sorts of
Diftractions, voluntary and involuntary.
'The former are very prejudicial to us:
Not fo the latter. Voluntary and finful
Diftractions are thofe which we willingly
admit, and entertain our Mind with in
Time of Prayer, and without attending to

H 5

what

we say or hear. Wilfully to give Occasion to them by gazing, staring about, and looking at every Body who comes into the Church, marking how they are dreſt, laughing and talking in Time of Service. No wonder if the Minds of ſuch are full of Diſtractions, and their Prayers inſtead of being pleaſing to God, offend him. The Prayers of ſuch are no more than vain Lip Labour, and a Mocking of God. All ſuch, it is to be apprehended, go from Church with no Fruit from where they have been.

Theot. This is a ſad Caſe. But, I hope it is not the ſame with thoſe who may have many Diſtractions, yet do what they can to avoid them.

Theoph. By no means. Some Diſtractions, as I ſaid, are involuntary, and to which the moſt devout Chriſtians are liable, for the Devil, the Enemy of all Good, when he cannot withdraw us from Maſs, or ſaying our Prayers, does all he can to diſturb us, by filling our Minds with a thouſand idle Thoughts and vain Imaginations, but theſe involuntary Diſtractions will not hurt us. They may be very profitable, as giving us Occaſion to humble ourſelves the more before God, confeſſing our own Miſery and Weakneſs, and our entire Dependance on his Grace, without which we cannot ſo much as produce one good Thought. Let us but ſeriouſly and ſincerely

do

do the beſt we can, and we may truſt in his Mercy and Goodneſs to ſupply the reſt.

Theot. This is comfortable and encouraging; but can't you preſcribe ſome Rules, by obſerving of which I may, in ſome Meaſure at leaſt, prevent thoſe Diſtractions, or the more eaſily drive them out of my Mind?

Theoph. The beſt I can propoſe is, Firſt, When in the Church, about to hear Maſs, ſeriouſly to reflect where, and in whoſe Preſence you are, in the Houſe of God himſelf, and in his Preſence, before whom the Powers of Heaven tremble, and the Cherubim and Seraphim proſtrate themſelves; that where the Bleſſed Sacrament is kept in the Tabernacle, there Jeſus Chriſt himſelf is truly and really preſent, requiring, and juſtly deſerving of our utmoſt reverential Attention, and humbleſt Acts of Adoration and Devotion. Secondly, Diligently to attend to all the Actions of the Prieſt at the Altar, the Rites, Ceremonies, and Prayers ordained by the Church to the Honour of God, and for the greater Solemnity of this auguſt and tremendous Sacrifice of the Maſs.

Theot. I am infinitely obliged to you, dear *Theophilus,* for the Pains you have taken with me. Let me beg one Favour more, which is, to tell me what Method, in your Opinion, is the beſt to hear Maſs devoutly, and with Advantage.

Theoph.

Theoph. This I will do with Pleasure; but, if you please, it shall be the Subject of our next Conference.

Theot. With all my Heart. At present farewel.

DIALOGUE XVII.

Method of Hearing Mass.

Theotime. IF my good Friend *Theophilus* is at Leisure, I shall be glad of a little Conversation with him this Morning, and on the Subject mentioned when I was Yesterday in his Company.

Theophilus. Good Day to you, *Theotime*, I am at leisure, and ready to oblige you in any Thing.

Theot. Consequently to this, you must now, according to my Request, tell me what Method, in your Opinion, is the best to hear Mass well.

Theoph. There are many pious and learned Authors, who have writ upon this Subject, and who have proposed various devout and excellent Methods of hearing Mass, and which every one may chuse as best suits their Inclinations and Devotions, as every one may not equally like the same; for it is in Regard of our Spiritual, as with our Corporal Taste, in which every one, in some Measure, differs from another, and each takes that Food or Liquor he likes best ; so in our spiritual Exercises, Prayers, and Books of Devotion, I would advise to make use of those which may be most adapted to us, and to affect us most with pious Sentiments and Devotion. The End of all these various Books and Methods is the same, to stir up in us a fervent Love of God, and to move us to serve him.   They are as so many beautiful Lines leading to the same Point.   Here then, *Theotime*, use your own Liberty, follow the Bent of your own pious Inclinations, and make use of that Method of hearing Mass, which may please you best, and is most accommodated to the Sacrifice, and to the Ends for which it is offered up. The common Manual has very good pious Prayers adapted to every Part of the Mass. A Treatise, called the *Sacrifice of the New Law explained by that of the Old*, is very good, and several others which are to be had.   In my Opinion, and not to derogate from the Excellency and Usefulness of others, the Methods of hearing Mass published by the truly pious and learned Mr. *Gother*, are admirable, and never to be too much recommended.   His first Method for Beginners is well adapted to them.   His second for the well instructed, and his third for the more advanced, are writ with equal

Judg-

Judgment and Piety, as is his fourth for the Abfent. I can't advife you better how to hear Mafs well, than by recommending his fecond or third Method, where you are taught how to accompany the Prieft, and to go along with him in every Part of the Mafs with proper and fuitable Affections, and I doubt not but you will find great Comfort and Advantage in obferving them.

Theot. I admire the Book, and always carry it with me when I go to hear Mafs. But, as you juft now faid, there is Variety in our fpiritual Tafte; I fhall efteem it a great Favour if you will give me a devout Method of hearing Mafs. This, added to the Explication you have given, will render your Inftructions compleat, and will be an additional Kindnefs to me.

Theoph. I think, *Theotime,* after recommending Mr. *Gother*'s excellent Methods of hearing Mafs, you might be very well content, nor, as I faid, can I give you better Inftructions on this Point; however, I will endeavour to fatisfy you; and may what I am about to fay be to the Glory of God, and to our mutual Inftruction and Edification.

When you are in the Church, and fee the Prieft at the Foot of the Altar, ready to begin Mafs, join with him, and offer up this Sacrifice, according to the Intention of the Church, and for thefe four Ends

for

for which it is offered. First, As a *Holocaust*, or Sacrifice of Oblation, to give supreme Worship or Adoration to God, as supreme Lord, Maker, and Governor of all Things, and consecrate yourself entirely to him and his holy Service. Secondly, As a *Euchariftick* Sacrifice of Praise and Thankfgiving for all his Benefits, spiritual and temporal, bestowed upon you. Thirdly, As a *Propitiatory* Sacrifice to obtain Pardon of your Sins. Fourthly, As an *Imprecatory* Sacrifice, to obtain all Graces and Blessings you stand in need of, and in all a Commemoration of Christ's Passion and Sufferings. Having thus devoutly prepared yourself, carefully attend to, and go along with the Priest in every Part of the Holy Sacrifice, as thus :

When he makes a profound Inclination to the Crucifix, do you with great Humility bow your Head, and give due Reverence likewife to it. Then sign yourself with the Sign of the Cross, and say with the Priest, *In the Name of the Father*, &c. then you may devoutly, jointly with the Clerk, recite the Pfalm, *Judica me Deus*; but take Notice, that here and elsewhere in the Mafs, whatever the People say jointly with the Priest or Clerk, they are to say it softly, and to themfelves. It is the Clerk only who is to answer aloud, and which he does in the Name of, and for the People, who speak by his Mouth, and which is

abun-

abundantly sufficient to express their Consent and joining with the Priest. The Reason why the Clerk is appointed to answer and to make the Responsories in the Name of all the Assistants, is to prevent all Noise and disagreeable discording Voices, some high, some low, which might cause Distractions to the Priest, and likewise to one another, that so the sacred Mysteries may be celebrated, and attended to in Silence, and with all interiour and exteriour Recollection possible.

While the Priest is saying the *Confiteor*, endeavour to stir up in your Soul a true Sorrow and Contrition for your Sins, humbly imploring the Mercy of Almighty God. When the Clerk recites the *Confiteor*, you may devoutly, but softly, say it with him, humbly striking your Breast at *Mea culpa*, and with a deep Sense of your many and grievous Sins, beg Pardon of God, through the Intercession of the Blessed Virgin and all the Saints, and that you may share in the Absolution pronounced by the Priest to the People after the *Confiteor*, then join as before, mentioned in the following little Verses and Responsories, and when the Priest says *Oremus, Let us pray*, endeavour to recollect your Thoughts, and dispose yourself to join in Prayer with all the Fervour and Attention you possibly can. At the *Introit*, which is properly the Beginning of the Mass, you may call to mind the

the earneſt Deſires of the antient Fathers, before Chriſt, for his Coming. Rejoice that he is come, and beg that he would come at this Time ſpiritually into your Soul, and make you fit to receive the Benefit of this holy Sacrifice. The *Kyrie Eleiſons* follow. Theſe you may ſay devoutly, but ſoftly, with the Clerk, and beg of Jeſus Chriſt to have Mercy on you: Join likewiſe with the Prieſt in ſaying the *Gloria in excelſis*; it is truly ſtiled the *Angelical Hymn*, and confiſts of moſt excellent Acts of Praiſe, Thankſgiving, and Adoration, better than which is not eaſily to be formed, and may here be very fitly ſaid, either in *Latin* or *Engliſh*, by the People.

After the *Gloria*, the Prieſt ſays the Collects. Seriouſly attend to them, joining your Intentions with his, praying for the ſame End he does, and in the Concluſion of them, with Heart and Voice ſay, *Amen*. While the Prieſt reads the Epiſtle, if you underſtand *Latin*, attend to what is read, and thoſe who do not underſtand *Latin*, or who cannot read, may ſilently give God thanks for revealing his holy Will to us in the ſacred Scriptures, and beg his Grace to do his holy Will in all Things. In like Manner, when the Goſpel is read, ſtand up and hearken to it, and in the End ſay devoutly with the Clerk, *Laus tibi Chriſte*; or, *Praiſe be to thee, O Chriſt, for this holy Goſpel*.

Theſe.

Theot. I beg Pardon for interrupting you. I observe many People read out of Books they have, the Epistles and Gospels, at the Time the Priest reads them. Is this proper?

Theoph. We have the Epistles and Gospels for the whole Year, published in *English*, and I can't discommend this Practice; but in my Opinion they had better read and reflect upon them at home some Time before they go to hear Mass, or in the Church before the Priest begins. This would imprint in their Minds the Substance of them, and help the Attention while the Priest reads them.

Theot. I am satisfied. Please to go on.

Theoph. After the Gospel, on *Sundays* and some other Festivals, the *Creed* is said, at which you may stand up, and recite it with the Priest, or make Acts of Faith, and of believing all and every Thing that God has revealed in his holy Word, and taught us by his holy Catholick Church. At the Words, *Et homo factus est*, reverently kneel dowu, and adore the divine Word made Flesh. The Creed being said, the Priest begins the Offertory, or Oblation of the Bread and Wine. Join with him, and lay your Heart upon the Altar, and with it your Body, your Soul, your Thoughts, Words and Actions, your whole Interiour and Exteriour, offering them all up to God, in Union with the Oblation

the

the Prieſt then makes, dedicating yourſelf wholly and entirely to the Service of God. When he ſays the *Orate Fratres,* anſwer with the Clerk, and devoutly join with the Prieſt in the ſecret Prayers, till you hear him about to begin the Preface, making the little Reſponſories before it. When the Prieſt recites the Preface with all poſſible Fervour and Devotion, ſay it with him, or mentally join with the Angels, and all the celeſtial Spirits, in praiſing and adoring God. At the *Sanctus, Sanctus, Sanctus,* bow down and humbly adore the ſacred, holy, and undivided Trinity.

When the Canon of the Maſs begins, attend with all the Silence and Recollection you can. This is the moſt ſolemn and the ſubſtantial Part of the Maſs, and being appropriated ſolely to the Prieſtly Function, or the Myſteries of this great Sacrifice, offered up by the Prieſt, is ſaid with a low and ſubmiſſive Voice, by him and by him alone, and is not to be ſaid by the People. During the Canon you may unite your Intention with the Prieſt, and uſe ſuch Prayers as correſpond to what the Prieſt prays for in the Canon, that is, pray for God's holy Catholick Church, for the ſupreme Paſtor of it, all Prelates and Paſtors, all Chriſtian Kings and Princes, for all who are in any Trouble or Neceſſity, or for any particular Bleſſing you may ſtand in need of; and at the firſt *Memento* remember

ber your particular Relations, Friends, and Benefactors. Thus entertain yourself till you hear the little Bell ring to give Notice of the Confecration, then recollecting all the Powers of your Soul, when the Prieft elevates the holy Hoft, bow down with all poffible Humility, and adore Jefus Chrift, truly and really there prefent, and the fame when he elevates the Chalice.

Theot. Many People, in Time of the Elevation, ftrike their Breafts very hard, and make their Acts of Adoration fo loud, and with fuch a Murmur, or Confufion of Voices, as rather caufes, in my Opinion, Diftractions, than excites Devotion. What do you think ?

Theoph. I muft think their Intention good, and that it is out of Devotion they do it; but it is rather to be difapproved. Strike your Breaft modeftly, and with Compunction, and make your Acts of Adoration in an humble and low Voice, or rather mentally, for in thefe facred Moments the greater Silence and Recollection is to be obferved, to avoid all Diftraction or Difturbance to the Prieft, during the Act of Confecration. Hence every one ought carefully to avoid all coughing, fpitting, hawking, or blowing their Nofes.

Theot. Is their Cuftom to be approved, who at the Elevation kneel but with one Knee, or only bend one Knee ?

Theoph.

Theoph. My anfwer to this is : Where Lamenefs, Weaknefs, or other Inability, hinders them from doing otherwife, they are neither to be cenfured nor condemned. Where this is not the Cafe, they are feverely to be cenfured and condemned for fhewing fo little Reverence to Jefus Chrift prefent, and muft anfwer for it, and for the Scandal and Difedification they give to others ; but I go on.

After the Elevation till the *Pater Nofter*, continue devoutly praying, and at the fecond *Memento*, pray for the Souls of the Faithful departed, for your particular Relations and Friends deceafed.   At the *Nobis quoque Peccatoribus*, modeftly ftrike your Breaft, and beg of God to be merciful to you. When the Prieft fays the *Pater Nofter*, you may fay it with him, and when the Clerk fays, *Sed libera nos à malo*, humbly beg to be delivered from all Evils and Dangers, efpecially the great Evil of Sin.   At the *Agnus Dei*, humbly addrefs yourfelf to the Lamb of God, Jefus Chrift, truly prefent on the Altar, faying foftly with the Prieft, *Agnus Dei qui tollis, &c.* ftriking your Breaft modeftly.   After that, entertain yourfelf in confidering the wonderful Love of Jefus Chrift to us, in the Inftitution of this moft holy Sacrament, giving us therein his own moft holy Body and Blood, to be the Food of our Souls, and to bring us to everlafting Life. While the Prieft com-

communicates, endeavour to make a spiritual Communion, and beg of Jesus Christ that you may spiritually receive him into the House of your Soul, and acknowledging your own Unworthiness, strike your Breast, and say the *Domine non sum dignus* with the Priest. At the Post-communion, and when the Priest says the last Collects, join with him and attend to them, saying, with the Clerk, at the End, *Amen.* When the Priest bows down, before he gives the Benediction, do you bow down humbly to receive the Benediction, begging of God, that as the Priest, in his Name, blesses you on Earth, he would vouchsafe to ratify that Benediction here, and give you an eternal Benediction hereafter. When the Priest reads the Gospel of St. *John,* stand up, and reverently attend to it, and at those Words, *Et verbum caro factum est,* kneel down and adore Jesus Christ made Man for our sake.

Mass ended, be not in a hurry to go out of the Church, as if you was tired with what you have been doing. Stay a little while; thank God for the Opportunity of hearing Mass; beg Pardon for all your Distractions and Indevotions, and that he would grant you to receive the Benefits of the holy Sacrifice you have assisted at. I have thus, *Theotime,* endeavoured to satisfy your Desire, and given a brief Method of hearing Mass: You may observe, it is

much

much upon the Plan of pious Mr. *Gother's*, and you may use either this, or that, or any other you may find in any approved Book of Devotion, as you like best yourself. One Thing I must now ask of you.

Theot. O! Sir, you have a right to command any Thing in my Power. Pray, what is it?

Theoph. When you go to hear Mass fail not to remember me, and let me have a Share in your good Prayers. In return, I will reciprocally pray for you.

Theot. I most willingly agree to the Proposal, and now be pleased to accept of my most grateful Thanks for your Goodness, in thus explicating to me the Holy Altar and Sacrifice. With this my Acknowledgment I take my Leave of you, and am your very humble Servant.

Theoph. I am equally your's, *Theotime,* Adieu.

Soli Deo Gloria. Amen.

INSTRUCTIONS

AND

DEVOTIONS

FOR

Hearing Mass.

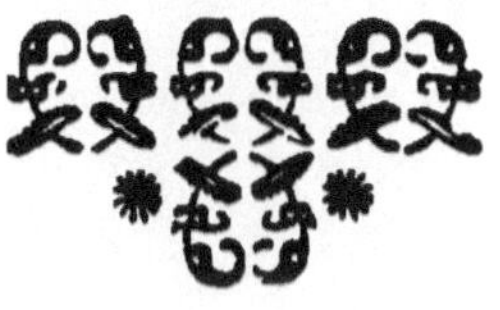

Printed in the Year MDCCLXVII.

THE
PREFACE.

THE greatest Sacrifice that has been of-fered to Almighty God, was that of Christ our Lord on the Cross; where, by the Effusion of his Blood, he cancel'd the Hand-writing that was against us, seal'd our Peace with God, and made such a lasting Provision of Merits and Grace, that whatever Blessings we receive from our Heavenly Father, come to us through him, and must be acknowledg'd the Effects of his Sufferings. By this Oblation of himself in our Behalf he became our Redeemer, and 'tis the Work of our Redemption he still car-ries on, not ceasing in Heaven to be our Advo-cate, and even from that holy Sanctuary, into which he is enter'd, applying to us the Merits of his Passion, and offering himself in our Cause for ever. For tho' Christ was crucify'd and died but once, yet the Oblation of Christ cruci-fy'd is eternal, and continues for ever, where-ever Christ is present; it continues in Heaven, because he is there; it continues on Earth, be-cause he is on our Altars; so that having once died for us on Mount Calvary, he still offers himself, as having been immolated for us on that

A 2

holy

holy Mount. But whether then on Mount Calvary, *or now in Heaven, or on our Altars, the Victim and the Oblation of the Victim are every where the same; it being no other than Jesus Christ, who is both the Oblation and the Offerer, in Quality of Priest eternal, as was foretold in the Psalms :* Thou art a Priest for ever, according to the Order of *Melchisedech.*

This Oblation then being not only a Memorial, but likewise a continual Application of the Merits of Christ's Passion to us, we have great Reason to bless our Redeemer for having made Choice of our Altars, there daily to offer himself to the eternal Father, and perpetuate the Oblation he made of himself on the Cross; and by this holy Expedient of his Love to excite us daily, not only with Gratitude to commemorate his Sufferings, but likewise powerfully move us to use all possible Endeavours for becoming faithful Servants to so good a Master, having there provided us the most effectual Means for obtaining of the Father all those Helps and Graces necessary to so great a Work. In this consists the Substance of our public Liturgy, where Christ is the invisible Offerer and the Priest performs the Ministry, to which he is called. Ministrorum vice sumus, *says St.* Chrysostom, qui vero hæc sanctificat & transmutat, ipse est *(*Christus.*)* We hold the Place of Ministers; but he that sanctifies these Gifts, and changes them, is Christ himself; he that wrought those Things at the last Supper, does what is done here. *This great Oblation then thus made by Christ and his Ministers, is the Subject*

f

of our daily Worship ; to this the Faithful are daily called, as having their Part too in this Offering, both in presenting it to Almighty God, and, by means of it, hoping for Blessings from the Divine Bounty : In what Manner they are to assist at it, is the Business of these short Instructions, in which, tho' there be nothing new, yet the Method may still be helpful to all Conditions ; to the Ignorant, in giving them some Light into this great Mystery ; and to the Well-instructed, by leading them still farther into this Abyss of Power and Goodness, in which the most Advanced have still farther to go.

But while I speak of this Oblation, I am very sensible of its being a Consequence of the real Presence of Christ in the Eucharist, and that there can be no Devotion expected here, but what is built on this Doctrine ; and therefore, for the laying a Foundation to this little Work, I think it very reasonable, by Way of Preamble, to clear some Difficulties belonging to this Point ; not that I pretend to explain the Manner how Christ is present in this Mystery, but in a Matter, where Reason is at a stand, to make this Wonder credible at least ; by laying before it some other wonderful Works of the Almighty, that one Incomprehensible may prepare the Way for another. 'Tis the Method St. Gregory used in explicating the Mystery of Christ's Resurrection and Apparitions, Hom. 26. in Evang. " The " Works of God, says he, would not be the " Subject of our Wonder, if they could be com- " prehended by our Reason ; nor has that Faith

" any Merit, where it has Experience to de-
" monstrate it. These Works then of our Re-
" deemer, which of themselves are above our
" Reason, must be consider'd by other Works of
" his; that so what is wonderful may gain
" Credit from other Things yet more wonder-
" ful." In this manner I shall, without Offence, touch at some Difficulties relating to
this Doctrine, and see how far the Works of
God will recommend the Truth of this Mystery
to our Belief.

I. Then, by what Power is it to be imagin'd,
that what was Bread and Wine, can be changed
into the Body and Blood of Christ?

By the divine Power, of which we have so
many Instances in H. Scripture; that Power
by which the Waters were turn'd into Blood,
Exod. vii. 20. the Dust into Lice, Exod. viii.
17. Lot's Wife into a Pillar of Salt, Gen.
xix. 26. the Water into Wine, at the Mar-
riage in Cana of Galilee, John ii. 9. that
Power which the Devil owned in Christ, Mat.
iv. 3. when he said to him, If thou be the
Son of God, command that these Stones
be made Bread. That Power may be easily
conceiv'd sufficient to change the Bread and
Wine into Christ's Body and Blood. 'Tis the
Power of God, whom in our Creed we believe
Almighty: He who made all Things of nothing,
can, whenever he pleases, change one Thing
into another. He spoke in the Creation, and all
Things were made; he speaks afterwards, and

by

*by his Word Things are changed, because he
has Power to make Things be what he says
they are:* As *therefore Christ says to the No-
bleman,* John iv. 50. *whose Son was sick at*
Capernaum, Go thy Way, thy Son liveth;
*by his Power made him to be as he said he
was; so here Christ saying,* This is my Body, This is my Blood; *his Power and Truth
make it to be, what by his Word he says it is.
Christ says it, and because we can neither
question his Power nor Truth, we therefore
believe it to be what he so solemnly asserts it.*

II. *How can the Body of Christ be contain'd
whole and entire under the Compass of a Piece
of Bread or Wafer.*

*We don't apprehend Christ's Body to be in
the Sacrament after that* grofs, carnal and corporal Manner, *as some of the Disciples seem'd
to understand it, when they cry'd out,* John vi.
60. This is a hard Saying, who can hear it?
but after a more perfect *and* spiritual Manner
*of Being. To conceive this aright, you must
observe out of St.* Paul, 1 Cor. xv. 42, 43.
*there are two very different Manners of Be-
ing proper to a human Body, according to its
different States; for it may be either corruptible or incorruptible; mortal or immortal;
natural or spiritual. Thus St.* Paul, *discoursing of the Manner in which our Bodies shall
be at the Resurrection, says,* v. 53. *that then*
this Corruptible must put on Incorruption,
and this Mortal must put on Immortality.

A 4

And

And, v. 44. It is fown a natural Body, it is raifed a fpiritual Body. There is a natural Body, and there is a fpiritual Body. *Now, tho' it be not poffible to imagine how a human Body, when it is in its* corruptible, mortal, *and* natural *Manner of Being, that is fo extended and grofs as here it is, can be truly and really contained under the Form of a Wafer: Yet, when this fame Body has put on its other more perfect Manner of Being, and is now become* incorruptible, immortal, *and even* fpiritual, *there is not then that Difficulty of apprehending it ; becaufe being now become in its Qualities like a Spirit, and a Spirit requiring no Extenfion or Greatnefs of Place for its Being ; fo neither does a* Body, *when it is become* fpiritual. *As therefore you can eafily conceive, how a Spirit may be really under the Compafs of a Wafer, fo likewife may it be underftood of Chrift's Body, which is not imagined to be there in its corporal and natural Manner of Being, but as it is incorruptible, immortal, and a fpiritual Body.*

By keeping clofe to this Thought, feveral other Difficulties may be folv'd, relating to this Subject. For Chrift's Body being in the Sacrament according to this perfect Manner of Being, even like a Spirit, it may be apprehended how the Sacrament may be broken without injuring or breaking his Body : As when a Man's Body is broken, or a Limb cut off, the Soul remains ftill entire, becaufe it is a Spirit, and not fubject to fuch Accidents as thefe. Thus likewife may it be

con-

*conceiv'd how the Body of Christ may be whole
and entire in every Part of the Sacrament, after
the sacred Host is divided ; as also how it may
be in many Places at once : For tho' we cannot
easily understand this possible to an extended
Body, and in its corporal Manner of Being,
there's no such Difficulty in relation to a Spirit,
or other Thing in its Manner of Being like a
Spirit, because a Spirit has no Dependance on
Place, nor is confined either to it or by it.*

III. *How then is it the same Body of Christ
which was born of the Virgin* Mary, *and crucify'd, since it is so very different from it ?*

'Tis the same true and real Body of Christ,
which was born and crucify'd, the same, I say,
in Substance, but different as to its Manner of
Being : *As the very same Bodies, in which we
now live, shall rise again, the same in Substance, but very different in their Manner of
Being, as being then to be glorified, and become
immortal and spiritual : Upon which Words of*
St. Paul, *the* English *Bible, printed at* Cam-
bridge, 1629, *observes, that however this sup-
poses a Change in the Bodies, yet 'tis* not
changing the Substance ; *which Explication
being allow'd of in our Case, it clears this
Difficulty : And there's Reason enough to admit it, if it be consider'd, how Christ enter'd in
amongst his Disciples, the Doors being shut ;
that he was born without Injury to his Mother's
virginal Integrity ; that he passed thro' the
Multitudes more than once, without being seen*

er

or perceiv'd; in which Instances there are Grounds to believe Christ assumed this preternatural and spiritual Manner of Existence, not only after his Resurrection, when his Body was glorify'd, but likewise before.

IV. *How can this be reconciled with the Senses, for our Seeing and Tasting tell us the* Eucharist *is Bread and Wine after Consecration; and must not we believe them, since God has given us these very Powers for this End?*

This must be answer'd by asking another Question. What did Mary Magdalene *see at the Sepulchre,* Mark xvi. 5. *The Scriptures say,* She saw a young Man sitting at the Right Side, cloath'd in a long white Robe, *and no Question her Eyes told her it was a young Man, from what she saw, and her Ears from what she heard him speak. And after all this Information of her Senses, was it a young Man? No; for,* Matt. xxviii. *we are assured it was an Angel; and the* English *Bible now mentioned, in the Margin in* Mark xvi. *says,* It was the Angel of God in the Likeness of a young Man. *Now, how is this to be reconciled with the Senses? The same Difficulty may be made in the Dove seen over* Christ *at his Baptism, and the* fiery Tongues *over the Apostles at* Pentecost. *For tho' the Information of* Sense *in these Cases was, that they were* young Men, *a* Dove, *and* fiery Tongues; *yet you see, our* Faith *goes otherwise, and we believe they were not in Substance*

what

what they appeared to be, but an Angel and the Holy Ghoſt, *under thoſe Forms. And if it be examined why we believe there was really an Angel, and the Holy Ghoſt, and not a young Man, a Dove,* &c. *the Reaſon is, becauſe God has revealed it in Holy Writ, and expreſly aſſured us what they were; and therefore upon his Word we make no Difficulty of believing it, notwithſtanding all the Information of* Senſe *to the contrary. Thus we do in our Caſe: Our Senſes tell us, as yours do, that the Sacrament appears to be nothing but Bread and Wine, and yet we believe there is really preſent in it Chriſt's Body and Blood; becauſe God has reveal'd it in Holy Writ, and expreſly ſaid,* It is his Body that was given for us, and his Blood that was ſhed for us. *And are we to be cenſured for believing what he ſo ſolemnly tells us? Some indeed are here greatly concern'd for the* Senſes, *and ſeem troubled for the queſtioning their Authority, and not acknowledging their Infallibility; when in Reality we do no more here than others, without the leaſt Difficulty, in the ſeveral Inſtances abovementioned. We have as great a Deference for the* Senſes, *as others, and confeſs their Authority; but, 'tis true, we have a much greater for* God's *ſacred Word, and the* Truth *of what he ſays; and therefore, whenever theſe ſeem to interfere, and we have one Sort of Information from the* Senſes, *and another from* God's Word, *we confeſs our Reſolution of preferring* God's Word *before the* Senſes, *and own ourſelves bound to maintain*
his

his Authority *and* Infallibility *rather than
theirs: So that if one must give Way, it is
evident which it is to be, and likewise on
whom our Faith is to depend, that is, on God,
rather than Man, on what God says, rather
than on the contrary Information of Sense:
And this is the Rule followed above, tho' here
reproved by some.*

*But now to reconcile this whole Matter, I
think 'tis plain the* Senses *are not here deceiv'd
at all; for the* Eyes *and* Tongue *say, in regard of the* B. Eucharist, *it has the* Colour
and Taste *of Bread and Wine, and this is certainly true, for it has so; here's no Mistake in
this: But now, when the* Judgment, *from this
Report made by those two* Senses, *presently and
peremptorily pronounces,* It is Bread and Wine,
*here is the Mistake in this over-hasty Proceed-
ing of the* Judgment, *which, to pronounce a-
right, in many* Cases *is under a Necessity of
examining and consulting the* Hearing, *and
taking Advice with this* Sense *too; and without this, it is most certainly exposed to many
gross Mistakes, and must be censured as very
rash and precipitate.*

*This we see it is bound to, in regard of many
Things which are natural, especially such as
are not very obvious and common, as in* Stones
and Metals: *For how many of this kind do we
daily meet with, which, when we have examined with our* Eyes, *with our* Taste *and
Feeling, we yet know not what they are, and
cannot frame a certain and true* Judgment *of
them:*

them: Till, by our Hearing, we are informed from some more experienced Person, what they really are? Here our Eyes may tell us indeed, what the Colour *is, and the* Tongue *what* Taste; *but if the Judgment should hence pretend to declare with Assurance,* what the Things *are, how easily might it run into Mistakes; not because these* Senses *are deceived, but because it takes not its Information from the Sense that is proper in this Case to give it; because it attends to the Report of the* Eyes, *which is insufficient when it should have regard to the* Ears? *And now if we turn to such Things, in which Art is concerned, which makes an Alteration beyond Nature, such are the Compounds of the Apothecary, the Chemist, the Perfumer, of almost all Trades in their Kind; nay, even of Cooks too: All these know how to mix and disguise Things with that Art, and give them many Qualities of* Colour, Taste, *and* Smell, *which belong not to them, that they are Kinds of* Mysteries: *And to judge by the* Eyes, *by the* Tongue, *by the* Touch, *or the* Smell, *would be many times to go out of the Way: And there is no surer Means of avoiding* Mistakes, *than to hear from the Artist, and from this* Sense *conclude what they are; and this is not to contradict or lay aside these Senses, but only to consider, which of them is most proper in every Case to inform the Judgment, and follow that.*

And is it not thus too, in all those Cases, where God is pleased to intervene with his extraordinary and miraculous Power? We know

he

be can change, whenever he pleases, the Nature of Things beyond all human Arts, and make spiritual *and* infinite *Beings appear under* material *and* corporeal Forms. *And now, tho' in* ordinary Cases *our* Eyes, &c. *give sufficient Direction to our Judgment ; yet in such as are the Subject of* an extraordinary Power, *it is impossible they should give any other Account, than of* what they appear to be. *But as to the concluding* what they really are, as to their Nature and Substance, *the Judgment must first consult with what is heard from the* Word of God, *the* Divine, *and the* Church : *And hence it may have such Information for its coming to an Issue, as the other Senses of themselves could never pretend to. Thus, tho' from the Report of the Eyes the Judgment can in* ordinary Cases *with Assurance pronounce, which is* a Dove, *or* young Man; *yet when, by an* extraordinary Power, God is pleased to present, under those Forms, other *spiritual or* infinite Beings, as of Angels, or the Holy Ghost, *then must the Judgment call in some other Help, and not proceed by what* these see, *but by what is* heard *from* Faith *and the* Word of God, *in this Point; and thus only can we judge aright. And why, but because as in Things of* Art, *the* Artist gives the most *certain* Account, *and it would be a Rashness to adhere to the Senses in* Contradiction to him; *so in Things that are* spiritual, *and the* extraordinary Works of God, *'tis God himself gives the best Direction to the* Judgment : It must *attend to what it*

hears

hears from him, *and not what is seen in the Object: And to adhere to the* Eyes, *in Con*tradiction *to him, would not be Reason, but Madness.*

Is it not Reason then, that in the blessed Eucharist, which the Scripture informs us to be the Subject of a miraculous Power, we should not only enquire what the Eyes see, and Mouth tastes, but likewise what the Word of God, what Faith and the Church declare in this Case; and rather frame our Judgment from what we thus Hear, *than from* Seeing *and* Tasting *? And this without any Discredit at all to these Senses: For tho' these are to be regarded, about their proper Objects of Colour and Taste, yet when the Question is,* What we are to believe, *they must give Leave to the Ears to take place; because, as the Apostle says,* Faith comes by Hearing. *Thus we render to every one their Due; to God, what belongs to God, and to every Sense, in their kind, what belongs to them: But to let our* Faith *be directed by what we* see, *rather than by what we* hear from God, *that we cannot do; because none knows the Things of God, but the Spirit of God.*

Thus having given some Light to these Difficulties, which are the common Grounds from whence arise all the Doubts and Disbelief concerning this Mystery, I hope on the one Side it may be an Encouragement to Reason and Sense readily to submit to this Divine Truth; and on the other, be a Means of raising the Devotion of those, who already believe it; that so with
greater

greater Fervour of Mind and Admiration of God's wonderful Goodness, they may attend to every Part of the great Sacrifice of Christ's Body and Blood daily offered for them on our Altars: For the doing of which in particular, I now proceed to the following Instructions.

Instruc-

Inſtructions *and* Devotions

FOR

Hearing M A S S.

What the Mass *is: What the beſt Way of hearing it.*

Q. *W*HAT is the beſt Way of hearing Maſs?

A. To accompany the Prieſt, in offering with him to Almighty God, the Sacrifice of the Body and Blood of *Chriſt*, under the Forms of Bread and Wine.

Q. *Then 'tis neceſſary every One ſhould know what the Prieſt does, for otherwiſe, how can we accompany him? Pray tell me therefore what that is.*

A. Without this there is no hearing Maſs with Profit; and therefore 'tis a Point in which every Chriſtian ought to be well in-

B   ſtructed.

structed.   You are for this End to imprint well in your Mind, that Priests at the Altar do the same which Christ did at his *Last Supper*, and which he commanded his Apostles and their Successors to do after him, when he said to them, *Do this in Remembrance of me.*   In Obedience to which Command, they do what he then did; that is, they take Bread and Wine to the Altar; they bless and consecrate it by the Power here given them, into his Body and Blood, and offer up this holy Victim to the eternal Father in Remembrance of him once offered upon the Cross for our Redemption; *Do this in Remembrance of me.*   This it is they do.

Q. Then I see the Mass is, as you have already said, an Oblation of the Body and Blood of Christ, *under the Forms of Bread and Wine, made in Remembrance of his Death on the Cross. And is not this what you call a Sacrifice?*

A. Yes, it is the Sacrifice of the new Law, in which are fulfilled all the Sacrifices of the Law of *Moses.*   And here you will do well to observe, that God has always been worshiped by Sacrifice, as you may see in *Abel,* in the Beginning of the World, and afterwards in *Moses,* when God himself established the Order of Priests and prescribed the Sacrifices, which were all Types of the Sacrifice that was to succeed in the Law of Grace.   And therefore as in the old Law there were two Sorts of Sacrifices; one which was offered up *entire,* and wholly consumed on the Altar, and

and was called an *Holocauſt*; the other, offer'd and conſumed in Part only, the other Part being divided between the Prieſt and the People, and might therefore be called a *Communion at Sacrifice:* ſo here in this one Sacrifice is Chriſt wholly offered up an Holocauſt for Men; and yet ſo that both Prieſt and People partake of the Victim: and thus is the old Law fulfilled in the new, as to all its Parts and Figures.

Q. I am to remember then, that as in the Law of Moſes, *were offered upon the Altar Birds and Beaſts, as Turtles, Oxen, Lambs, &c. Theſe Sacrifices were all aboliſhed by Chriſt, and in their Place has ſucceeded by his Command, the Oblation of* Chriſt *himſelf, the true Lamb of God, that takes away the Sins of the World, and this is the Sacrifice of the new Law. Now I can eaſily apprehend how the Prieſts are to make this Oblation, becauſe they bleſs and conſecrate the Bread and Wine: But how are the People to do it, whoſe Office is ſo different from the Prieſts?*

A. "Tis the Prieſt alone that conſecrates but 'tis not to be imagined, it is he alone that is to offer the Victim ; no, the Maſs is the Sacrifice of the whole Church, that is, both of Prieſt and People ; and therefore as the Prieſt offers it to Almighty God, ſo ought likewiſe the People to offer it, both with the Prieſt and by him. For as in reſpect of the *Conſecration*, the Prieſt is the Miniſter of Jeſus Chriſt, who has given him Power to conſe-

crate,

crate, and who with him confecrates the Victim; fo in regard of the Oblation, the Prieſt is deputed by God for the People, who with him ought to offer it to God; And this St. *Paul* hints, *Heb.* v. 1. *Every Prieſt being choſen from among Men, is appointed for Men in thoſe Things that belong to God, that he may offer Gifts and Sacrifices for Sins.*

Q. *'Tis the Prieſt then alone is to* confecrate, *but the People are to join with him in* offering *up to Almighty God, the ſacred Hoſt and deſiring him to accept it. Was not there ſomething of this Method practiſed in the old Law ?*

A. Yes, the People having brought to the Prieſt what was to be offered, did afterwards in time of Sacrifice, while the Prieſt was at the Altar, offer it there to God by the Hands of the Prieſt ; and on this their own Offering, as well as on the Prieſts, depended the good Acceptance it was to have with God. Something of this Practice you fee, *Luke*, i. 9, 10. where 'tis related, while *Zacharias* was burning Incenfe at the Altar, the whole Multitude of the People were without in Prayer, *viz.* in the Body of the Temple. Thus in all their Sacrifices the Office of the Prieſts was to offer them at the Altar, while the People affiſting at the Oblation, at the fame Time offered them to God, by the Hands of thoſe his Miniſters, either for the Remiſſion of their Sins, for a Thankſgiving, &c. And thus in our Chriſtian Sacrifice, ought the People ever to join with the Prieſt, in offering it to Almighty God.   This

This Method was earneſtly recommended by St. *Chryſoſtom* to the Faithful of his Time, *Hom. in 2 Cor.* exhorting them to bring an earneſt Attention with them, to the Celebration of the dreadful Myſteries, and to conſider that Prieſts and People make up but one Body; that therefore they ought to join with one another, and not to caſt off all from themſelves, and throw it wholly upon the Prieſts. The ſame is urged by the learned *Roderigus, Par. 2. tr. 8. c.* 15. where he ſays, that tho' it be the Prieſt only that ſpeaks, and with his Hands offers this Sacrifice, yet all the Faithful offer it likewiſe with him; which being ſuppoſed I declare, ſays he, the beſt Method of hearing Maſs is to go on jointly with the Prieſt, offering up the Sacrifice and doing as much as may be, the very ſame that he does; making this Account with ourſelves, that we all will meet there, not only to hear Maſs, but likewiſe to make and offer up the Sacrifice together with the Prieſts; for in Reality and in Truth the Thing is ſo.

Q. *Well, but does the Church require this of the People?*

A. That this is imported in *hearing Maſs* may be plainly ſeen in the Liturgy itſelf, throughout which it is manifeſt, the Sacrifice there offered is *common,* and that the People are to offer it with the Prieſt.

In the Beginning of Maſs, you ſee the *Publick Confeſſion* is made by the People, as well as the Prieſt. The *Kyrie Eleiſons* are ſaid by both. The *Gloria in Excelſis* is ſaid aloud and all in the plural Number, as including the People. Before every Prayer is ſaid *Oremus,* whereby the Prieſt calls on the whole Aſſembly to join with him. The *Epiſtles, Goſpels* and *Creeds,* are ſaid in a low Voice, to ſhew they belong to all preſent.

As to what follows, tho' ſaid in a low Voice, 'tis plain the People are concerned in it. In the *Oblation* of the *Bread,* the Prieſt mentions himſelf and all preſent. In the *Oblation* of the *Wine,* he ſays in the Name of all, *We offer to thee, O Lord,* &c. He repeats the ſame in the following Prayer; and after waſhing his Fingers he prays thus, *Receive, O Holy Trinity, this Oblation we make thee,* &c. And then turning to the People he ſays, *Brethren pray that my Sacrifice and yours, may be acceptable in the Sight of God,* &c. And then calls on all to join with him in Thankſgiving, requiring them to *lift up their Hearts, and give Thanks to God.*

In the *Canon,* all is expreſſed in the plural Number; as in the firſt Prayer, *We humbly beſeech thee, to accept and bleſs theſe Gifts and Sacrifices we offer thee.* In the Second, *Be mindful, O God, of thy Servants, and of all here preſent, for whom we offer, or who offer to thee this Sacrifice.* In the third and fourth the People are included with the Prieſt.

And thus ſtill he goes on after the Elevation, *Wherefore we thy Servants, and alſo thy*

holy

*holy People, mindful of thy Paſſion, &c.
And ſo in all the following Prayers; We
humbly beſeech thee, &c. And to us Sinners,
&c. Deliver us from all Evils. Lamb of
God have mercy on us, &c.*

Thus conſidering the whole Liturgy, 'tis
evident the Maſs is a Sacrifice common both
to Prieſt and People ; and while we behold the Spirit of Chriſt and his Church in
the Inſtitution of it, it may be eaſily concluded, the Manner of aſſiſting at it, which
is moſt conformable to this Spirit, muſt neceſſarily be the beſt.

On which Grounds it follows, that as
many of the Faithful, as deſire to conform
to this Spirit of the Church, when they go
to Maſs, ought to go with the Intention of
offering to Almighty God, with the Prieſt,
this great Sacrifice of the Body and Blood
of Chriſt, and conſequently be very careful
to accompany him, if not in all, at leaſt in
the principal Parts, that ſo by this Means they
may more effectually partake of the fruits of it.

*Q. I don't ſee this is the general Method of
the Faithful, for they ſeem to underſtand that
the making the Oblation belongs only to the Prieſt;
and their Part is only to aſſiſt at it with Devotion, that ſo they may have ſome Share in its
Effects, and in the Prayers there ſaid by the
Prieſt; for this End we ſee ſome ſaying their
Beads all the Time of Maſs, others their Morning Prayers, others the Offices of the Day, or
ſome private Devotion and but with very little*

 Regard

Regard to what the Priest does; and is not this very far from what you speak of?

A. 'Tis different, but yet I question not, but as many as are there with their Souls truly raised to God, partake in some Degree both of the Offering, and of the Effects of this holy Sacrifice; and therefore, without condemning their Devotions, I only propose a Method, which is judged the best, and may be most for our spiritual Advantage; such as is generally observed by as many as perfectly understand their Duty and would be followed by others were they better instructed. For this End I make it here my Request, to the Generality of *Catholicks* not to content themselves with some *general Notions*, concerning the Mass, but to take Pains themselves, and engage some charitable Friend to give them a more particular Instruction, and make them sensible of the true Nature of it and all its Parts, that so they may lose none of those Advantages otherwise to be reaped in this divine Instruction; and that thus may be avoided many prophane Indecencies and irreligious Levities, too often seen at that holy Time and which most certainly arise from a Want of due Knowledge and Instruction of what is there done, and of what is their Duty to do.

And now as to those, who, in Time of this divine Sacrifice, are wholly taken up in saying the *Rosary*, or other *particular Devotions*; I only desire them to remember

they

they have a great Part in the Sacrifice there offered; that it belongs to them to offer it to Almighty God with the Prieft; as likewife in fome Manner to partake of the Victim: that fince their heavenly Father has called them to fo great a Dignity, they would fpare fo much Time from their private *Devotions*, as to comply with this greater Duty, than which, none can poffibly be more acceptable to God. And therefore if they cannot be perfuaded to change their Method that they would make fuch Interruptions, at leaft, in their other Prayers, as may give them Liberty in fome Degree to perform this; that is, lay them by at the more effential Parts of the Mafs, to which they ought to give their Attention.

Q. Well, I underftand you now, that the Mafs is the Oblation of the Body and Blood of Chrift, *made to Almighty God, that the Prieft is deputed to confecrate and make this Oblation, and that the People are likewife to offer it with him. But now you muft tell me in what Manner they are to do this.*

A. I'll fhew you the beft Method I can: but I muft firft lay before you the *chief Ends* for which this Sacrifice is to be offered by all *Chriftians.*

Of the Principal Ends, *for which the Sa-crifice of the Body and Blood of* Chrift *is to be offered: And of the* General Difpofitions in the Offerers.

1. THE firft Duty of a *Chriftian* is *to render to God that fupreme Honour and Worfhip which is due to him as the Sovereign Being.* And this being not poffible to be more effectually done, than by offering to him the Sacrifice of his only Son; infomuch as this is an Oblation of infinite Value, being God equal to himfelf; therefore it is that the *firft and principal End of every* Chriftian in going to Mafs, ought to be *to acknowledge God the Supreme Being, and give him that Honour and Worfhip, which is due to him alone.*

2. Another principal Duty of a *Chriftian* being *to give Thanks to God for all his Bleff-ings,* and there being no more acceptable Of-fering, we can make him, than of his only Son, in whom he is well pleafed; therefore it is, every *Chriftian,* in going to Mafs, ought to remember, that another *principal End* is, to offer to Almighty God this Sacri-fice of his only Son, *in Acknowledgment and Thankfgiving for all Benefits and Bleffings re-ceived whether general or particular, publick or private.*

3. Since in the Mafs is offered to God the fame Body and Blood of *Chrift* which be-ing facrificed on Mount *Calvary* were a full Satisfaction for Sin; therefore it is that the

daily

daily Oblation of the same on our Altars ren-
ders God propitious, by being a daily Application of the Merits of his Son's Paſſion, and
moves him to grant Grace, and the Gift of
Penance, in order to the Remiſſion of the
greateſt Sins; and for this End every *Chriſtian*
going to Maſs, ought to lay before the Father
*the Merits and Paſſion of his only Son who is there
offer'd, with a firm Hope of obtaining thro' him,
that Grace, which may be the effectual Remedy
of all his Offences*

4. This Oblation of the Body and Blood
of *Chriſt,* being thus a Means of daily laying
before the eternal Father, the infinite Value of
his Son's bitter Paſſion; therefore it is a daily
Application of the Merits of *Chriſt* to us,
likewiſe for the Relief of our Neceſſities, and
the obtaining new Graces and Bleſſings for us:
and for this Reaſon, every *Chriſtian,* in going to Maſs, ought to offer it to Almighty
God *for the obtaining all Bleſſings, whether
temporal or ſpiritual,* whether for himſelf,
Friends, Governors, or Church; and *for the
Remedy of all Miſeries and Neceſſities, publick
or private.*

These are the *four principal Ends,* for which
all the Faithful ought to offer up the holy Victim *Chriſt Jeſus,* in the Maſs, to the eternal
Father, for his greater Glory, and their
Good; ever remembering beſides, in this Oblation, to renew daily the Memory of *Chriſt's*
Death and Paſſion, as he himſelf commanded.

Q. So

Q. *So then as often as the Faithful go to Mass, they ought to join with the Priest and offer up the Body and Blood of* Christ. 1. *For the giving* supreme Worship to God. 2. In Thankſgiving for all Benefits. 3. *For the* obtaining Pardon of their Sins. 4. For the procuring new Graces and Bleſſings, *and even in* Remembrance of *Chriſt's* Paſſion. *Is there any Thing more on that Subject?*

A. Only my Requeſt again to all *Catholicks,* ſo ſeriouſly to reflect on theſe *general Ends,* for which they go to Maſs, as to let this be a Means of regulating their Devotion, of raiſing their Spirits to God and keeping up that true *Chriſtian* Behaviour and Reverence, as ſeem abſolutely neceſſary for thoſe who deſire to diſcharge themſelves well of theſe great Duties.

Q. *How do you mean in Particular?*

A. That while Chriſtians in the Maſs offer to Almighty God the Body and Blood of *Chriſt,* thus to pay *Sovereign Homage* to him they would look on *Chriſt* on the Altar, as their Model, and there conſecrate themſelves daily to God, by making a Sacrifice of their Body and Souls according to that Pattern before their Eyes, and there heartily endeavour to give Honour to God, by offering not only *Chriſt* but themſelves likewiſe to him.

2. That as often as they offer *Chriſt* in *Thankſgiving* to God for all his Benefits, they would likewiſe join themſelves to that Sacrifice and make an Oblation of their own

Hearts

Hearts to God; remembering the beft Acknowledgment on their Part, of Bleffings received, is a true Chriftian Life, and the employing all that to his Honour, which has been the Gift of his Goodnefs.

3. That in offering *Chrift* on the Altar as a *Propitiation* for their Offences, they would remember, that Chrift there offered became a Remedy for Sin, by prefenting himfelf to the eternal Father, to fuffer whatever Punifhment his Juftice fhould appoint, for the making due Satisfaction for the Tranfgreffions of Men: And confequently if they defire to partake of the Effect of this Oblation, in the Pardon of their Sins, they would there prefent themfelves before the Altar, in the *Spirit of Penance.* 1. Humbling themfelves at the Sight of their Offences, with a contrite Heart; befeeching God to grant them a fincere Repentance. 2. Offering themfelves according to the Example before them, to fuffer whatever God's Juftice fhall determine. And, 3. Refolving, that as they offend daily, fo their Life fhall be a *daily and continual Penance*; not doubting but Chrift's infinite Satisfaction fhall be thus effectually applied to them, and fupply all their Defects.

4. That in offering Chrift on the Altar for the *obtaining new Bleffings*, they be careful to put up all their Prayers to God *in his Name*; depending entirely on Chrift as their Redeemer, as their Mediator, and as their Head; and putting themfelves in fuch a Difpofition of
Soul,

Soul, that they be truly his Members, and defire to live by his Spirit.

Thus if the Faithful prefent themfelves before the Altar in this Manner, to offer up that holy Victim, Chrift Jefus, to his eternal Father, it will moft certainly be for God's Honour, and the great Advantage of their own Souls. For if they think nothing of thefe *interior Difpofitions*, but run to Mafs out of Cuftom; without any Concern of thus raifing up their Thoughts to God, or apply-ing them, as the Nature of this Sacrifice re-quires; being there in a formal Way, like fo many Statues, without praying or thinking, I can't tell what Benefit they expect, or even what they do there. And then for many others, who, in that lazy Pofture of kneeling on one Knee, feem to be paying their Duty to fome Demi-god; others who are gazing and ftaring about; others who are prophane-ly whifpering and converfing; others in their Vanities, and even in the State of Sin, with more ftill of this Kind; what can I fay of them, but that they abufe or neglect the Bleffings of Heaven; make void the Defigns of Mercy, and difhonour God in that divine Inftitution, which was ordained for the giv-ing him the higheft Worfhip? Can thefe hope to obtain Pardon of their Sins, through that Holy Victim, who in the Time of its offering are giving new Provocations to Hea-ven, in the Addition of their Sins; or, who think fo little of Repentance, that knowing them-

themselves to be in a wicked State they are resolved to go home as they came? Will God accept this Offering from them, in the Odour of Sweetness, who has declared he will receive no Sacrifice from polluted Hands? Certainly, there is little Ground to flatter them with such Hopes: They have more Reason to consider, what Part of that Company they resemble which surrounded Christ upon the Cross; for as, when he was nailed to the sacred Wood, there wanted not some, who reproached and blasphemed him in his Sufferings; so here, being now offered an unbloody Victim, 'tis not without some, who by their irreligious Behaviour and criminal Lives, like those wicked *Jews*, cast out Blasphemies against him; who are yet so much worse than they, inasmuch as their Knowledge and Belief is an Aggravation of their Crime, beyond that of the *Jews*, who had Ignorance to plead for them, in knowing not what they did.

Q. Then I see, to run to Mass and see it ended, is not sufficient to partake of the Effects of it, unless a Person be careful to assist there with great Attention, Application and Devotion. What then will become of many that think not of this?

A. 'Tis every one's Duty to be informed and instructed in such Obligations as belong to their State, as to do them well, and if they are wanting in this, they have so much to answer for. Now a little Reason is

sufficient

sufficient to make them sensible of it.   For if they once reflect, that in going to Mass they go to *honour God, to thank him for his Benefits, to beg Pardon for their Sins, to pray for new Blessings,* and to *commemorate the Death of Christ,* does it not immediately appear, that a *religious Behaviour, a sincere Devotion and Repentance,* are the most suitable Dispositions for those that come to offer to God the very same Victim which was sacrificed for their Sins upon Mount *Calvary.*

Q. I see the Reason of what you say, and wish all duly considered it, for their own Good. But having now understood the principal End, and general Dispositions, with which we are to hear Mass, you must now comply with your Promise, and lay before me an easy Method for the joining with the Priest in making this Oblation.

A. That I will do; but you must give me Leave to speak to more than yourself: For there being, amongst the Faithful, Persons of very different Capacities, some that understand little, others that are better instructed, there is no one Method proper for all; and for this Reason I intend to propose three, answerable to the three different Degrees or Orders, in which all the Faithful may be ranked. One for young Beginners, who being wholly Strangers to this Publick Service of the Church, desire to be instructed in it: Another for the Generality of Catholicks, who by Education or Practice are better acquainted

ed with it: A third for such whose Learning, Piety or Parts, raise them something above the rest: And a fourth may not be improper, for such as are *absent:* And thus I shall include the whole Body of the Faithful.

First Method of hearing MASS, *for young Beginners.*

Q. *WHAT Directions do you give to such who as yet know nothing of the Mass, and desire to be instructed in it? What would you have them do at first, when they are present at it?*

A. My Advice is, that at first, when they go to Mass, they would for the first eight or ten Days use no Book at all; but bend their whole Endeavours to observe what the Priest does, by only looking on. By this Means, in a Week or Fortnight (it being every Day the same) they will begin to observe the more remarkable Parts of it: As, 1. The removing of the Book. 2. The uncovering the Chalice. 3. The putting Wine into the Chalice. 4. The lifting up the Host and Chalice. 5. The Priest Receiving. 6. His giving the Benediction, &c.

Having observed something of this, it will be then a great Help to have some charitable Friend kneel by, and inform them how these Parts are called, or what is then done; but so, as not to burthen them with too much at first. They may let them know

when

when the Prieſt ſays the *Confiteor,* or publick Confeſſion : That at the firſt Removal of the Book is read the *Goſpel :* At the uncovering the Chalice, or putting Wine into it, is the *Offertory :* At the lifting up the ſacred Hoſt and Chalice, is the *Elevation :* When the Prieſt receives, is the *Communion,* &c. By this Means, being thus acquainted with what is thus done, and the *Names* by which theſe Parts are called, they will ſoon be fit to uſe Books of Devotion, and ſay the Prayers proper, as in them directed by their Titles over them, and by theſe be prepared to underſtand all the reſt.

Being come thus far, it may be proper here again to inform them, as before, that the Prieſt at Maſs conſecrates the Bread and Wine into the Body and Blood of Chriſt : That he offers this Holy Oblation to God, for his Honour and Glory, for the Good of his own Soul, and of all preſent. That the Prieſt knowing how unworthy he is to perform this ſolemn Action, dares not approach the Altar, till by ſaying the *Confiteor* he has firſt humbled himſelf in the Confeſſion of his Sins before God : And that ſince the People are to join with the Prieſt in offering to God the Body and Blood of his only Son, 'tis but reaſonable they ſhould likewiſe humble themſelves with the Prieſt, in the Confeſſion of their Sins, by ſaying the *Confiteor* with him, or ſome other Prayer anſwerable to it, in the true Spirit of Humility and Contrition.　　　　　　　　　　At

At the *CONFITEOR,*

That is, in the very Beginning of the Mass, when the Priest stands bowing down, before he goes up to the Altar; the People may say the same with him, or as follows,

O Lord God, Father Almighty, I confess to thee in the Presence of thy holy Angels and blessed Saints, that I have provoked thy Anger, by committing Evil both negligently and wilfully: In thy Sight I have sinned; Lord, I have sinned: I acknowledge my Iniquity: But thou, of thy Goodness, hast promised Pardon to those that truly repent. Wherefore, behold I now bow down before thee, and heartily detesting all my Wickedness, with the penitent *Publican,* I thus humbly implore thy Mercy: *O God be merciful to me a Sinner;* deal not with me, I beseech thee, according to my Iniquities, nor reserve me for everlasting Punishments; but, according to the Multitude of thy tender Mercies, save thy unworthy Servant, that I may serve thee all the Days of my Life, and join with all the Powers of Heaven to praise thee, to whom belongs all Honour and Glory, and Adoration for ever. *Amen.*

When

When the Priest goes up to the Altar.

ALmighty and everlasting God, look down, I beseech thee, on thy Servants here met together in the same Spirit and Faith; and mercifully give ear to the Prayers now offered at thy Altar in our Behalf. And as for me in particular, grant me Pardon of all my past Offences, give me a new Spirit, that I may carefully observe my own Ways, diligently reform whatever is corrupt and sinful, and courageously resist all the Enemies of my Salvation. Give me Patience in all Difficulties, Charity to forgive all Injuries, Constancy to perform all Duties. Be thou ever with me, direct and govern me, both as to Soul and Body, for behold I now deliver whatever belongs to me into thy Hands: Let me therefore be thine now and for ever.

At the G O S P E L,

That is, when the Book is removed to the other Side of the Altar, and all the People stand up.

LORD Jesus Christ, who camest from Heaven to instruct us in all Truth, and continuest still daily to teach us by the holy Gospels, and the Preachers of the Word, grant me me Grace, that I may be wanting in no Care neceſſary for my being inſtructed in thy ſaving Truths: Let me be as induſtrious in my Soul's Concern, as I am for my Body, that while I take Pains in the Affairs of this World, I may not, through Stupidity or Neglect, let my Soul ſtarve and periſh everlaſtingly. Let the Rules of the Goſpel be the Direction of my Life, that I may not only know thy Will but likewiſe do it, that I may obſerve thy Commandments, and reſiſting all the Inclinations of corrupt Nature, only follow thee, who art the Way, the Truth, and the Life: For thus only can I be truly thy Diſciple; and thus only, O Jeſus, canſt thou be my Maſter.

At the OFFERTORY.

That is, when the Prieſt uncovers the Chalice, and offers up the Bread, on a little Plate, and putting Wine into the Chalice, offers that likewiſe in the Middle of the Altar.

THE Prieſt now offers to thee, O God, the Bread and Wine, which are to be bleſs'd and conſecrated into the Body and Blood of thy only Son: He offers to thee the Holy Victim, Chriſt Jeſus, which he deſires thee to accept for thy Honour and our Good. I likewiſe, thy unworthy Servant, join with him in making this Oblation to thee, deſiring thee to accept it in Memory of that free Obla-

tion

tion, which our dear Redeemer made of him-ſelf to become a Sacrifice for our Sins. And as for myſelf, behold I now offer my Body and Soul, and all that belongs to me, with theſe Gifts, upon thy Altar, heartily be-ſeeching thee, that by thy Grace it may be all ſanctified this Day, and conſecrated to thy Service and Glory. Lord, I confeſs I am a Sinner and Nothing; but give me now thy Bleſſing, and I ſhall be thine for ever.

When the Prieſt has waſhed his Hands at the Corner of the Altar.

LORD Jeſus, 'twas thy infinite Love for Man, and Deſire of his Salvation, which moved thee to leave us thy Body and Blood to be daily offered on our Altars: that ſo we might have a perpetual Memorial of thy moſt ſacred Paſſion, and by laying before the Father the infinite Value of thy Sufferings, we might powerfully move him to grant us all Bleſſings neceſſary for our Salvation.

Behold then, according to thy holy Ordi-nance, I now join with the Prieſt in offering this holy Sacrifice, in Remembrance of thy Paſſion and Death on the Croſs. I humbly offer it to the Eternal Father, in Adoration of his Sovereign Majeſty, and in Acknow-ledgment of his Supreme Being; I offer it him in Thankſgiving for his Bleſſings be-ſtowed on me and his whole Church; I of-fer it him, that in Virtue of thy Sufferings on

the

the Cross, I may obtain Pardon of all the Offences I have committed against him, and that thro' the infinite Value of thy Merits I may receive all those Helps, which are necessary for my Well-being here and hereafter.

Moved likewise by the grateful Oblation of this spotless Lamb, and the Memory of his Passion, I beseech thee, O God, to pour forth thy Blessings on thy Church, on this Nation, on my Friends and Benefactors; shew Mercy likewise to 'my Enemies, be found by those that seek thee; comfort the Afflicted, and reclaim all Sinners from their evil Ways, and help all according to their different Necessities.

At the ELEVATION,

That is, just in the Middle of the Mass, when the Priest, having consecrated, lifts up first the sacred Host, and then the Chalice over his Head, in Memory of Christ being lifted up on the Cross.

I Adore thee, O Jesus my Redeemer, who wast crucified for the Sins of Men. I confess thee to be the Son of the living God: Thou wast once lifted up on the Cross, and now, in Memory of thy Passion, is thy Body and Blood daily offered up under the Forms of Bread and Wine. Have Mercy on me, dear Jesus, and grant that thy Sufferings and Death may not be lost on me, thro' my Wickedness or Neglect. This thy

sacred

facred Blood was fhed for my Redemption.
O grant by this thy Mercy, I may rather
chufe to lay down my Life, and fhed my
Blood, than wilfully offend againft thy infinite Goodnefs.

At the ELEVATION,

They may go on praying thus :

I Love thee, dear Jefus, the Saviour of my
Soul, who diedft on the Crofs a Sacrifice
for the Sins of the whole World. I moft
firmly believe, that by Virtue of Confecration, thou, Lord, true God and true Man,
art really prefent in a moft wonderful Manner on the Altar. I believe thou art here
prefent, who art the affured Hope, and only
Salvation of Sinners ; who art the fovereign
Remedy of all our Neceffities, the Comfort
in our Troubles, and Support in our Diftrefs.

Hallowed be thy Name, my fweet Saviour Jefus Chrift, and may all Creatures give
thee Praife, for that infinite Love which
brought thee from Heaven to offer up thyfelf
on the Crofs for our Redemption.

Hallowed again be thy Name, moft bleffed
Jefus, for that infinite Love which moved
thee to leave us in this venerable Sacrament
thy Body and Blood under the Forms of
Bread and Wine, fo to become our daily
Oblation, and renew in us the Memory of
thy Death and Paffion.

Lamb

Lamb of God, that takeſt away the Sins of the World, have Mercy on us and grant us thy Peace.　Look on us with the Eyes of Compaſſion and heal all our Infirmities. Behold I am miſerable, weak and ſubject to ſin, but if thou wilt, thou canſt make me whole: Heal me then O Lord, and I ſhall be healed.　Be now to me a Saviour, and give me thy Grace, whereby I may conquer all my evil Inclinations, and ſerve thee more faithfully to the End of my Life.

Refreſh my Soul with this ſpiritual and heavenly Eood, and ſtrengthen me continually with thy Aſſiſtance, that neither in Life nor Death I may depart from thee, nor ever be deprived of thy Grace and Bleſſing, who liveſt and reigneſt with God the Father, in the Unity of the Holy Ghoſt, One God, world without End.　*Amen.*

At the C O M M U N I O N,

That is, when the Prieſt communicates and receives the Body and Blood of Chriſt.

NOW the Prieſt receives this holy Banquet; but as for me, I am unworthy to partake of it: I am moſt unworthy Lord, thou ſhouldeſt enter under my Roof; but ſince by thy Word thou waſt pleaſed, even abſent to heal the Centurion's Servant, ſpeak now the Word and my Soul ſhall be healed.

I acknowledge thee to be the Bread of Life who cameſt down from Heaven to be the Food of our Souls; and that whoever eats of this Bread, shall live for ever: I wish I were truly disposed to partake of it as I ought, that so my Soul might be refreshed and comforted. Despise not, I beseech thee, this my Desire; and tho' I am frail and weak, yet still let my Soul be sensible of thy Sweetness; come then Lord, and command that my sinful Soul may be healed, preserve me from all Temptation and from the Dangers of my own Weakness, and abide with me for ever.

At the *BLESSING*,

That is, when the Priest at the End of the Mass, maketh the Sign of the Cross with his Hand over the People.

MAY the Blessing of Almighty God, Father, Son and Holy Ghost, descend upon me, and keep me for ever. And thou, O heavenly Father, pardon, I beseech thee, all my Distractions and Negligence in this Time of Prayer. I offer thee the infinite Merits of thy Son's bitter Passion to supply all my Defects and beg of thee through him to grant me that Grace whereby I may be enabled to serve thee all my Life. I here purpose this Day to watch over myself, and especially to avoid those wonted Failings, into which I so easily fall; and for all the Actions of this Day, I here consecrate them to thy Service and to the Honour of thy Name;

Name; for thou art my Lord, and if I live not to thee, I shall be for ever miserable: be with me therefore my *Jesus*, and protect me for ever. *Amen.*

Q. WHEN *a Person understands indifferently well so far, what is he to do still, to improve himself and know farther?*

A. I would have him be attentive still to other Parts of the Mass, and endeavour to know the *English* of some Expressions which being used every Day, he may soon learn with a little Care, and they will be very helpful in order to perfect him in a true Understanding of the Whole: such are these which follow.

1 *Kyrie*

1 *Kyrie eleison.*
2 *Christe eleison.*
3 *Gloria in excelsis Deo.*
4 *Dominus Vobiscum.*
5 *Et cum Spiritu tuo.*
6 *Oremus.*
7 *Deo Gratias.*
8 *Gloria tibi Domine.*
9 *Laus tibi* Christe.
10 *Credo in unum Deum.*
11 *Et Homo factus est.*
12 *Orate Fratres.*
13 *Per omnia Sæcula Sæculorum.*
14 *Sanctus, Sanctus, Sanctus.*
15 *Surfum Corda.*
16 *Pater noster.*
17 *Et ne nos inducas in Tentationem.*
18 *Sed libera nos à Malo.*
19 *Pax Domini sit semper vobiscum.*

20 *Agnus Dei qui tollis peccata Mundi, miserere nobis.*
21 *Domine non sum dignus ut intres sub Tectum meum sed tantum dic Verbo, & sanabitur Anima mea.*
22 *Ite, Missa est.*
23 *Benedicamus Domino.*
24 *Requiescat in Pace.*
25 *Benedicat vos omnipotens Deus,* Pater, *&* Filius, *&* Spiritus Sanctus.
26 *Et Verbum Caro factum est.*

1 Lord have Mercy upon us.
2 *Chrift* have mercy upon us.
3 Glory be to God on high.
4 The Lord be with you.
5 And with thy Spirit.
6 Let us Pray.
7 Thanks be to God.
8 Glory be to thee O Lord.
9 Praife be to thee, O *Chrift.*
10 I believe in one God.
11 And he was made Man.
12 Brethren, pray.
13 World without End.
14 Holy, Holy, Holy.
15 Lift up your Hearts.
16 Our Father.
17 And lead us not into Temptation.
18 But deliver us from Evil.
19 The Peace of our Lord be always with you
20 Lamb of God, that takeft away the -Sins of the World, have Mercy on us.
21 Lord, I am not worthy thou fhouldeft enter under my Roof; fay but only the Word and my Soul fhall be healed.
22 Depart, Mafs is done.
23 Let us blefs our Lord.
24 Let him reft in Peace.
25 Almighty God, Father, Son, and *Holy Ghoft* blefs you.
26 And the Word was made Flefh.

Wheu

The Ordinary of the Mass.

**The Prieſt, at the Foot of the Altar, be-
gins thus ;**

*In the Name of the Father, and of the Sin,
and of the* Holy Ghoſt. *Amen.*

P.	*I will go to the Altar of God.*

A.	*To God who rejoices my Youth.*

P.	*Judge me O God, and diſcern my Cauſe
from the Nation not holy ; from the unjuſt and
deceitful Man deliver me.*

A.	*Becauſe*

When a Person by Industry and Observation is come to understand thus far, he ought by Degrees to take notice of these Parts of the Mass; as when the *Kyrie eleison* is said, when *Credo in unum Deum*, or the *Credo*; when *Orate Fratres*, when the *Preface*; when *Sanctus, Sanctus,* when the *Canon* begins; when the Priest makes the *Mementos*; when he says the *Pater noster*; when *Agnus Dei*; when *Domine non sum dignus*; when St. *John's Gospel*; which may be done in a short Time, with the Help of some charitable Friend kneeling by: and then it may be proper to look over the whole Mass and see the Method of it, and thus fit himself for it with a distinct Application to every Part as here follows, translated from the *French,* tho' with some considerable Alterations and Additions.

Second Method of hearing Mass, by accompanying the Priest in every Part of it; and proper for such as are well instructed.

People.

The People may answer the Priest as is set down in the other Page, or say as follows:

In the Name of the Father and of the Son, and of the *Holy Ghost. Amen.*

I will draw near thy Altar, O my God, there to gain new Strength and Vigour to my Soul, and by thy Grace separate me from those Unbelievers who have no Trust in thee.   C 4   'That

A. Because thou art my God, my Strength, why hast thou rejected me? And why do I go sorrowful, while the Enemy afflicts me?

P. Send forth thy Light and Truth; they have conducted and brought me to thy holy Hill and to thy Tabernacle.

A. And I will go to the Altar of God, to God who rejoices my Youth.

P. I will praise thee on the Harp, O God, my God; Why art thou sorrowful, my Soul, and why dost thou trouble me?

A. Hope in God, because I will still praise him; he is the Salvation of my Countenance and my God.

P. Glory be to the Father and to the Son, and to the Holy Ghost.

A. As it was in the Beginning, is now and ever shall be, World without End. Amen.

P. I will go to the Altar of God.

A. To God, who rejoices my Youth.

P. Our Hope is in the Name of our Lord.

A. Who made Heaven and Earth.

The Prieſt bowing down, ſays the *Confiteor.*

I Confeſs *to Almighty God, to the Bleſſed Virgin* Mary, *to the bleſſed* Michael *the Arch-Angel, to the bleſſed* John Baptiſt, *to the holy apoſtles* Peter *and* Paul, *to all the Saints, and to you Brethren, that I have very much ſinned in Thought, Word and Deed, thro' my Fault, thro' my Fault, thro' my moſt grievous Fault, Therefore I beſeech the bleſſed Virgin* Mary,

bleſſed

That Grace which comforts me, when the Remembrance of my Sins afflicts and casts me down.

That Grace which lets me know there's an everlasting Refuge in thy Goodness, and that thou art ready to forgive even our greatest Sins, as soon as we sincerely acknowledge them.

The People may say the Confiteor, *after the Priest, or as follows:*

I Confess then and acknowledge, O my God, not only to thee, to whom the Secrets of my Heart are already known, but also to that sacred Assembly of Saints which are eternally blessed with thy Presence, and to all about me that are here present groaning under the Burthen of Sin; that I have infinitely offended thee in my

C 5 Thoughts.

blessed Michael *the Archangel, blessed* John
Baptist, the holy Apostles, Peter *and* Paul, *and
all the Saints and you Brethren, to pray to our
Lord God for me.*

A. *Almighty God be merciful to you, and
forgiving you your Sins, bring you to Life
everlasting.* R. Amen.

Then the Clerk, in the Name of the People
having said the *Confiteor,* the Priest prays
as follows for them.

*A*Lmighty *God be merciful to you, and forgiving you your Sins, bring you to Life
everlasting.* R. Amen.

*Almighty and merciful God, grant us Par-
don, absolution and Remission of our Sins.* R.
Amen.

P. *Looking towards us, O Lord, thou wilt
give us Life.*

A *And thy People will rejoice in thee.*

P. *Lord shew us thy Mercy.*

A. *And grant us thy Salvation.*

P. *Lord hear my Prayer,*

A. *And let my Cry come to thee.*

P. *Our Lord be with you.*

A. *And with thy Spirit.*

The

Thoughts, in my Words, and in my Actions; and that nothing but thy infinite Mercy can equal my Sins; Therefore I beſeech thoſe Favourites of Heaven, that are always attending thy Divine Majeſty, to intercede for me: And firſt that glorious and perpetual Virgin, thy ever bleſſed Mother; then thy pure and holy Angels, and all thy Saints who are inflamed with divine Charity; and laſtly, all thoſe, who here below are endeavouring, tho' at a Diſtance, to follow their great Example.

After the Confiteor.

O My God, who haſt commanded us to pray for one another, and in thy holy Church haſt given even to Sinners, the Power of abſolving from Sin; receive with an equal Bounty the Prayers of thy People for the Prieſt, and thoſe of thy Prieſt for the People.

The Prieſt going up to the Altar, ſays in a
        low Voice :

*TAKE from us our Iniquities we beſeech thee
    O Lord, that we may be worthy to enter
into the Sanctuary with a clean Heart ; thro'*
Chriſt *our Lord.*   Amen.

Being come up to the Altar, he kiſſes it
            ſaying :

*WE beſeech thee, O Lord, by the Merits of
    thoſe Saints whoſe Relicks are here,
and of all the Saints, to forgive us all our
Sins.*   Amen.

The Prieſt goes to the Book, and having read
    two or three Verſes of the Scripture, call-
    ed the *Introit of the Maſs,* which being
    every Day proper or different, cannot be
    ſet down, he then goes to the Middle of
    the Altar, and ſays:

P. *Kyrie eleiſon.* ⎫
A. *Kyrie eleiſon.* ⎬ Lord have Mercy on us.
P. *Kyrie eleiſon.* ⎭
A. *Chriſte eleiſon.* ⎫
P. *Chriſte eleiſon.* ⎬ Chriſt have Mercy on us.
A. *Chriſte eleiſon.* ⎭
P. *Kyrie eleiſon.* ⎫
A. *Kyrie eleiſon.* ⎬ Lord have Mercy on us.
P. *Kyrie eleiſon.* ⎭
                        The

When the Priest is going up to the Altar.

UNite, O Lord, our Hearts and our Wills, and remove from us every Thing that may any Ways make us unfit for our appearing in thy Sanctuary.

Tho' we are unworthy of ourselves, yet our Comfort is, we are the legitimate Posterity of those blessed Saints whose sacred Relicks are placed near thy H. Altars: Grant then, thro' their Prayers, what thou may'st justly refuse us thro' the slothful Tepidity of ours, and forgive us all our Sins.

At the Introit,

Or when the Priest goes first to the Book.

GRant, Lord, we may be truly prepared for the offering this great Sacrifice to thee this Day; and because our Sins alone can render us displeasing to thee, therefore we call aloud to thee for Mercy.

At the Kyrie eleison.

HAve Mercy on me, O Lord, and forgive me all my Sins; and tho' I have nothing of my own to move thy Goodness, yet let my Importunity prevail: Have Mercy on me, O Lord, have Mercy on me.

At

Then he begins *Gloria in Excelfis Deo,* as
follows ;

GLORY *be to God on high, and Peace on
Earth to Men of Good-will.　We praife
thee, we blefs thee, we adore thee, we glorify
thee, we give thee Thanks for thy great Glory,
Lord God, Heavenly King, Father Almighty.
Lord* Jefus Chrift, *the only begotten Son, Lord
God, Lamb of God, Son of the Father, who
takeft away the Sins of the World, have Mercy
on us; who takeft away the Sins of the World,
hear our Prayer; who fitteft at the Right-hand
of the Father, have Mercy on us; for thou only
art holy; thou only art our Lord; thou only,*
O Jefus Chrift, *together with the* Holy Ghoft,
art moft High in the Glory *of* God *the* Father.
Amen.

He turns to the People and fays:

P. *Our Lord be with you.*
A. *And with thy Spirit.*

Then goes to the Book, and having faid *O-
remus, Let us pray,* he begins the Collects,
or Prayers of the Day; which being every
Day different, cannot be here fet down.
Place of the Collects.

The

At the Gloria in excelsis.

THE Glory, O my God, which may any Ways be proportion'd to thy Greatness, can only be paid thee in Heaven; my Heart, however, desires to give thee what Homage it can upon Earth: And therefore with this thy Servant at the Altar, and the whole Congregation, I praise thee, I bless thee, I adore and glorify thee, and give thee Thanks, Almighty *Father*, Eternal *Son*, and *Holy Ghost*, most high God and only Lord. All I expect is from thee, and I desire no longer to live, than I am to live in thy Service.

When the Priest turns to the People, and says, Our Lord be with you.

BE thou always with us, O my God, and let thy Grace never depart from us.

While the Priest is saying the Collects, *or Prayers of the Day, the People may thus join with him.*

ALmighty and Eternal *God*, we humbly beseech thee mercifully to give Ear to
the

The *Collects* being ended, the Priest, laying his Hand on the Book, reads the *Epistle* or *Lesson*; which being every Day different, cannot be set down here.

The

the Prayers of thy Servants, which he offers thee in the Name of thy Church, and in Behalf of us thy People: Accept them to the Honour of thy Name, and Good of our Souls; and grant us all those Blessings which may any Ways contribute to our Salvation; thro' our Lord *Jesus Christ, &c.*

On a Sunday *or* Feria, *may be said.*

O God, who never forsakest those that put their Trust in thee, mercifully hear our Prayers, and since our Weakness is such that without thee we can do nothing, grant us the daily Assistance of thy Grace, that in observing thy Commandment, we may be ever acceptable to thee, thro' our Lord *Jesus.*

On the Festival of a Saint.

GRant, we beseech thee, Almighty God, that the Example of thy Saints may effectually move us to reform our Lives, that while we celebrate their Festivals, we may also imitate their Actions; thro' our Lord *Jesus Christ.*

At the Epistle.

THou hast taught us, O Lord, by thy *Prophets* and *Apostles;* grant we may so improve, by their Doctrine and Example, in the Love of thy holy Name, that we may manifest in our Lives, whose Disciples.

we

The *Epistle* being ended, the Clerk answers, *Deo Gratias, Thanks be to God;* and then the Priest goes on with the *Gradual,* which is composed of some few Verses of the Holy Scripture, and is every Day different.

This being ended, the Book is removed; and while it is carry'd to the other Side of the Altar, the Priest stands bowing down at the Middle of the Altar, and says,

CLeanse my Heart and Lips, Almighty God, *who didst cleanse the Lips of* Isaiah *the Prophet with a burning Coal, Vouchsafe, thro' thy gracious Mercy, so to purify me that I may worthily declare thy Gospel;* thro' Christ *our* Lord. Amen. *Bless me, O Lord.*

Our Lord be in my Heart and Lips, that I may worthily and fitly publish his Gospel. Amen.

After

we are; that tho' we live amidft Corruption, we may not follow the Inclinations of Flefh and Blood; but having mafter'd all their Paffions, we may be directed by thy Light, be ftrengthen'd by thy Grace, walk in the perfect Obfervance of thy Law, and ferve thee with clean Hearts.

At the Gradual.

HOW wonderful, O Lord, is thy Name thro' the whole Earth! I will blefs our Lord at all Times; his Praife fhall be ever in my Mouth: Be thou my God and my Protector: In thee alone will I put my Truft, let me not be confounded for ever.

When the Prieft ftands bowing down before the Middle of the Altar, and the Book is removed to the other Side.

WHat Ears, O Lord, are fit to hear thy Gofpel, or Heart to receive it, except they are firft prepared by thy fanctifying Grace? Let the Fire then of thy Love have the fame Effect on us, as the Fire of thy Altar had on the Prophet *Ifaiah*; for thus only, O Lord, will thy holy Word be to us a Means of Life, and never rife in Judgment againft us.

At

After this the Priest goes to the Book, and
reads the Gospel, which is different every
Day; first saying, *Dominus Vobiscum, Our
Lord be with you: Sequentia Sancti Evangelii secundum,* &c. *The Sequence of the Holy
Gospel.* To which the Clerk answers, *Gloria tibi Domine, Glory be to thee, O Lord.*

At the End of the Gospel the Clerk answers,
Laus tibi Christe, Praise be to thee, O Christ;
and *the Priest going to the Middle of the Altar,*
says the Nicence Creed, *beginning thus,* Credo in unum Deum.

I *Believe in one God, the Father Almighty,
Maker of Heaven and Earth, and of all
Things visible and invisible; and in one Lord
Jesus Christ, the only begotten Son of God, and
born of the Father before all Ages, God of God,
Light of Light, True God of true God; begot-
ten, not made; consubstantial to the Father,
by whom all Things were made; who for us
Men,*

At the Gospel.

IMprint, O Lord, we beseech thee, the Maxims and Rules of thy Gospel deep in our Hearts, that while we profess ourselves Christians, we may not live like Heathens: What will it profit me, if I know thy Will and do it not ? If I hear thy Law and keep it not ? This will be only to turn the Food of Life into Poison, and make seeing the Way to Happiness be the Increase of my Damnation. Deliver me, O God, from this Error, and so perfectly at present possess my Heart, that my rebellious Appetites being over-ruled by thy Grace, I may henceforth live in the Denial of myself, and like thy true Servants, only hear and follow thee.

At the Creed.

The People may say it with the Priest, or make a short Profession of their Faith, as follows:

I Believe O Lord, all thou hast taught me by thy holy Church: In this Faith, by the Assistance of thy Grace, I desire to live and die, O Lord, help my Unbelief, I adore all I apprehend in these adorable Mysteries, and likewise what I am not able to comprehend; for since my Understanding is so narrow, that I know but
very

Men, and for our Salvation, came down from Heaven; and was incarnate by the Holy Ghost of the Virgin Mary, and WAS MADE MAN; was crucified also for us, suffered under Pontius Pilate, and was buried; and the third Day rose again, according to the Scriptures; and ascended into Heaven; sits at the Right-hand of the Father, and shall come again with Glory to judge the Living and the Dead, of whose Kingdom there shall be no End. And in the Holy Ghost, the Lord and Giver of Life; who proceeds from the Father and the Son, who together with the Father and the Son is adored and conglorified; who spoke by the Prophets: And One holy Catholick and Apostolick Church. I confess One Baptism for the Remission of Sins; and I expect the Resurrection of the Dead, and the Life of the World to come. Amen.

After the Creed (and likewise on all Days on which the Creed is not said) the Priest turns to the People and says, *Our Lord be with you;* and having read the *Offertory,* being a Verse of the Holy Scripture, he then uncovers the Chalice, and offers the Bread on the Patin, &c. saying,

ACcept, O holy Father, Almighty and Eternal God, this unspotted Host, which I thy unworthy Servant offer thee, my living and

true

very little even of myself, 'tis neither just nor poſſible I ſhould perfectly comprehend thee, O my infinite and incomprehenſible God: By th. divine Grace I am convinced of the Sincerity and Wiſdom of thoſe who have delivered theſe divine Myſteries to us. Their miraculous Succeſs is a ſufficient Proof: Thy Goodneſs and Promiſes are my Security: Theſe comfort my Heart, and ſupport my Faith.

Where ſhall I go, my Lord? Thou haſt the Word of eternal Life.

Of thy Truths thus deliver'd my Reaſon and Will ſhall never doubt, tho' my Senſes and vain Imagination ſhou'd.

I aſk not the removing of Mountains: How little ſoever my Faith be, ſince it is true and ſincere, vouchſafe, O Lord, to accept it. I believe, O Lord; help my Unbelief.

At the OFFERTORY.

When the Prieſt uncovers the Chalice, and offers the Bread on the little Plate, the People ought to offer it with him.

ACcept, O Eternal Father, this Offering we make thee; 'tis only Bread as yet, but by a Miracle of thy Power and Grace, thou art going to make of it a holy and eternal Hoſt, who offers himſelf to thee, for the Salvation of all the Faithful, true God; for my innumerable Sins, Offences and Negligences, for all here present, and for all faithful Christians, living and dead, That it may avail me and them to Life everlasting. Amen.

When the Priest puts Wine and Water into the Chalice, he says,

O GOD, who, in creating human Nature, hast wonderfully dignify'd it, and reformed it again by a yet greater Miracle, grant, by the Mystery of this Water and Wine, we may partake of his Divinity, who vouchfafed to take upon him our Humanity, namely, Jesus Christ thy Son, our Lord, who with thee, in the Unity of the Holy Ghost, liveth and reigneth God, World without End. Amen.

Then offering the Wine in the Chalice in the Middle of the Altar, he says,

WE offer thee, O Lord, the Chalice of Salvation, beseeching thy Clemency, that it may ascend before thy Divine Majesty, as a sweet Perfume for our Salvation, and for that of the whole World. Amen.

Bowing

ful, abfent and prefent, living and dead. Regard not O Lord, our Mifery, except it be with an Eye of Pity; but look on that eternal Prieft, Chrift Jefus, who being innocent and fpotlefs, is continually our Advocate before thee, pleading for the Remiffion of our Sins, and Relief of our Neceffities.

When the Prieft, at the Corner of the Altar, puts Wine and Water into the Chalice.

IN thy Incarnation O Lord, thou haft united thy Divinity to our frail human Nature; but go on ftill daily, we befeech thee, with thy Works of Mercy, and grant that we thy People may be fo truly united to thee, that neither Intereft, Pleafure, or Neglect may be ever able to divide us from thee.

When the Prieft offers the Chalice in the Middle of the Altar.

THOU only, O Lord, canft render this Offering worthy of thee, and capable of giving Salvation to the World: Accept it we befeech thee, and purify our Souls, that we may be acceptable in thy Sight.

When

Bowing down his Head, says,

*A*Ccept us, O Lord, in the Spirit of Humility, and a contrite Heart; and so may our Sacrifice be made this Day in thy Sight, that it be pleasing to thee, O Lord God.

Then, blessing the Bread and Wine, he says,

*C*Ome Almighty and Eternal God, the Sancti-fier, and bless ✠ this Sacrifice, prepared for the Glory of thy holy Name.

He then goes to the Corner of the Altar, and washes his Hands, saying, *Ps.* xxv.

I Will wash my Hands among the Innocent, and encompass thy Altar, O Lord.

That I may hear the Voice of Praise, and declare all thy wonderful Works.

Lord, I have loved the Beauty of thy House, and the Place where thy Glory dwells.

Destroy not my Soul, O God, with the Un-righteous, nor my Life with bloody Men:

In whose Hands are Iniquities, their Right-hand is filled with Gifts.

As for me, I have walked in my Innocency: Redeem me, and have Mercy upon me.

My

When he bows down.

WE can add nothing here, but the Sacrifice of an humble and contrite Heart, which thou, O Lord, wilt never despise.

When he blesses the Bread and Wine, which he has offered, making the Sign of the Cross over them.

THere remains now this to be done by thee, my Lord, that thou come, O most Holy and Almighty God, and bless and sanctify what already begins to belong to thee.

When the Priest washes his Fingers at the Corner of the Altar.

THou Lord, who once vouchsafed'st to wash thy Disciples' Feet before their Invitation to thy holy Table, wash us also, we beseech thee, O Lord, and wash us again; not only our Feet and Hands, but our Hearts, our Desires, our Souls, that we may be wholly innocent and pure.

When

My Feet have stood in the right Way : In thy Congregations I will bless thee, O Lord.
Glory be to the Father, and to the Son, &c.

The Priest goes to the Middle of the Altar, and bowing down, says:

REceive, O holy Trinity, this Oblation we make thee, in Memory of the Passion, Resurrection and Ascension of our Lord *Jesus Christ*; and in Honour of blessed Mary ever Virgin, of blessed John Baptist, of the holy Apostles Peter and Paul, of these and of all the Saints; that it may be available to their Honour and our Salvation. And may they vouchsafe to intercede for us in Heaven, whose Memory we celebrate on Earth; thro' the same Christ our Lord. Amen.

Then, kissing the Altar, he turns to the People, and says, *Orate Fratres,* &c. that is,

BRethren, pray that my Sacrifice and yours may be acceptable to God the Father Almighty.

When the Priest in the Middle of the Altar stands bowing down, they may say the same with him, or as follows.

MOST Holy and Adorable Trinity, vouchsafe to receive this our Sacrifice, in Remembrance of our Saviour's Passion, Resurrection and glorious Ascension; and grant it may sensibly work in our Souls the Effects of these Mysteries.

Let those Saints whose Memory we celebrate, not forget us in Heaven. They found Help in this Divine Mystery; Grant, O Lord, it may likewise contribute to our Salvation.

When he turns about and says, Orate Fratres, *the People ought to pray, as he desires, saying.*

MAY our Lord receive this Sacrifice from thy Hands, to the Praise and Glory of his Name, for our Good, and the Benefit of his whole Church.

 When

He then goes on with some Prayers, which being said in a low Voice, are called *Secreta*; and being different every Day, cannot be set down; And as many *Collects* as he said-before the *Epistle,* so many Prayers he says here answerable to them.

SECRETA.

When the Priest is saying the Prayers in the Book, proper to the Day, in a low Voice, the People may thus join with him.

MErcifully hear our Prayers, O Lord, and graciously accept this Oblation, which we thy Servants are making to thee, that as we offer it to the Honour of thy Name, so it may be to us here a Means of obtaining thy Grace, and in the next Life, everlasting Happiness.

On a Sunday, *or* Feria, *may be said;*

ACcept, O Lord, we beseech thee, both our Offering and Prayers, and by this holy Sacrifice work such a Change in our Hearts, that our Affections being taken off from the Things of this World, our Desires may be wholly fixed on Heaven.

On the Festival of a Saint.

SAnctify, O Lord, we beseech thee, these Gifts which we offer thee, in this Solemnity of thy holy Servant, and so strengthen us by thy Grace, that both in Prosperity and Adversity, our Ways may be ever directed to thy Honour. Through our Lord Jesus Christ thy Son, who liveth and reigneth with thee, in the Unity of the Holy Ghost, one God, &c.

D 4   *The*

Then he goes on, saying with a loud Voice;
Per omnia Sæcula Sæculorum; that is,

WOrld without End.
　　A. *Amen.*

Preface begins.

　　P. *Our Lord be with you.*
　　A. *And with thy Spirit.*
　　P. *Lift up your Hearts.*
　　A. *We have lifted them up to God.*
　　P. *Let us give Thanks to our Lord God.*
　　A. *It is meet and just.*

IT is *verily meet and just, right and available to Salvation, that we always, and in all Places give Thanks to thee, holy Lord, Father Almighty, eternal God, through Christ our Lord; by whom the Angels praise thy Majesty, the Dominations adore it, the Powers tremble in its Sight, the Heavens and heavenly Virtues, and blessed Seraphims with common Jubilee glorify it; together with whom we beseech thee, that we may be admitted to join our Voices in an humble Manner.*

Holy, holy, holy, Lord God of Sabbath. The Heavens and Earth are full of thy Glory. Hosanna in the Highest. Blessed is he that comes in the Name of our Lord, Hosanna in the Highest.

After

The Prayers being ended, he begins again in a loud Voice; thus, Per omnia Sæcula Sæculorum; *and so begins the* Preface, *which the People may say with him, or as follows:*

RAise our Hearts, O Lord, we beseech thee, above the Thoughts of earthly Things, and lift them up to thee. Where our Treasure is the Treasure of Salvation, there let our Hearts also continually be. As our Life is but one continued Series of thy Favours towards us, so let us continue our daily Thankfgivings to thee.

Behold the whole Hierarchy of thy holy Angels, who stand always trembling in thy Presence, are now with us going to adore thee on this Altar. Permit us, O Lord, to join our weak and tepid Praises in Concert with their divine Hymn, and say,

Holy, holy, holy, is the Lord of Hosts: How great is the Distance of his infinite Majesty from us poor Worms below! Heaven and Earth are full of thy Glory: Grant, Lord, that our Hearts may be also full of it. Let Heaven and Earth bless him that comes in the Name of our Lord; 'tis our Lord himself is coming, tho' after an invisible Manner; blessed be his Name.

When

After this he begins the *Canon,* or chief Action of the Sacrifice, in a low Voice, bowing down, and saying,

THerefore, most merciful Father, we humbly pray and beseech thee, through thy Son Jesus Christ our Lord, to accept and bless these ✠ Gifts, these ✠ Presents, these holy ✠ unspotted Sacrifices, which in the first Place we offer to thee, for thy holy Catholick Church, that thou wouldst be pleased to grant her Peace, to preserve unite, and govern her through the whole World, together with thy Servant N. our chief Bishop, N. our Prelate, and N. our King, as also all orthodox Believers and Professors of the Catholick and Apostolick Faith.

Then joining his Hands before his Breast, he in Silence makes his *Memento,* praying for such in particular as are recommended to him, *&c.* beginning thus,

BE mindful, O Lord, of thy Servants, Men and Women, N. N. Here he prays in Silence.

Having

When the Priest begins the Canon, *bowing down,
and in a low Voice.*

MOST merciful Father, who haſt given
us thy only Son to be our daily Sacrifice, we beſeech thee, in the Name of this
holy Victim, incline thy Ear to our Prayers,
and favour our Deſires.

Thou who art the Paſtor of all Paſtors,
protect, unite, and govern thy holy Church
through the whole World, pour forth thy
Bleſſings on his preſent Holineſs, and on that
Prelate who has a particular Charge over us.
Preſerve and ſave our King: Render him both
Good and Great in this Life, and eternally
happy in the next, and give a Bleſſing to his
Subjects.

While the Priest makes his Memento, *ſtanding
with his Hands joined before his Breaſt, the
Faithful ought at the ſame Time to make their*
Memento, *praying in particular for them-
ſelves and Friends, &c. ſomething after this
Manner.*

I Offer thee, O Eternal Father, with this
thy Miniſter at the Altar, this Oblation
of the Body and Blood of thy only Son, to
thy Honour and Glory; in Remembrance of
my Saviour's Paſſion, in Thankſgiving for
thy Benefits, in Satisfaction for all my Sins,
and

Having ended the *Memento*, he opens his
Arms, and goes on.

*AND for all here prefent, whofe Faith and
Devotion is known to thee, for whom we
offer, or who offer thee, this Sacrifice of Praife,
for themfelves, and for all theirs; for the Redemption of their Souls; for the Hope of their
Salvation and Safety; and who now pay their
Vows to thee, the eternal, living, and true God.
Communicating with, and Honouring the Memory, in the firft Place, of the glorious ever Virgin
Mary, Mother of our Lord God Jefus Chrift;
as alfo of the bleffed Apoftles and Martyrs, Peter and Paul, Andrew, James, John, Thomas, James, Philip, Bartholomew, Matthew,
Simon,*

and for the obtaining thy Grace, whereby I
may be enabled to live virtuously, and die
happily. I desire thee likewise to accept it,
O God, for *N. N.* my Parents, Friends and
Benefactors; grant them all Blessings spiritual and temporal; likewise for all such as
are in Misery; for those I have any ways injured in Word or Deed; for all my Enemies;
for the Conversion of Sinners, and Enlighten-
ing all that sit in Darkness. Pour forth thy
Blessings on all, according to their different
Necessities, through the Merits of thy only
Son our Lord.

*Here every one may add their particular Necessi-
ties, as likewise of their Friends, &c.*

GIVE Ear, we beseech thee, to the
Prayers of thy Servant, who is here
appointed to make this Oblation in our behalf, and grant it may be effectual for the
obtaining of those Blessings, which he asks
for us.

Be thou, O Lord, the Eternal Bond of
all our Friendships and Societies. And as
thou hast vouchsafed to join us not only in
Communion with thy sacred Houshold of
Faith here below, but also with those who
are now triumphing in Heaven with the
Martyrs, and Apostles, and thy blessed Virgin Mother, be thou the Sacred Bond to
fasten and preserve us therein for ever.

When

Simon *and* Thaddeus, Linus, Cletus, Clement, Xyſtus, Cornelius, Cyprian, Laurence, Chryſogonus, John *and* Paul, Coſmas *and* Damine, *and of all thy Saints; by whoſe Merits and Prayers, grant we may in all things be defended by the Help of thy Protection.* Thro' *the ſame* Chriſt *our Lord.* Amen.

The Prieſt, ſpreading his Hands over the Oblation, ſays,

*W*E *therefore beſeech thee,* O Lord, *graciouſly to accept this Oblation of our Servitude, and of thy whole Family: Diſpoſe our Days in thy Peace, preſerve us from eternal Damnation, and command us to be numbered amongſt thy Elect.* Through Chriſt our Lord. *Amen.*

Which Oblation we beſeech thee, O God, *to render in all things bleſſed, approved, effectual, reaſonable and acceptable: That it may be made to 'us the Body and Blood of thy moſt beloved Son, our Lord* Jeſus Chriſt.

Who, the Day before he ſuffered, took Bread into his ſacred and venerable Hands, aud having lifted up his Eyes towards Heaven, to thee, God, *his omnipotent Father, and giving Thanks to thee, he bleſſed it, and broke it, and gave it to his Diſciples, ſaying,* Take and Eat you all of this ; For this is my Body.

Here

When the Priest holds his Hands spread over the Chalice.

BEhold, O Lord, we all here, tho' of different Conditions, yet united by Charity, as Members of that one Body, of which thy dear Son is the Head, present to thee, in this Bread and Wine, the Symbols of our perfect Union. Grant, O Lord, that they may be made for us, who are here below, the true Body and Blood of thy dear Son; that being consecrated to thee by this Holy Victim, we may live in thy Service, and depart this Life in thy Grace.

He that is Almighty, he that is Truth itself, has said with his holy Mouth, *This is my Body.* And how then can we doubt the Truth of it? He that has made all Things of Nothing by his Word; is he not to be believed, when he says, he has changed one Thing into another? Yes, I believe and adore.

Here the Prieft kneels down, and adores Chrift in the Eucharift, and then he lifts up the Sacred Hoft, in Memory of Chrift's Body lifted up on the Crofs.

Then taking the Chalice, he fays,

IN like manner, after he had fupped, taking this excellent Chalice into his facred and venerable Hands, giving thee alfo Thanks, he bleffed it, and gave it to his Difciples, faying, Take and Drink you all of this, For this is the Chalice of my Blood, *of the New and Everlafting Teftament, a Myftery of Faith which fhall be fhed for you, and for many, to the Remiffion of Sins.*

He kneels down and adores, and then lifts up the Chalice, faying,

AS often as you do thefe Things, you fhall do them in Remembrance of me.

Then goes on.

WHerefore, we thy Servants, as alfo thy holy People, O Lord, being mindful of the bleffed Paffion of the fame Chrift thy Son, our Lord, and of his Refurrection, as alfo of his glorious Afcenfion into Heaven, offer to thy moft excellent Majefty, of thy own Gifts and Favours, a pure ✝ *Hoft,*

At the Elevation of the Host.

MOST admirable Body, I adore thee with all the Powers of my Soul. Lord who hast given thyself entire to us, grant we may become entirely thine.

THE same Eternal Word, who brought all Things at first out of Nothing: He that said, *Let there be Light*, and there was Light: *Let the Earth bring forth its Fruit*, and it was so: The same Eternal Word now says, this is my Blood, and speaks it from the highest Heavens, at this very Moment, by the Voice of this Servant.

At the Elevation of the Chalice.

MOST adorable Blood, that washest away all our Sins, I adore thee: Happy we, if we can return our Life and Blood for thine.

After the Elevation.

'TIS now, O Lord, with grateful Hearts, we call to Mind the sacred Mysteries of thy Passion and Death; thy Resurrection and Ascension. Here is thy Body, that was broken; here is thy Blood, that was shed for us, of which these exterior Signs are but the

Figures,

✠ *Hoſt, a holy* ✠ *Hoſt, an unſpotted* ✠ *Hoſt,
the holy* ✠ *Bread of eternal Life, and Chalice*
✠ *of eternal Salvation.*

*On which vouchſafe to look with a propi-
tious and ſerene Countenance, and accept them
as thou waſt pleaſed graciouſly to accept the
Gifts of thy juſt Servant* Abel, *and the Sacrifice of our Patriarch* Abraham, *and that
which thy High-Prieſt* Melchiſedech *offered
thee, a holy and unſpotted Hoſt.*

Bowing down, he ſays,

W E moſt humbly beſeech thee, Almighty God,
command theſe Offerings to be carried by
the Hands of thy holy Angel, to thy Altar above,
in the Preſence of thy Divine Majeſty, that as
many of us as, by this Participation of the
Altar, ſhall receive the moſt ſacred Body ✠
and Blood ✠ of thy Son, may be filled with
all heavenly Bleſſings and Grace. Thro' the
ſame Chriſt our Lord.   Amen.

Then

Figures, and yet in reality contain the Substance. It is now we truly offer thee, O Lord, that pure and holy Victim, which thou hast been pleased to give us, of which all the other Sacrifices were but so many Types and Figures.

If with a favourable Eye thou hast regarded the Sacrifices of *Abel,* of *Abraham,* and *Melchisedech,* look likewise on ours; for however weak our Faith may be, yet our Sacrifice is greater than theirs, and only worthy of thy heavenly Altar.

When the Priest bows down.

ALmighty God, who art infinitely Good, look not on our Sins, but on the infinite Ransom paid for them. And now, while it is offered on our Altars here below, do thou receive it on thy Altar above: Here from our Hands; but there from the Angel of thy great Council, that eternal Priest, who is himself both Priest and Victim, all in thee, as thou art all in him. Bless all those who here partake of this Holy Sacrifice, either by their Lips or Hearts.

While

Then with his Hands joined before his Breast, he in Silence makes his *Memento,* or Commemoration for the Dead.

BE mindful also, O Lord, of thy Servants N. and N. who are gone before us, with the Sign of Faith, and rest in the Sleep of Peace.

Here he mentions such in particular whom he intends to pray for.

Having ended the *Memento,* he says,

TO these, O Lord, and to all that rest in Christ, grant, we beseech thee, a Place of Refreshment, of Light and Peace. Through the same Christ our Lord. Amen.

Then striking his Breast, he says in a loud Voice.

AND to us Sinners, thy Servants, hoping in the Multitude of thy Mercies, vouchsafe to grant some Part and Society with thy holy Apostles and Martyrs, with John, Stephen, Matthias, Barnaby, Ignatius, Alexander, Marcellinus, Peter, Felicitas, Perpetua, Agatha, Lucia, Agnes, Cecilia, Anastasia, *and with all*

While the Priest makes his Memento for the Dead, standing in Silence with his Hands joined before his Breast, the Faithful ought likewise to make their Memento thus,

I Offer thee again, O Lord, this Holy Sacrifice of the Body and Blood of thy only Son, in behalf of the Faithful departed, and in particular for the Souls of *N. N.* my Parents, Relations, Benefactors, Neighbours, *&c.* Likewise of such as I have any ways injured, or been the Occasion of their Sins; of such as have injured me, and been my Enemies; of such as die in War, or have none to pray for them, *&c.* For these and all others, as many as are yet in the State of Penance, waiting for their Discharge, we beseech thee to hear us: Grant them Rest, O Lord, and eternal Salvation; admit them to the Company of thy blessed Saints.

When the Priest strikes his Breast, and in a loud Voice says, Nobis quoque Peccatoribus: *And to us Sinners.*

V Ouchsafe to grant the same one Day to us, poor and miserable Sinners as we are; and judge us not according to our Demerits; but through the infinite Multitude of thy Mercies, in which we hope, liberally extend to us thy Grace and Pardon.

We

all thy Saints; into whose Company, we beseech thee, admit us, not considering our Merit, but as granting us Mercy.   Thro' Christ our Lord.

By whom, O Lord, thou dost always create, ✠ sanctify, ✠ quicken, ✠ bless, and give us all these good Things.

Here kneeling down, and then taking the Sacred Host in his Hand, he makes the Sign of the Cross with it, over the Chalice, thus,

BY him, ✠ and with ✠ him, and in ✠ him, is to thee, God the Father ✠ Almighty, in the Unity ✠ of the Holy Ghost, all Honour and Glory.

Having kneeled down, he says,

For ever and ever.

A. Amen.

Let us pray.

INstructed by thy wholesome Precepts, and following thy divine Institution, we presume to say,

Our Father who art in Heaven, Hallowed be thy Name; thy Kingdom come: Thy Will be done on Earth as it is in Heaven: Give us this Day our daily Bread; and forgive us our Trespasses, as we forgive them that trespass against us.   And lead us not into Temptation.

A. But

We ask it of thee in the Name of thy dear Son, who lives and reigns eternally with thee, and in that Form of Prayer, which he himself hath taught us.

At the Pater Noster; *or,* Our Father.

TReat us, O Lord, as thy Children; and grant we may always truly respect thee, as our Father.

That we may be more devoted to thy Glory, and thy Will, than to our own.

Nourish us daily, O Lord, with thy heavenly Bread, as well as with thy temporal.

Dispose us so far to pardon others, that we may deserve a Pardon from thee.

Defend

A. *But deliver us from Evil.*   P. Amen.

Deliver us, O Lord, we beseech thee, from all Evils past, present and to come: And by the Intercession of the blessed and glorious ever Virgin Mary, *Mother of God, and of the holy Apostles* Peter *and* Paul, *and of* Andrew, *and of all the Saints; favourably grant us Peace in our Days; that, through the Assistance of thy Mercy, we may be always free from Sin, and secure from all Disturbance. Through the same* Jesus Christ, *our Lord, thy Son; who, with thee, liveth and reigneth, in the Unity of the Holy Ghost, God, World without End.*

A. Amen.

P. *The Peace of our Lord be always with you.*

A. *And with thy Spirit.*

Having broken the Host, he puts a Particle of it into the Chalice, saying in a low Voice;

MAY *this Mixture and Consecration of the Body and Blood of our Lord* Jesus Christ, *be to us that receive it, effectual to Life everlasting.* Amen.

Having

Defend us from the World, from the Devil, from ourselves, and from all Sorts of Evil.

After the Our Father.

Deliver us from those Evils, which we labour under at present; from past Evils, which can be nothing but our manifold Sins; and from the Evils to come, which will be the just Chastisement of our Offences, if our Prayers, and those more powerful ones of thy Saints, who intercede for us, intercept not thy Justice, or excite not thy Bounty.

When he breaks the Host, and puts a Particle of it into the Chalice.

THY Body was broken, and thy Blood shed for us: Grant that the Commemoration of this Holy Mystery may obtain for us Peace: And that those, that receive it, may find everlasting Rest.

Having kneeled down, he says, striking
his Breast,

*L*AMB of God, that takeſt away the Sins
    of the World, have Mercy on us.
    Lamb of God, that takeſt away the Sins of
the World, have Mercy on us.
    Lamb of God, that takeſt away the Sins of
the World, Grant us thy Peace.

Then ſays the following Prayers.

*L*ORD Jeſus Chriſt, who ſaidſt to thy Apo-
    ſtles, I leave you Peace, I give you my
Peace; regard not my Sins, but the Faith of
thy Church, and vouchſafe her ſuch Peace and
Union, as may be agreeable to thy Will, who
liveſt and reigneſt for ever and ever. Amen.
    Lord Jeſus Chriſt, Son of the living God,
who, according to the Will of the Father, haſt by
thy Death given Life to the World, thro' the
Co-operation of the Holy Ghoſt; deliver me, by
this thy moſt ſacred Body and Blood, from all my
Iniquities, and from all Evils; and make me
always obedient to thy Commandments; and
never ſuffer me to be ſeparated from thee, who
with the ſame Father, and Holy Ghoſt, liveſt
and reigneſt, God, World without End. Amen.
    Let not the Participation of thy Body, O
Lord Jeſus Chriſt, which I, unworthy, preſume
to receive, turn to my Judgment and Condemnation;

When the Priest, bowing down, strikes his Breast, and says thrice, Agnus Dei, Lamb of God ; *the People may say the same, or as follows :*

O Lamb of God, who takeſt away the Sins of the World, waſh away all ours in thy Blood. Lamb of God, give us thy Sweetneſs and Innocence, that we may be better diſpoſed to receive thy Peace.

After Agnus Dei, *or* Lamb of God, *&c.*

IN ſaying to thy Apoſtles, my Peace I leave you, my Peace I give you, thou haſt pro-miſed, O Lord, to all thy Church, that Peace which the World cannot give : Peace with thee, and Peace with ourſelves.

Let nothing, O Lord, ever interrupt this holy Peace ; let nothing ſeparate us from thee, to whom we heartily deſire to be united, thro' this bleſſed Sacrament of Peace and Reconciliation. Let this Food of Angels ſtrengthen us in every Chriſtian Duty, ſo as never more to yield under Temptations, or fall into our common Weakneſſes.

But alas! who does not tremble at this holyTable! ſince 'tis true, as we are differently diſpoſed, we may receive either Life or Death ; and that the unworthy Receiver draws upon himſelf, not a Bleſſing, but thy

E 2

juſt

nation; but let it, through thy Mercy, be an effectual Security and Cure both of Soul and Body; who liveſt and reigneſt with the Father, in the Unity of the Holy Ghoſt, God, World without End.   Amen.

He kneels, and having taken the Hoſt into his Hands, ſays in a low Voice,

I *Will take the Bread of Heaven and call on the Name of our Lord.*

Then ſtriking his Breaſt, he ſays in a loud Voice: *Domine non ſum dignus.*

Lord, I am not worthy   *Thou ſhouldeſt enter under my Roof, ſay only the Word, and my Soul ſhall be healed.*

Lord, I am not worthy

Lord, I am not worthy

juſt Wrath. Help us therefore, O Lord, and ſo prepare us by thy Grace, that in this holy Myſtery we may find the effectual Remedy of all our Evils.

At Domine non ſum dignus, Lord, I am not worthy.

Say it with the Prieſt, and then go on thus:

KIng of Kings, Lord of Lords, whom the Heaven and Earth cannot contain, how great is thy Goodneſs, thus to become our Sacrifice and our Food! But I, miſerable Sinner, am not worthy to receive thee. Speak therefore the Word, and my Soul ſhall be healed.

Lord, I am not worthy to receive thee: 'Tis thou muſt firſt fit and prepare my Soul: Say but the Word then, and it ſhall be ready for ſo great a Gueſt: Speak, Lord, and I ſhall be healed.

 Ma)

Receiving the Sacred Hoſt, he ſays,

THE Body of our Lord Jeſus Chriſt preſerve my Soul to Life everlaſting. Amen.

Having pauſed a while, he kneels down, and then ſays,

WHAT ſhall I return to our Lord for all he has given me; I will take the Chalice of Salvation, and call on the Name of our Lord. I will call on our Lord in praiſing him; and I ſhall be ſafe from my Enemies.

Then taking the Chalice, he ſays,

THE Blood of our Lord Jeſus Chriſt preſerve my Soul to Life everlaſting. Amen.

Then Wine is put into the Chalice, for the firſt Ablution, and he ſays,

GRant, O Lord, that what we have taken with our Mouth, we may receive with a pure Heart: and that of a temporal Gift, it may become to us an everlaſting Remedy.

Wine and Water is put into the Chalice, for another Ablution, and he ſays,

MAY thy Body, which I have received, O Lord, and thy Blood, which I have drank, abide within me: And grant, that no Pollution

of

May then this Body and Blood of my Lord and Saviour Jesus Christ, be the eternal Life of my Soul.

Thou art the Food of Life, O good Jesus, and 'tis by thy Power and Grace my Soul must live to thee. Communicate then to me, at present, thy divine Blessings, and let my weak and hungry Soul be now comforted and strengthened by this heavenly Food, that it may be an effectual Remedy of all my Weaknesses, and make me faithful in thy Service for ever.

At the second Ablution.

GRant, O merciful Jesus, that when ever I shall receive this precious Body and Blood, they may for ever abide in me, and become a heavenly Nourishment to my Soul.

When

of Sin may remain in me, who have been re-
freshed by thy pure and holy Sacraments; who
livest and reignest for ever and ever. Amen.

Having wiped his Fingers and the Chalice,
he covers it, and then going to the Book,
reads the Communion, which is a Verse
out of the Holy Scripture, and is different every Day : Then goes to the Middle of the Altar, and turning to the
People, says,

P. *Our Lord be with you.*
A. *And with thy Spirit.*

Then going to the Book he says the Prayers
called the *Postcommunion,* which are different every Day, and therefore cannot be
set down here.

Postcommunion.

P. *Our*

When the Chalice is covered, he goes to the Book, and reads the Communion.

LET it be now, O Lord, the Effect of thy Mercy, that we, who have been present at this holy Mystery, may find the Benefit of it in our Souls.

At the Postcommunion, *when he goes a second Time to the Book.*

WE give thee Thanks, O God, for thy Mercy, in admitting us a Part in offering this Sacrifice to thy Holy Name: Accept it now to thy Glory; and be ever mindful of our Weakness.

On a Sunday, *or* Feria.

SAnctify us, O Lord, we beseech thee, by the powerful Effects of these divine Mysteries; may we be cleansed by them from all Sin, delivered from all Adversities, and confirmed in thy Grace for ever.

E 5

On

P. *Our Lord be with you.*
A. *And with thy Spirit.*
P. *Depart, Mass is done ;* or, *Let us bless our Lord.*
A. *Thanks be to God.*

Bowing before the Altar, he says,

*L*ET *the Performance of my Duty, O Holy Trinity, be pleasing to thee; and grant, that the Sacrifice, which I, unworthy, have offered in the Sight of thy Majesty, may be acceptable to thee ; and thro' thy Mercy be Propitiatory to me, and all those for whom I have offered it. Thro' Christ our Lord.* Amen.

He turns to the People, and gives them the Blessing, making the Sign of the Cross over them with his Hand, saying,

*A*Lmighty God, Father, Son, and Holy Ghost, *bless you.*
A. *Amen.*
P. *Our Lord be with you.*
A. *And with thy Spirit.*
R. *The Beginning of the Gospel according to St.* John.
A. *Glory be to thee, O Lord.*

At

On the *Festival of a Saint.*

HEAR us, O merciful God, and by the Interceffion of this thy holy Servant, may the Effects of thefe thy Bleffings ever appear in our Lives, that while we celebrate his Memory, we may be in Hopes of partaking of his Reward.

When the Prieft bows before the Middle of the Altar.

MOST Holy and Adorable Trinity, without Beginning, and without End; it is through thee, and by thee, we began this Sacrifice, and by thee we ought to finifh it. Vouchfafe therefore to accept it: And as thou art an Abyfs of Majefty hidden from us, be thou alfo an Abyfs of Pity and Mercy to us.

While

At the Corner of the Altar he reads St. *John's* Gospel.

IN the Beginning was the Word, and the Word was with God, and God was the Word. This was in the Beginning with God. All Things were made by him, and without him was made nothing that was made. In him was Life, and the Life was the Light of Men: And the Light shined in Darkness, and the Darkness did not comprehend it. There was a Man sent from God, whose Name was John. *He came for a Witness to give Testimony of the Light, that thro' him all might believe. He was not the Light, but was to give Testimony of the Light. He was the true Light that enlightens every Man, that comes into this World. He was in the World, and the World was made by him, and the World knew him not. He came to his own, and his own received him not. But as many as received him he gave them Power to be made the Sons of God, to those, who believe in his Name; who not of Blood, nor of the Will of the Flesh, nor of the Will of Man, but of God, are born. And the Word was made Flesh, and dwelt in us: And we saw his Glory, as the Glory of the only Begotten of the Father, full of Grace and Truth.*

 A. *Thanks be to God.*

While the Priest reads St. John's Gospel at the Corner of the Altar.

O Eternal Word, fpeak to my Soul, which adores thee in a profound Silence: Thou art the great Creator of all Things; abandon not, I befeech thee, thy own Creature; be thou my Life, my Light, and my All.

O Light eternal, enlighten me as to this prefent Life and in the Life to come.

Chafe away, by thy Prefence, thofe thick and unhappy Clouds that hover over my Soul, and hinder me from underftanding thee.

That I may always know and underftand thee, whenever thou vouchfafeft to come to me.

Reign in me, as in thy own Inheritance: For thou, Lord, haft made me; thou haft redeemed me; may I be ever thine.

I have finned too much againft Heaven, and before thee, and am not worthy to be called thy Son.

If thou yet receiveft me as a prodigal Son, grant, Lord, that my Love and Obedience may fomething correfpond with that high Birth, where Flefh and Blood are not concerned; where my Will may defire nothing but as directed by thine.

Thou God incarnate, have Pity on my frail and mortal Flefh, and grant it may one Day fee what it here adores below. *Amen.*

IN this Method of hearing Mafs, it may be eafily obferved, how exactly the Faithful acompany the Prieft, almoft in all he fays; it being generally the fame, as to the Subftance, only accommodated to them, in Confideration of the Part they bear in the folemn Act of Worfhip.

And now while the Church feems to require the Faithful to join with the Prieft, may not they, who follow this Method, fatisfy themfelves, that they have complied with their Obligation, and likewife hope to obtain large Bleffings from the Hand of God, who have wholly applied their Thoughts in this great Myftery, and permitted nothing to divert them from it? And tho' others chufe at this Time, to fatisfy themfelves with private Devotions; is it not to be feared, that a Want of due Underftanding of the Mafs is too often the Occafion of it? Let them reflect at leaft, whether the folicitude of finifhing the Tafk of thofe Prayers, they purpofe to themfelves, does not often take off their Thoughts and Devotion from fuch principal Parts of the Mafs, to which they ought moft particularly to attend. How often do they quite pafs over the *Creed*, the *Offertory*, the *Mementos*, the *Communion*, &c. without any Sort of Application? And if they lay by their Books at the *Elevation*, they fnatch them up again with fo much hafte, that 'tis plain, they allow not themfelves that Time which is

suitable

ſuitable to the Greatneſs of the Myſtery, or
may be moſt beneficial to their own Souls.
What I have therefore to recommend to theſe,
is to reflect on this Matter a little, and conſider whether it be reaſonable, to make the
greater Act of Religion give Way to the *leſſer*;
and ſince the hearing Maſs, in the Method
here propoſed, includes, in an eminent Manner, all other private Devotions, whether it
be not moſt juſt, to allow to the Maſs the
Time that belongs to it; and not borrow
from that, for the ſatisfying other Duties.
This I ſay to ſuch as truly underſtand it;
For as to others, who have only a very groſs
and imperfect Knowledge of it, 'tis not to be
wondered, if they take another Way, and
make uſe of a Staff, who are ſo weak as not
to be able to go without it. But then let theſe
too conſider, how far they are bound to labour for their Improvement, and not be at a
Stand in a Matter which, being ſo much to
their Soul's Diſadvantage, muſt neceſſarily be
cenſured as a State of Sloth and Neglect.
But now leaving theſe, I turn to ſuch as are
advanced in the ſpiritual Life, and know how
to ſpeak to God, without the immediate Help
of Books; having ſome Directions to lay before them, which likewiſe may not be improper for others to read, who are not yet
come to this Degree.

But firſt, I think, it may not be improper
here to give a ſhort Glance at the chief Ceremonies uſed at Maſs; becauſe thoſe who
under-

underſtand euough to follow this ſecond Method, may make ſome Reflections on them, ſuch as may be a great Help to direct them in their Devotion.

Firſt then, *Bowing down,* is a Poſture often uſed by the Prieſt in Time of Maſs, *viz.* as often as he ſays ſuch Prayers, in which he *acknowledges his Unworthineſs, humbly makes his Offering to Almighty God, begs for Mercy,* &c. And this he is ordered to do, that by this external Humiliation he may be put in Mind of that interior Humility of Spirit, with which he ought ever to perform thoſe Actions; as likewiſe to direct all preſent then to humble themſelves before Almighty God, while they ſee the Prieſt thus bowing down.

2. *Kneeling,* is generally in the Maſs an Act of Adoration, by which the Prieſt gives ſovereign Worſhip to Chriſt our Redeemer, really preſent in the Euchariſt: And therefore this the Prieſt performs with all the Powers of his Soul, adoring before his Lord, and ſhews the Faithful how they ought ever to adore in Spirit, as often as they ſee the Prieſt kneeling before the holy Euchariſt. He kneels likewiſe once in the Middle of the Creed, when he pronounces theſe Words, *Et Homo factus eſt : And he was made Man.* And once at the End of St. *John*'s Goſpel, when he ſays, *Et Verbum Caro factum eſt ; And the Word was made Fleſh.* Both Times to ſignify the ſecond Perſon of the Bleſſed Trinity coming down from Heaven, to take on him our Nature,

ture, so to become our Redeemer: In Acknowledgment of which Mystery, all Christians ought to bow, both Priest and People, so to testify their Sense of that infinite Mercy, and give Thanks for it.

3. *Striking the Breast*, is a Ceremony delivered in Scripture, as an Expression of a sincere Repentance, in the poor *Publican*. And this the Priest uses, as often as he professes a Repentance for his Sins; as in the *Confiteor :* Or begs for Mercy; as at *Agnus Dei :* Or confesses his Unworthiness; as at *Domine non sum dignus.* And if he does this, not as using a bare Ceremony, but with a truly humble and contrite Heart, there's no Question, 'tis what is very Christian, and may serve likewise to move the Faithful to a hearty Contrition and sincere Acknowledgment of their Unworthiness, as often as they practise the like Action. And if they would thus seriously return to the Heart, as often as they strike their Breast, they might reasonably hope with the *Publican* to go home justified.

4. *Turning to the People*, is what the Priest does, as often as he gives a Blessing to them, in saying, *Dominus vobiscum ; Our Lord be with you*, &c. or desires their Prayers, as at *Orate Fratres ; Brethren pray*, &c. For as when he makes his Offerings and Prayers to God, he stands with his Face to the Altar, which is the Place of Worship; so when he addresses himself to the People, he turns to them.

5. *Making*

5. *Making the Sign of the Cross*, is used in Blessing the Bread and Wine as an Acknowledgment of our Belief, that all Grace and Benediction is to come to us through the Merits and Passion of Christ crucified.

6. *Kissing the Altar*, is what the Priest does before he blesses the Offering, or the People, &c. to signify again, that all Peace and Blessing is purchased for us by Christ's Suffering on the Cross, which is represented by the Altar: And that all Good is to come from his sacred Merits. Thus far of some general Ceremonies. The several Parts of the Mass may be likewise here very well observed. The first Part is from the Beginning, till the Priest unveils the Chalice: And this is a Preparation of Priest and People for the great Action of the Sacrifice, and consists in Humiliations, in confessing of Sins, begging for Mercy; of Prayers, and reading Part of the holy Scripture in the Lesson and Gospel; and of a Profession of Faith in the Creed. The second Part is from the unveiling the Chalice till 'tis again covered with the Veil: And in this is performed the Sacrifice; the Bread and Wine being first prepared at the *Offertory*, then blessed and confecrated into the Body and Blood of the Lamb, and then confummated at the *Communion*. The third Part is from the Communion, or second Veiling of the Chalice, to the End: And this is a Thankfgiving. This being observed, we turn now to the Persons already mentioned.

Third

Third Method of Hearing Mass, proper for such as are more advanced.

TO those, who know how to govern their Thoughts, and are well acquainted with the Way of the Spirit, the Hearing of Mass is but one continued Exercise of the Soul, in all the Acts of Christian Virtues : When applying herself to every particular Part, she is led from one Virtue to another with great Variety and Sweetness, but without Disorder. This is done by an inward Light communicated by Almighty God, not only to Men of Learning, but often to such who, being otherwise Weak and Ignorant, have nothing but Humility, and seeking God with sincere Hearts, to prepare them for these Favours of Heaven.

All these, when they go to hear Mass, go as to a School of Virtue, where they are to meet their divine Master, by whom they are to be instructed in all the Rules of a Christian Life, to be reproached of all their Failings, and encouraged in all those great Duties, which are required of them.

1. They behold, in this Mystery, Christ our Lord, in the Flames of divine Love, offering himself a Sacrifice every Day to the Glory of his Father. Which is a Lesson to them, that if they design truly to belong to God, they ought daily to offer themselves to him, to make their Lives a perpetual Sacrifice

fice, and endeavour to live no more themselves, but to him.

2. They fee an Excefs of that other Branch of Charity, which regards our Neighbour in the Holy Euchariſt, where Chriſt gives himſelf to the Faithful under the Form of Bread and Nouriſhment, by Means of which they may be changed and transformed into him. And this is a Rule to them, of the Love they ought to bear to their Neighbour; and a Reproach, as often as they confider, how Intereſt and Self-love makes them neglect this great Duty, and lay a Ground for Mifunderſtandings, Complaints and Quarrels

3. They fee him there in a State of Humility, under the Sacramental Species: This is to them a Condemnation of all Pride, and by his Example, fuppreſſes all vain Eſteem they can have of themſelves.

4. They behold in him a wonderful Patience, bearing not only with the Blafphemies of Unbelievers, but alfo with the Sacrileges of unworthy Receivers. This confounds their exceffive Nicenefs, who cannot, without Diſturbance, bear the leaſt Injury or Contempt.

5. They confider him there in a State of Poverty: This condemns all Thoughts of Covetoufnefs, and encourages them to caſt off all vain Solicitude, and ſubmit to Inconveniencies without murmuring.

6. They fee him there as it were in a State of Penance, covered with thofe fenfible Accidents, as with Sackcloth and Afhes, and thus

offering

offering himself to his Eternal Father as an Host of Propitiation for our Sins: This shews them how to repent of their Sins; and with what Charity they ought to pray for all those who are separated from God by their Offences, and are under the Tyranny of vicious Habits.

7. They see him there an Advocate for all, even for those who have offended him. This forcibly moves them to cast off all Sorts of Animosities, Ill-will, or Hatred, from their Hearts, and to let no Kind of Injuries be a Confinement to their Charity, which ought to be, like their Master's, extended to all.

Infinite other Lessons of this kind they hear from their Divine Master in this School of Piety; such as the World cannot understand: Whilst placing themselves at his Feet, like holy *Magdalene*, with Humility they say to him in their Hearts, *I will hear what our Lord shall speak:* And there receive as many Instructions as there were eminent Virtues practised by our Redeemer. I will here propose some Method of this interiour Exercise, for the Help of such as desire to be acquainted with this Way. But first shew you a Form, in which they offer this Holy Sacrifice to God, before the Priest comes to the Altar.

An Oblation of the Mass, as it gives supreme Worship to God.

HOLY Trinity, one God, whose Power, Wisdom, Goodness, and Mercy, is incomprehensible, here prostrate in Body and Soul, I adore thee; and present myself now before the Altar, to join with thy Servant in offering to thee, the Sacrifice of the Body and Blood of our Lord Jesus Christ, to the greater Glory of thy Name, in Acknowledgment of thy supreme Dominion over all Creatures, and our entire Dependence on thee: In Confession of thy infinite Perfection, Happiness and Glory. And with the Sacrifice of Praise, I likewise offer thee, all that Adoration, which he gave thee, while yet on Earth; as also all that Honour, Praise and Homage, which have been paid thee by the Blessed Virgin, and all the Angels and Saints. For as to myself, what am I, but a miserable Sinner, a poor Worm of the Earth, unworthy to appear before thee, and therefore wholly confiding in the Merits of thy Son our Lord, I cast myself before thy Throne of Majesty, confessing to the whole World, that I am the Work of thy Hands, and as nothing before thee. I wish that as many as thou hast created in all Nations, were now adoring on their Knees before thee, and giving sovereign Honour to thy Name. But because there are infinite Numbers, that know thee not, and of those that know thee, too many that adore

thee

thee not, therefore for all these I now adore thee; and humbly beseech thee to accept this Oblation, in order to their Deliverance from all the Sins and Blasphemies by which they offend against thy Laws. To thee, O God, all Honour and Glory, thro' Christ our Lord. *Amen.*

An Oblation of the Mass, as it is a Thanksgiving for all Blessings.

I Give thee Thanks, O Lord, Fountain of all Good, for all thy Blessings: But because no Creature is capable of rendering thee the Thanks due to thy infinite Goodness, therefore, behold, I now come to offer thee, with the Priest, the Sacrifice of thy only Son in Thanksgiving for all thy Benefits: And in particular I now desire thee to accept it, in Return for all those Mercies thou hast shewn us by the Hands of our Redeemer, in his being made Man, and suffering for us; for that infinite Love, by which thou hast given him to me to be a Father, a Protector and Teacher, and for all the Fruit of his Life, of his Passion and Death. Accept it likewise in Thanksgiving for all that Treasure of Graces poured forth on the Blessed Virgin-Mother of our Lord Jesus Christ, and on all thy chosen Servants, especially those whose Memory and Virtues we honour this Day. Let it be a Thanksgiving for all those Gifts, by which thou raisest so many, while yet on Earth, to

an

an eminent Degree of Holiness, for thy wonderful Patience in bearing with Sinners, and granting them Time to repent ; for all thy Favours bestowed on all Men whatever, whether Friends or Enemies, Faithful or Unbelievers ; for thy Protection and Assistance given to thy Church ; for that Love, by which thou hast made me a Member of it ; for thy wonderful Providence in delivering me from so many Dangers both of Soul and Body ; for Strengthening me in Temptations, Directing me in Difficulties, Comforting me in Afflictions ; for all thy Light and Grace, by which thou hast conducted me in the Way of thy Commandments, and givest me Hope of persevering to the End ; for all Temporal Blessings, by which thou hast encouraged me ; for all thy Scourges, by which thou hast instructed and corrected me : For these and infinite others thy Mercies, I now desire to return thee the poor Tribute of a grateful Mind : But what kind of Return can I make, who am nothing but Misery, Sin and Ingratitude ? I will therefore now offer thee the Sacrifice of thy only Son : His Merits are infinite, and in them only can I find a just Proportion with thy Blessings, the Effects of thy Goodness : Accept then this, O Lord, from the Hands of thy Servant ; but to all thy other Favours, add now this one of thy Grace, whereby my Heart may go along with the Offering.

An Oblation of the Mafs, as it is available for the Remiffion of Sins.

COvered with Shame and Confufion, I now appear before thee; O Lord, the Thoughts of my Unworthynefs, the Guilt of my injured Confcience, the Confideration of my Ingratitude, of my great Neglects of Eternity, of my Self-love, of my Omiffions, and the Weight of all my other Crimes, is now a Terror to me, for the Divifion they have made betwixt my Soul and thee, O God, my only and everlafting Good; thefe have hid thy Face from me: But, behold, fenfible of my Offences, I now return to thee, humbly befeeching thy Goodnefs to difcharge me from the Guilt of all my Sins: And becaufe no Creature is able to fatisfy thy infinite Goodnefs, for the Injuries and Contempts offered thee in my Tranfgreffions, but only the Blood of thy beloved Son, our Lord Jefus Chrift: Therefore I now come to offer him to thee a Sin-offering, that laying before thee his infinite Merits, I may obtain of thee a fincere Contrition of Heart, for the Pardon of all my Sins, thro' his bitter Paffion and Death, who being once offered a Sacrifice on the Crofs, I now offer again on thy Altar. For it is in him I behold, as it were, a great and fpacious Sea of Merits, fufficient not only to cover, but even to fwallow up all my Offences; it is in him I fee an infinite Treafure of Satisfaction, for

the

the Releafe of all my Crimes. Be not therefore angry with thy Servant, tho' in himfelf moft unworthy, but hear the Voice of thy Son's Blood crying out to thee, not Revenge, but Mercy and Pardon. Give Ear to it, O Lord, and forgive me my Sins: Grant me new Grace to amend, and Perfeverance in Good, and I fhall for ever fing forth the Praifes of thy Mercies.

An Oblation of the Mafs, for the obtaining God's Bleffings.

I Come now, O Lord, to join with thy Minifter whom thou haft chofen, and with him to offer thee the moft grateful Sacrifice of thy only Son, in whom thou art will pleafed; that, through his Paffion and Death, thou mayeft be moved in thy tender Mercy to have regard to the Neceffities of all, and pour forth thy Bleffings on them, for their Relief according to their different Wants. Accept then, O God of infinite Goodnefs, this Sacrifice we offer, and let this open thy heavenly Treafures. Have Mercy on all, whom thou haft created; fill them with the Knowledge and Faith of thee. Shew forth thy Light to thofe Nations who know thee not, to all Infidels, Turks, Jews, Heretics, and Schifmatics; deliver them from their Blindnefs, Obftinacy and Errors, that they may be perfectly united to thee. Sanctify thy Church, which thou haft planted with
thy

thy Right-hand, and watered with thy Blood; remove from her all Scandals, Abuses, Diffensions, and Schisms, that there may be one Fold, and one Shepherd. Grant to our chief Bishop, to all Prelates and Pastors, that they may faithfully watch over and feed the Flocks committed to them, both by Word and Example; being ever mindful of the Charge they have undertaken, and performing it without Reproof. Shew thy Mercy to all Ecclesiastical Orders, that by their Virtues and good Discipline, they may be as Lights shining before Men: Revive in them their first Fervour; give Zeal to their Governors, Obedience to Inferiors, that all may live up to their Profession. Excite in the Preachers of thy Word a true Apostolic Spirit, that they may seek nothing but thy Honour, and the enlarging thy Kingdom: Grant to all Kings, Princes and Magistrates, Wisdom, and a Strength of Mind, that they may be Protectors of thy People, and the Supporters of Justice. Defend all the Faithful from Famine, Plague and War, from Persecution and all Distress, whether spiritual or temporal: Help all that are under any Trouble or Affliction, and send them thy heavenly Comfort. Deliver those who are in Danger of Sin, and protect them by thy Grace. Stand by those, I beseech thee, who are now in their Agony; grant them true Contrition, and secure them against all Snares of their Enemy.

 Have

Have Compaſſion on all thoſe unhappy Sinners, who live in the State of Sin; touch them with thy powerful Grace, that they may ſee their Miſery, amend, and return to thee. Be merciful to all my Enemies, and forgive them; remove from them all Paſſion, ſoften their Hearts with true Charity, and deliver us from all Evil. Look on all thoſe to whom I have given any Scandal, Offence, or ill Example. Remember all my Relations, Friends, and Benefactors: Repleniſh them with all neceſſary Succours from above, that faithfully ſerving thee, they may live in thy Favour, and die in thy Grace. Preſerve the Juſt in thy Ways, and grant to the Tepid and Imperfect a daily Increaſe of Faith, Hope and Charity. Have Mercy on all faithful Souls departed this Life, releaſe ſuch as ſuffer, admit them to thy Preſence, and give them Reſt everlaſting. And forget not me, O Lord, the moſt unworthy of all Sinners, who every Moment ſtand in need of thy Help: Extinguiſh in me all earthly Deſires, and enflame my Heart with the Fire of thy Love: Direct me in the Way of thy Truth, preſerve me from all Evil, and grant me final Perſeverance, thro' Chriſt our Lord, thy only Son, and my Redeemer. *Amen.*

A ſhort

A short Oblation of the Mass, in these four Ways, for such as are strengthened in Time.

LORD of Heaven and Earth, see here an unworthy Sinner comes to offer thee this Day the Sacrifice of thy only Son ; and I now offer it to thee, together with all the grateful Sacrifices that have been offered thee from the Beginning of the World, in Union with that wonderful Sacrifice, which my Redeemer instituted at his last Supper, and consummated on the Cross : To thy greater Praise and Glory : In Protestation of thy supreme Dominion, and our Dependance on thee : In Remembrance of the Death and Passion of my dear Saviour : In Thankfgiving for all thy Blessings, whether bestowed on me, or on thy Church, or on all thy Creatures : For the obtaining Pardon for all my Sins, which I now desire to abhor, in as much as they are displeasing to thee : For the Relief of my Necessities, spiritual and temporal, and of all Christian People, Friends and Enemies : For all the World, and for the Faithful departed. Accept it, Lord, from thy holy Altar, by the Hands of thy Servant ; and tho' I am of all Sinners most unworthy, yet let not my Unworthiness make void the Effects of thy Goodness, but hear my Prayers, and let the Offering, I now make thee, find Acceptance in thy Sight. *Amen.*

Having

Having in this Manner prepared themselves, they thus proceed.

At the Beginning of Mass.

AT the Priest's making the Sign of the Cross they begin, 1. With an Act of Faith in the Blessed Trinity. 2. Offer the Sacrifice then beginning to the Glory of God, in Remembrance of Christ's Passion. 3. Hope, thro' the Merits of Christ crucified, to obtain Grace, for the well performing this Devotion, to God's Honour, and the Good of their Souls.

At the Glory be to the Father.

THey bow with the Priest with all Humility, adoring God in their Souls, and profess a Desire of submitting to all his Appointments.

At the Confiteor.

THey recite it in the Spirit of Humility, and in saying those Words, *Through my Fault,* &c. endeavour to pronounce them with true Contrition, joined with a firm Hope of Mercy and Pardon for their own and others Sins; and so continue in this State of Humility, Repentance and Hope, while the Priest says the *Misereatur,* and gives the *Absolution.*

At

At the Kyrie eleison.

THey again raise up their Hearts, with the same interiour Disposition, and beg for Mercy, for their own and others Sins.

At the Gloria in Excelsis.

THey in Spirit join with the Angels, in giving Glory to God, and go on with those other Affections of Praise, Adoration, Thanksgiving, Faith, Hope, Love, Petition, *&c.* according to the Tenor of that sacred Hymn.

At the Dominus Vobiscum.

THey bow down in Humility to dispose themselves for the receiving that Blessing the Priest then gives; and beg of Allmighty God to abide with them, both then and for ever; and this they do as often as he repeats these Words.

At the Collects.

THey join with the Priest in recommending to God the Necessities of the Church and their own: And as often as the Conclusion is repeated, *Per Dominum nostrum,* &c. they repose their whole Confidence of obtaining their Requests, in the Merits of our Lord Jesus Christ.

At

At the Epistle *and* Gospel.

THey either humbly attend to them, if they understand *Latin*; or otherwise, raise up their Thoughts in Thanksgiving to God, for those holy Instructions he has left them in the Holy Bible; pray for Grace, whereby they may be enabled to observe them; and resolve that no Care or Endeavours shall be wanting on their Parts, necessary for their being directed by such holy Maxims.

At the Creed.

THey make a Profession of their Faith, giving Thanks to God for his Mercy, in bringing them to the Knowledge of it; resolve to live and die in it; pray for the Enlightning all that are in Darkness: And when the Priest kneels at those Words, *Et Homo factus est*, never fail to adore, with Thanksgiving, the Son of God becoming Man for our Salvation.

At the Offertory.

THey offer up the Host and Chalice with the Priest; and forget not to do it, in Remembrance of Christ's offering himself to his eternal Father, to become our Redeemer: And then encouraged by this their Lord's Example, offer themselves to him, with all that belongs to them, Body, Soul, Reputation, Health, Estate, &c. And putting their

Hearts

Hearts on the Paten with the Bread, and in the Chalice with the Wine, they pray, that, as the Bread and Wine are soon to be changed into the Body and Blood of Christ, so their Hearts may be truly converted or changed into him, that so Christ may live in them.

When the Priest washes his Fingers.

THey give Thanks that they have been washed by the Blood of Christ, pray for a clean Heart, and that they may be purified even from all lesser Defects.

At Orate Fratres.

THey pray, as the Priest desires, that God would be pleased to accept that Oblation, that it may be for his Honour, and their Salvation.

At the Preface.

THey raise up their Hearts to God, according to the Summons of the Priest: Then endeavouring to comprehend all his Blessings bestowed on them and all Creatures, pour forth their Souls in *Thanksgiving*. And desirous to give him due Praise, call on all the blessed Spirits in Heaven; and beg Leave, that Dust and Ashes may join with them, in adoring before the Throne of God, and pronounce, tho' unworthy, that sacred Hymn of Praise, *Holy, Holy, Holy, Lord God of Sabbath*, &c. In saying which they place

F 5

them-

themfelves in Spirit before the Lamb : And being at the fame Time fenfible, how unworthy their Sins rendered them of this divine Function, they therefore bow down, and ftrike their Breafts, in Acknowledgment of this their Unworthinefs.

At the Memento.

THey again join with the Prieft, in offering the holy Sacrifice to God for all thofe, whom they defire to be benefited by their Prayers, befeeching God to accept it, 1. For themfelves, for the Remiffion of all their Sins; for obtaining fuch particular Virtues as they want, and final Perfeverance. 2. For the Church, its chief Bifhop, Prelates, Paftors, &c. 3. For the King and fecular Magiftrates. 4. For Parents, Friends, Benefactors, &c. 5. For all in Neceffity, Poor, Sick, Prifoners, Captives, Diftreffed, &c. 6. For Enemies. 7. For all in mortal Sin. 8. For all Heretics and Unbelievers. 9. For all the true Servants of God. Adding fuch other Neceffities, whether public or private, as Circumftances fuggeft to them.

When he fpreads his Hands over the Oblation.

THey then lay their Hearts and Souls on the Altar, that they may be there fanctified with thofe Gifts, and become a Sacrifice to God, pure and undefiled.

At

At *the* Confecration.

HAving prepared themfelves with all poffible Devotion, when the Prieft kneels,
they bow down, and with all Reverence
adore Chrift the Son of God, under the
facramental Species; and this they obferve
afterwards, as often as the Prieft kneels
down, ever accompanying him, kneeling
and adoring with him in their Hearts.

In the time of Confecration *and* Elevation,
*the Faithful ought to avoid all unneceffary
Spitting, Blowing the Nofe, &c. which
often give Difturbance to the Prieft, and
argue a Mind not fo well recollected, as it
truly ought to be, at that Time.*

At *the* Elevation.

THey contemplate Chrift exalted on the
Crofs for Man's Redemption, and with
all their Power endeavour to raife their
Hearts to him, in feveral Acts of Virtue;
by Faith, Hope, Love, Adoration, Humility, *&c.* and ftriking their Breafts, fay,
*Jefus be merciful to me a Sinner; Jefus, Son
of* David, *have Mercy on us. I love thee,
my God, I adore thee with all my Heart.*
And at the *Elevation of the Chalice,* are
ever mindful (with a Senfe of Gratitude
and Grief) of that Blood Chrift fhed for
them,

them, Offering their Lives to him, to become an unbloody Sacrifice at least, in suffering such Troubles as he shall appoint for them. *Benedic anima mea Domino, & omnia quæ intra me sunt, Nomini Sancto ejus.*

At the Elevation.

WITH the Priest, they here offer the holy and immaculate Lamb to the eternal Father, in Memory of his Passion, Resurrection and Ascension; hoping, thro' his Merits, to be Partakers one Day of his Glory. And here reflecting who it is that lies before them on the Altar, and what infinite Charity he shewed while on Earth, to such as were afflicted with any Distemper; hence encouraged, they lay before him all the Infirmities of their Souls, and with the Blind and Lame in the Gospel cry out, *Jesus, have Mercy on me; Lord, if thou wilt, thou canst make me whole.* Or otherwise, imagining themselves to be on Mount *Calvary,* they there, at the Foot of the Altar, exercise their Souls in all those Acts of Love, Thanksgiving, Contrition, Hope, Resignation, *&c.* as they would have done, had they been at the Foot of the Cross; since here is the very Lamb, who offered himself there a Sacrifice.

At the Second Memento.

THey lay before their heavenly Father this holy Victim, in Behalf of the Faithful departed.

departed. 1. For the Souls of their Relations, Friends, &c. 2. For Enemies. For any lately· dead, or particularly recommended. *Lastly*, For all departed in the Christian and Catholic Unity. That so, by this general Commemoration, as St. *Augustine* says, all such as have no Parents, or Children, or Relations, or Friends to pray for them, may have this Charity performed them, by their pious and common Mother the Church.

At Nobis quoque Peccatoribus,

THey pronounce those Words with the Priest in all Humility, earnestly begging to have a Share in the Effects of this Sacrifice, and being pardoned thro' the Merits of Christ, to be at length admitted to the Glory of the Blessed.

At Omnis Honor & Gloria,

THey make a profound Act of Adoration, giving God all Glory, through Christ our Lord.

At the Pater Noster,

THey say it devoutly with the Priest, with great Confidence in their Redeemer.

At the Breaking the Host,

THey remember, with Gratitude, Christ's Body, that was broken for them on the Cross ;

Crofs; and thro' his Sufferings, pray here for a threefold Peace, *viz.* with God, their Neighbours, and themfelves; and fuch a Peace in all Troubles, as the World cannot give.

At Agnus Dei.

HAving faid this thrice with the Prieft in the Spirit of Humility and Contrition, they continue their Addreffes to the Lamb of God, to be delivered from all the Evils of Sin, and efpecially from thofe to which they perceive themfelves moft inclined.

At Domine non fum Dignus,

THey repeat this with the Prieft, but as the Centurion did, with an humble Heart. And then while the Prieft is communicating, they endeavour, in the beft manner they can, to partake of the Victim that has been offered either really, or at leaft in Spirit, by making a fpiritual Communion. Exciting in their Souls a fervent Defire of receiving this holy Food, bewailing their Unworthinefs, and that their Hearts are fo unprepared for entertaining fo great a Gueft: Then having performed many Acts of Faith, Hope, and Charity, towards their loving Redeemer, there really prefent, they with all Humility beg of him, that fince they receive not his precious Body by a facramental Participation of this Sacrifice, they

may

may receive, at least, a large Portion of his Spirit, by the Participation of his Grace: And hope, according to the Degree of Charity wherewith they perform this, they may partake of the divine Blessings in their Souls.

After the Communion,

THey give God Thanks for the Benefit received in this holy Mystery, and most particularly for the Death and Passion of his only Son here commemorated. Then in receiving the Benediction, they open their Hearts, with Humility, and a Confidence in God, that he will please to fill them with Abundance of heavenly Graces. Then begging Pardon for all Distractions and Negligences in Time of their Devotions, they recommend themselves to the Divine Protection, offering all the Actions of the Day to his Honour: And when the Priest is gone into the Sacristy, if their Devotion keeps them no longer, then they depart with Reverence.

Here I have given a just Taste of the interior Sweetness those experience, who follow this more spiritual Way; in which there is not one Christian Virtue but what becomes the Exercise and Refreshment of the Soul before the End of Mass: And tho' this be not a Method to be recommended to all, because it requires a true Understanding

ftanding of every Part of the Mafs, and befides this, a great Compofure and Command of Thoughts; yet it may be proper
for moft to read over and perufe, that fo they
may know how to embrace and purfue thofe
good Thoughts to their own Advantage,
which occafionally may be fuggefted to
them in Time of this divine Offering. For
fince there are but few fo very dull, but
they know how to *think ferioufly* in a Sub
ject of their worldly Interefts, methinks it
is very reafonable, they fhould learn how
to think when they have God's Mercies, and
the Concern for their Salvation before them.
But in this. every one as well as he can.
Now I muft turn a little to thofe, whofe
Circumftances will not permit them to be
prefent at Mafs, on Days of Obligation.

Fourth

Fourth Method of Hearing MASS:
Being Instructions for the Absent.

IT is but too common a Fault of such as
cannot observe the Church Precept, in going
to Mass, to sit down at Home contented,
and think no more of it, as if they had no
Concern, or could be no ways advantaged by
it, because they cannot personally be there.
For the removing which Mistakes, so prejudicial to them, I desire them to consider,

1. That wherever Mass is said, it is most
certainly offered by the Priest and the Church,
*for all faithful Christians, that it may avail
them to Life everlasting,* as it is expressed in
the *Offertory :* So that, tho' those that are
present, have great Advantage over others,
yet the *Absent* are not excluded from partaking of its Benefits.

2. That since the Mass is offered for those
of the Faithful that are *absent :* those also
may receive Advantage by it, if they take
care to dispose themselves, by joining their
Devotion with it, and being there in Spirit
and Desire, when their Occasions will not
permit them to be otherwise present. Since
'tis most certain, God will accept this great
Offering, which in their Hearts they make to
him, and their fervent Piety supplying all
Wants of corporal Presence, they will be refreshed with divine Graces, especially thro'
the

the Merits of Chrift, applied by this Sacrifice, which are not confined to Place.

From thefe Confiderations, every good Chriftian, that is folicitous for his eternal Welfare, will be careful on fuch Days of Obligation, on which he is lawfully hinder'd from going to Mafs, to take half an Hour to himfelf, and in his Clofet hear Mafs in Spirit; and if he has a Family, he will not fail to fummon them together, for the performing this Devotion in common; firft feeing they be inftructed how to do it.

And the firft Thing they ought to do, is to bewail their Misfortune, in not being prefent at this holy Sacrifice, by which they are deprived of many fpiritual Advantages to their Souls. And if Chriftians did but a little confider the many mournful Expreffions of *David* in his Banifhment, of the *Jews* in their Captivity, lamenting their Abfence from the Tabernacle and Temple, and the Want of Sacrifice; I think they would not fit down fo unconcerned, as too commonly they do, in their Abfence from this adoreable Sacrifice; which being fo much greater than what the *Jews* had, is fo much more confiderable in the Loffes thofe fuffer who are banifhed from it. How then might they figh with *David*, *Pfalm* lxxxiii.

How lovely are thy Tabernacles, O Lord of Hofts! My Soul has a Defire and Longing to enter into the Houfe of our Lord.

My

My Heart and my Flesh, rejoice in the living God.

The Sparrow has found her Abode, and the Turtle a Nest for her Young.

Thy Altars, O Lord of Hosts, *is the Place of my Rest*, my King, and my God.

Blessed are they that dwell in thy House, O Lord, they shall praise thee for ever.

Look on us, O God and Protector, and have Regard to the Face of thy Christ.

For one Day in thy House is better than a thousand *here*.

'Tis better to be the least in the House of my God, than to dwell in the Company of Sinners.

As the Hart pants after the Fountains of Water; so my Soul sighs after thee my God.

My Soul thirsts after the God of Strength and Life: When shall I come and appear in the Presence of my God?

I have wept Day and Night; because they daily insult over me, and say, where is thy God?

This came to my Mind, and I poured forth my Soul in Grief; because I desire to go to thy wonderful Tabernacle, even to the House of God.

Hope then in thy God, for I will still sing Praise to him; for he is my Saviour, and my God.

Having thus bewailed their Misfortune, in not being present at this holy Sacrifice, and fervently expressed their Desires of being there,

there, they ought in Spirit to place themfelves there, where they commonly hear
Mafs : And having in general begged of
Almighty God, to accept of that holy Oblation, which is there offered to his Name,
and that they may partake of it; they then
apply themfelves to the fame Devotions
they commonly ufe in the Time of Hearing
Mafs.

And as for thofe who are fo well inftructed, as to know every Part of the Mafs, and
commonly hear it without the Help of Books,
they may begin and go on from one Part of
it to another, with all thofe Exercifes, as fet
down above in the *Third Method*, and, no
Queftion, will thus perform a Devotion very
acceptable to God, and beneficial to themfelves. And for others, who make ufe of
Books in Time of Mafs, they may ufe the
fame Prayers here, according to the *Second
Method*, or fuch like ; being careful never to
omit the principal Parts of it. For however
the Prieft be not really with them, yet they
are, in Spirit, prefent before the Altar with
him; they are before Almighty God, and
where the Merits of Chrift's facred Paffion
may be applied to them : And will not he
moft certainly hear them, if with the Prayer
at the *Confiteor* they humbly acknowledge
their Offences: If at the *Kyrie eleifon*, they
heartily cry out for Mercy: If at the *Gloria
in Excelfis*, they give Adoration and Glory
to God: If at the *Collects*, they recommend
their

their own and the Church's Necessities: If at the *Gospel,* they make Profession of living according to the Maxims of God's Word; and so proportionally on with all the other Parts of the Mass, as the *Creed, Offertory, Sanctus, Mementos, Elevation,* &c. Will not this be a very commendable Devotion on any Day, especially on those which are commanded to be kept holy; since by this Method the Soul is awakened and raised up to God, and united to him in the Exercise of those Virtues, which make up a true Christian Life, and render it, as much as may be, like the State of the Blessed?

And tho' this Method may not please some, who are willing to suspect every Thing that seems to streighten the broad Way they are in, and to oblige them to retrench some of their Liberties, which are the Effects of their Sloth and Indevotion; yet considered by pious and well-meaning People, I believe they will find it very suitable to the Spirit and Practice of the Church in other Duties: For is it not thus in *Fasting, Prayer,* and *Alms?* When a *Christian,* thro' *Sickness,* &c. is disabled from the performing these penitential Works, must he not perform them, at least, in *Spirit* or *Desire?* Is it not thus with *Baptism* and *Confession* too? So that when a Priest cannot be had, and the Precept urges, must not the Penitent confess in *Desire* at least? Must he not examine himself, and call to mind his Sins? Must he not excite in himself a true Sorrow and

and Contrition, and thus, on his Part, do al-
moſt every Thing, as if the Prieſt were there?
This ought certainly to be done at the Hour
of Death ; and at other Times too, it would
be the moſt aſſured Means of obtaining
God's Grace, by thus giving Teſtimony, that
nothing is wanting on his Side, for the diſ-
charging that Duty God has laid on him.

And the Ground of this is declared by St.
Peter Damian, who ſhewing that this Oblation of the Body and Blood of Chriſt, is the
Sacrifice of all the Faithful, who make but
one Body, infers this Conſequence ; that therefore tho' we are abſent from the Church,
when theſe divine Myſteries are celebrated,
yet we ſtill aſſiſt there, and in ſome Manner
are there preſent, by Reaſon of that invio-
lable Unity, by which it is effected, that what
belongs to all is the Concern of every one in
particular ; and what ſeems to belong to ſome
in particular, is common to all, by Means of
that Bond of Faith and Charity, which unites
all. I. *Dom. Vcb.* c. 10. Now tho' this
ought to be no Encouragement for any to
make it indifferent, whether they go to Maſs
or no, or to omit that Duty, which is ſo
ſtrictly enjoin'd by a Church Precept, and is
moſt certainly accompanied with many Advantages and Bleſſings, yet when any are
lawfully hinder'd from perſonally attending,
this ought to mind them, that they may ſtill
partake of the Effects of that holy Sacrifice ;
and therefore, that 'tis their Buſineſs to diſpoſe

pose themselves in the best Manner they can, that so they may not be unworthy of those Blessings intended for them ; and as they are united to the rest of the Faithful by Faith and Charity, so, at that Time, they may be more particularly united to them by Prayer and Devotion.

Among all these several Ways, may all the Faithful, of what Capacity soever, find one proper for them, for the Hearing Mass with Devotion and Benefit. And it were to be wished, that all would so seriously consult this Matter both with themselves and their Director, as to come to a good Understanding of this great Mystery, and see what Method would be most beneficial to them ; and not rest satisfied, till they know how to accompany the Priest thro' every Part of the Mass, and apprehend the true Meaning of the Whole. This I am confident would be a Remedy against many Indecencies, and the great Irreverence too often met with in public Assemblies, where many come punctually indeed, and with a Design of complying with a Duty, but profit very little, thro' their affected Ignorance ; and give ill Example and Scandal to others, thro' their Lightness, and too remarkable Indevotion, which is never to be removed till they take more Care and Pains to be better informed of their Duty : Which I pray God, by his effectual Grace, to inspire all to undertake and do.

Here,

Here, for the Sake of such as desire more exactly to accompany the Priest, and observe the Devotion of every Day, I will set down some Prayers which may be easily apply'd to every particular Festival, and be said in their proper Places, for such as use the *Second Method.* One is for the *Collect*, to be said in its due Place, just before the *Epistle*: The Second is the *Secreta*, just after *Orate Fratres*: The Third is the *Postcommunion*, after the Priest has received.

On the Festivals of our blessed Redeemer.

Collect.

O God, by whose Mercy and Goodness, we are here met to celebrate this Mystery of our Blessed Redeemer: Grant, by the Merits of his Passion, we may here faithfully serve him on Earth, and enjoy him hereafter in Heaven. Thro' the same Lord Jesus Christ thy Son, &c.

Secreta.

ACcept, O Lord, we beseech thee, the Oblation of this present Solemnity, that thro' thy Grace, and the Effect of these holy Mysteries; we may truly live in him, who was pleased, for this End, to take on him our Nature: Who liveth and reigneth with thee, &c.

Post-

Postcommunion.

GRant, O Lord God, that we, who celebrate this Festival of our Lord Jesus Christ, in the Oblation of this Holy Victim, may, through the Effect of thy Grace, daily increase in Virtue, and come at length to the Possession of that Happiness, which he has purchased by his Blood, who liveth and reigneth, &c.

On the Festival of our Blessed Lady.

Collect.

STrengthen us, O God of Mercy, against all our Weakness, and grant, that we, who celebrate the Memory of the Blessed Virgin *Mary*, Mother of our Lord, may, by the Assistance of her Prayers, forsake all our Iniquities: Through our Lord Jesus Christ, thy Son, &c.

Secreta.

MAY this holy Oblation, O Lord, by the Effect of thy Mercy, and the Intercession of Blessed *Mary*, ever Virgin, obtain for us the Blessing of Peace and Prosperity, both now and for ever. Through our Lord Jesus Christ, &c.

Postcommunion.

INfuse, O Lord, we beseech thee, thy Grace into our Hearts; that we, who, by the Message of the Angel, have known the Incar

G

nation

nation of Chrift thy Son, may, by his Paffion and Crofs, be Partakers in the Glory of his Refurrection. Through the fame Lord Jefus Chrift, thy Son, who liveth, &c.

On the Festival of Apostles.

Collect.

ALmighty and everlafting God, who haft called us here this Day to celebrate with Joy the Feftival of thy holy Apoftle *N.* Grant this Bleffing to thy Church, that we may ever love what he believed, and believe what he taught. Through our Lord Jefus Chrift, &c.

Secreta.

GRant, we befeech thee, O Lord, that in the Solemnity of the holy Apoftle *N.* we may, by his Affiftance, partake of thy Bleffings, in Memory of whofe Victories we make this Oblation to thee. Through our Lord Jefus Chrift, &c.

Postcommunion.

MAY this holy Sacrifice, O Lord, which has been here offered, be to us a Defence in this prefent Life, and by the Interceffion of thy bleffed Apoftle *N.* a Means of fe-curing to us the next. Through our Lord Jefus Chrift, thy Son, &c.

Of

Of one Martyr.

Collect.

HAVE Regard to our Weakness, Almighty God; and because we sink under the Weight of our Offences, may the powerful Intercession of this holy Martyr *N.* be our Support and Protection. Through our Lord Jesus Christ, thy Son, &c.

Secreta.

SAnctify these Gifts, O Lord, which are offered to the Honour of thy Name, and by the Intercession of this thy Martyr *N.* may they be a Means of obtaining for us thy Mercy. Through our Lord Jesus, &c.

Postcommunion.

MAY this holy Victim, O Lord, which has been here offered, be an effectual Means of purifying us from all Sin, and of bringing us to everlasting Happiness. Through our Lord Jesus Christ, thy Son, &c.

Of many Martyrs.

Collect.

O God, who comfortest us by the yearly Solemnity of these thy holy Martyrs *N.* and *N.* mercifully grant, that as we rejoice in their Virtues, we may be encouraged by their

 Example.

Example.   Through our Lord Jesus Christ, thy Son, &c.

Secreta.

GIVE Ear, O Lord, to these our Prayers, which we pour forth in this Solemnity of thy holy Martyrs ; that we, how unworthy soever, may find Help in the Sufferings and Prayers of those who have been well-pleasing to thee. Through our Lord Jesus, &c.

Postcommunion.

WE beseech thee, O Lord, that we, who have assisted at these holy Mysteries, may find Help in their Prayers, whose Memory we honour in this Solemnity. Through our Lord Jesus, &c.

Of a Bishop.

Collect.

GRant, O Lord, we beseech thee, that this Solemnity of thy holy Bishop *N.* may be to us an Increase of Devotion, and a Help to secure our eternal Happiness. Through our Lord, &c.

Secreta.

MAY the Festival of this thy Servant be to us a spiritual Comfort, that being here met in Thanksgiving for his Virtues, we may be sensible of the Effect of his Prayers. Through our Lord Jesus. &c.

Post-

Postcommunion.

O God, the bountiful Rewarder of all that faithfully serve thee, grant that, by the Prayers of this holy Prelate we may obtain of thee Pardon of all our Sins. Through our Lord, &c.

Of a Confessor.

Collect.

O God, who art pleased to refresh our Souls in the yearly Solemnity of thy holy Servant *N.* grant in thy Mercy, that as we keep his Festival, we may likewise imitate his Virtues. Through our Lord Jesus Christ, thy Son, &c.

Secreta.

WE offer thee, O Lord, a Sacrifice of Praise, in Memory of thy Saints, and we hope, by this holy Victim, to be delivered from all Evils, both present and to come. Through our Lord Jesus, &c.

Postcommunion.

WE beseech thee, Almighty God, that we, who have here offered to thee the holy Sacrifice of thy only Son, may by the Intercession of thy blessed Servant *N.* be delivered from all Adversities. Through our Lord Jesus, &c.

Of

Of a Virgin or Widow.

Collect.

HEar us, O Lord, our Salvation, and as we celebrate the Festival of thy holy Servant *N.* so may we find the Benefit in the Exercise of our Devotion. Through our Lord Jesus, &c.

Secreta.

ACcept, O Lord, this Oblation we make thee in this Solemnity of thy faithful Servant *N.* in whose Prayers we hope to find Assistance. Through our Lord Jesus Christ, &c.

Postcommunion.

THou hast blest thy People, O Lord in the Acceptance of this holy Victim ; grant we may be now assisted by her Prayers, whose Memory and Virtues we this Day honour. Through our Lord Jesus Christ, thy Son, &c.

For the Faithful departed.

On the Day of one's Departure.

Collect.

O God, whose Property is always to have Mercy and to spare, we humbly beseech thee, in behalf of thy Servant *N.* whom thou hast now called out of this World, that thou would'st please to secure his Soul from the

Hand

Hand of the Enemy, and not forget it for ever ; but command thy Angels to receive and conduct it to Paradise ; that for his Hope and Faith in thee he may escape the Pains of Hell, and enter into everlasting Joys. Through our Lord Jesus Christ, *&c.*

Secreta.

HAve Mercy, O Lord, we beseech thee, on the Soul of thy Servant *N.* for whom we offer thee this Sacrifice of Praise ; and we most humbly pray thy divine Majesty, that being reconciled by this Peace-offering, he may come to everlasting Rest. Through our Lord Jesus, *&c.*

Postcommunion.

GRant, we beseech thee, Almighty God, that the Soul of thy Servant *N.* being purified by this Oblation, and discharged from his Sins, may obtain thy Pardon, and be admitted to eternal Rest. Through our Lord Jesus Christ, *&c.*

On *an* Anniversary-Day.

Collect.

LORD God of Mercy, grant to the Soul, whose Anniversary we now keep, a Place of Refreshment, the Happiness of Rest, and the Light of thy Glory. Through our Lord Jesus, *&c.*

G 4

Secreta.

Secreta.

MErcifully héar our Prayers, O Lord, which we pour forth in behalf of this thy Servant's Soul, for whom we offer thee this Sacrifice of Praiſe, on this his Anniverſary-Day, and beſeech thee to receive it into the Number of the Bleſſed. Through our Lord Jeſus, &c.

Poſtcommunion.

GRant, O Lord, we beſeech thee, that the Soul of thy Servant, whoſe Anniverſary we keep this Day, being purified by this Oblation, may obtain thy Pardon, and be admitted to everlaſting Reſt. Through our Lord Jeſus Chriſt, &c.

On other Days throughout the Year.

For a Soul departed.

Collect.

HAve Mercy, O Lord, we beſeech thee, on the Soul of this thy Servant ; and having delivered it from the Miſeries of this Life, receive it now into thy eternal Happineſs. Through our Lord Jeſus Chriſt, &c.

Secreta.

Secreta.

MAY the Acceptance of this holy Oblation, effeĉtually move thee, O Lord, to
releaſe the Soul of thy Servant from all its
Sins, from which none has been wholly free ;
that by means of this Sacrifice, it may partake of thy everlaſting Mercy. Through our
Lord Jeſus Chriſt, &c.

Poſtcommunion.

ABſolve, O Lord, we beſeech thee, the
Soul of this thy Servant from all its
Sins ; that it may ariſe at the laſt Day in the
Glory of the Reſurreĉtion, among thy choſen
Servants. Through our Lord Jeſus Chriſt,
thy Son, &c.

G 5   *A Word*

A Word how the SUNDAY *ought to be kept.*

Q. *H*Aving *now been so charitable as to inform me in what Manner I ought to* hear Mass; *pray tell me, whether in* Hearing Mass *I have discharged the whole Duty of the* Sunday ? *Or whether, when Mass is done, I have still any farther Obligation on me, relating to that Day ?*

A. I could wish every one would take care to hear Mass well and devoutly on *Sundays.* But when that is done, 'tis most certain, the Duty of the Day is not then over; but there is still a due Regard to be had to the Institution of it.

Q. *The Church Precept enjoins nothing but* Hearing Mass *on* Sundays; *and seems to leave the rest to every one's Disposal.*

A. But can you imagine the Church Precept makes void the *Commandment* of God ? The Church indeed, by her Precept, declares to all her Members, that she requires them to *hear Mass* on *Sundays,* but she no where tells them this is the *whole Duty of the Day,* or pretends to absolve them from the Obligation God had laid on them in the *Commandments* given to *Moses.* This Command of God, *Remember thou keep holy the Sabbath Day,* (allowi ng only for the Change of the Day) stands still in Force: and, as God gave it by *Moses*

to

to his People, ſo he ſtill gives it to the Faithful by his Church. Therefore you ſee it ſtands recorded every where amongſt the Commandments, in all her Books of Inſtruction, Prayer Books and Catechiſms; and in all Examinations of Conſcience, preparatory for Confeſſion, 'tis in particular called over in ſeveral Points, beſides what belongs to hearing Maſs; and while the Church thus requires of all to learn the *Ten Commandments,* and beſides theſe to know her *Precepts,* ſhe plainly declares her Senſe, that no Precept of hers is intended to annul any Commandment of God; but only lets them know, that as the *Publick Worſhip* of the *New Law,* is diſtinct from that of the *Law of Moſes,* ſo ſhe requires of all her Members to be preſent at this *Publick Worſhip,* on all *Sundays,* &c. but no where tells them, they have no other Obligation on thoſe Days.

Q. What is it more they have to do?

A. The Commandment of God ſays, *Remember thou keep holy the Sabbath Day:* Every Chriſtian then has all that to do, which is neceſſary for the *ſanctifying* or keeping that Day *holy.* Now can you imagine, the employing *Half an Hour in hearing Maſs,* is a *ſanctifying the whole Day?* That is one thing indeed required; but when that is done, a Chriſtian may ſo eaſily miſpend the Reſt of the Time, that caſting up his Accounts at Night, he may find it has been rather *profaned* than *ſanctified;* that he has rather kept it *wickedly* than *holy.*

Beſides

Besides hearing Mass, 'tis expected the Faithful should assist at all the Publick Service, and Exercises of the Church: And where Circumstances permit nothing more than Mass, that this Misfortune be not turned to the Advantage of Idleness and Sloth; but that a proportioned Time be allowed to private Devotions, and spent in Praying and Reading. This seems to be a Duty; and besides this, it were to be wished, that all would be so careful in the well-employing this Day, not only in abstaining from servile Work and all scandalous Diversions, but likewise of duly attending to the great Concern of their Salvation; that upon viewing the main Body of their Actions, they may hope, they have not only sanctified the Day, but likewise been sanctified by it.

To this the Church encourages all her Children, and for this End in the Catechism *ad Parochos*, set forth by Order of the Council of *Trent*, Charge is given to all Parish Priests. 1. To take great Pains in often explicating and pressing this Commandment to the People, and gives this Reason, *Because the Observance of all the rest of the Laws of God, depends much on the due keeping of this.*

2. There it shews that the *Sunday* is a Day consecrated to religious Duties, to divine Actions, and holy Employments: 'Tis a Day consecrated to God himself, and therefore to be employed in such Actions, as become the Holiness of God.

3. It

3. It requires Parish Priests diligently to instruct the People what are the Duties proper for that Day.   Amongst which Hearing Mass is in the first Place. 2. Often frequenting the Sacraments, for the remedying the Distempers of their Souls, such are, Confession and Communion, Hearing Sermons or Exhortations where it may be. 3. Exercising themselves often on that Day in Prayers, in giving Thanks and Praise to God. 4. Taking great Care diligently to learn all those Things which are necessary for a true Christian Life. 5. Doing Acts of Charity, as relieving the Poor, visiting the Sick, comforting the Afflicted.   These Particulars are set down in this Catechism, as Exercises proper for the sanctifying this Day.

Every good Christian then may hence evidently discover, that the Design of God and his Church, in commanding this Day to be kept holy, is,   1. That in it he should give Adoration, Praise, Honour, and due Thanks to God. 2. Do such Things as may be for the Advantage of his Soul, either in the obtaining Pardon of his Sins, Improvement in Virtue, or Benefit to his Neighbour. That for the Discharging the *former Part* of this Duty, 'tis required of him he should hear Mass devoutly, and in this pay sovereign Homage to God: That at other Times of the Day he should Pray, give Praise and Honour to his Maker. And for performing the Second, that he should go to the Sacraments,

hear

hear Exhortations, read ſuch Books as may
be proper for his Inſtruction in the Knowledge of his Duty, Amendment of his Fail-
ing, Increaſe of Piety, and living the Life
of a true Chriſtian, anſwerable to his Condition, and doing ſuch Works of Charity,
as Occaſions ſhall preſent.

*Q. What think you then of all thoſe, who
content themſelves with hearing Maſs on* Sundays, *and without any more praying or reading, ſpend all the reſt of the Day in walking,
talking, dreſſing, formal viſiting,* &c.

A. And I aſk you, whether theſe do all
that God and the Church requires of them
on theſe Days? If they do, I have nothing
to ſay againſt them ; but if they are really
wanting in Duties, intended for God's Honour and their Soul's Good, then do you
tell me, whether they are Innocent ?

Thoſe pious Exerciſes abovementioned,
proper for ſanctifying the *Sunday,* are all ſet
down in the ſaid *Church Catechiſm,* with
this Recommendation: *Quibus Chriſtiani
homines exercere ſe debeant. Exerciſes in which
Chriſtians ought to employ themſelves.* And tho'
hearing Maſs be firſt mentioned, yet the
other Duties are very much urged: There
the *wilful Omiſſion of hearing Sermons* is cenſured as *a Contempt of Chriſt's Word*: When
it recommends *Praying,* this is mentioned,
as what ought to be the frequent Exerciſe
and Employment of the Day: *Exercitatio
atque Studium Fidelium in Precibus Frequens*

eſſe

esse debet. When it mentions the *learning such Things as are necessary for a Christian Life;* this is pressed as a principal Duty, and 'tis required to be done with the *greatest Care: Præcipua Cura:* And when it proposes *doing Works of Charity,* it presses that these be diligently performed: *Sedulo se exerceant:* And declares in the Words of St. *James* i. that this is the *pure and undefiled Way* of worshipping God. By which you see in what Manner the Church desires this Day should be employ'd.

Now if a Person only hears Mass on a *Sunday,* and spends all the rest of the Day, as proposed by you above, in conversing, walking, *&c.* does he not omit many Duties, which the Church (according to the Exposition of this Catechism) requires of him for the keeping of that Day holy? And do you think this can be without Offence?

Hence you see by the Doctrine delivered in this Catechism, all those are wanting to this Command of God, 1. Who, besides hearing Mass, do not apply themselves at other Times of the Day (if not lawfully hindered) to praying, reading, *doing good Works, &c.* but are wholly taken up in *going their own Ways,* and vainly pleasing themselves, when they are commanded to *walk in the Ways of God and his Church.* 2. All Parents, Masters, *&c.* who permit their Children, Servants, *&c.* thus to omit the Duties of the *Sunday,* and idly to spend the Day in vain Conversation, Visiting, running Abroad, *&c.* 3. All those,
who

who have the Charge of Souls, and take no
Care to employ this Day in Catechiſing, In-
ſtructing and Reforming theſe Abuſes, but
let every one go on, as ſeems good in their
own Eyes, to live and die in Ignorance, and
under the Slavery of many ill Habits, for
want of giving them their due Inſtruction,
and not obliging them to ſpend that Time
upon their Souls, which God requires of
them: And for as many of the Flock as ſhall
periſh, and God knows how many periſh,
on this Account, who is it muſt render an
Account of their Souls?

Q. If it be thus with thoſe, who paſs all the
Sunday *in* unneceſſary Viſits, Walking, &c.
What ſay you of thoſe, who ſpend a great Part
of the Day in Publick Houſes, *in* Drinking,
Gaming, &c.

A. Do you tell me whether this be a Way
of *keeping the Day holy,* as God commands it
to be kept. Are theſe any of the holy Duties
and Exerciſes mentioned above, proper for a
Day conſecrated to God's Worſhip and the
Good of our Souls? Compare but Sanctifying
and Drinking; *Worſhipping or Seeking God,* and
Gaming; and ſee how they agree together:
When one reads the Precept, and duly conſiders the End of it, 'tis not eaſy reconciling
theſe Actions with the Deſign of our heavenly Father, in laying this Command on us:
For that which is but a tolerable Employment on any Day of the Week, if it be not
enough to profane it; how can it be proper
for

for a *Sunday*, which ought to be kept holy to our Lord.

Q. *If there be no Excess where is the Harm?*

A. The very going into those Houses, to spend the Time in Drinking, seems a kind of Excess, on Days that are particularly consecrated to God: For they are Houses of Idleness, of Excess and Vice; they are Places profaned by all Manner of Wickedness, by Blasphemies. Atheism, the Ruin of Families, &c. And can it be well-pleasing to God, to spend a Day holy to him, in Places thus polluted with the Worship of Devils? A Person that has any Sense of Piety, and of the Reverence due to his Lord, ought to have a Dread, especially on such Days of approaching to them; the Thought of the Wickedness there committed, and of the War there daily made against Heaven, ought to raise an Abhorrence in his Soul, and to make him fly from those Seats of Pestilence, as truly at Defiance with the Worship of God.

And this the greatest Number of Men are particularly obliged to consider, for tho' they have no Design at all of any Kind of Intemperateness on this Day, yet how few are there that desire to go into Publick Houses on a *Sunday*, but who, on other Days of the Week, have in those Places offended God in their Excesses, either of Drinking, Idle-talking, Swearing, ill Example, or immoderate Expence of Money or Time! And if this

has

has been their Caſe, ought not they to de-
cline thoſe Houſes on a *Sunday*, out of a juſt
Deteſtation of their former Offences? Becauſe
this is a Day, in which they ought to call
themſelves to an Account for all the Miſcar-
riages of the Week, and expreſs their ſincere Repentance of them; ſo to make their
Peace with God. For believe me, an Abhorrence of Sin ſeems not very real, where
there's yet a Love of the Occaſions and
Places where they were acted: As thoſe *Iſ-
raelites* did not heartily deteſt their Idols,
who had yet a Love to the High-places,
where they had worſhipped them.

Q. *But we'll ſuppoſe now, for the Sake of
others, who ſeem more pious, that there has
been nothing of all this in their whole Lives:
May not ſuch as theſe take this Liberty, and
divert themſelves with moderate Drinking,
Gaming, Shews, &c.*

A. Even this ſeems not agreeable to the Intent of this Commandment: For as the Day
is holy, ſo if there be any Diverſion neceſſary
on it, it ought to be ſuch as is in ſome Manner
holy too; ſuch as, being innocent, and leaſt
expoſed to all Danger of offending either
God or Man, is in ſome Kind ſuitable to a
Day that is ſacred. For as Churchmen, who
are conſecrated to the Service of God, when
they ſtand in need of any Diverſion, ought
not to conſider only what in itſelf is lawful,
or what is an allowable Diverſion in the
Laity; but are in Prudence bound to look
farther,

farther, and make Choice of what is expedient for them, and agreeable to their State ; .
that so they lessen nothing of the Reputation of their Profession, or give Scandal to any little ones; but in all Things shew what they are, as well in the Relation of their Minds, as in the Practice of their Duties: So certainly on Days that are sacred, 'tis not every Thing lawful that is expedient, but there may be great Indiscretions, if not Offences, by admitting of such Diversions as are unsuitable to the Circumstance of the Time.

And amongst these may be justly reckoned those above-mentioned, as being of that dangerous Nature, that even sober People have not that true Command of themselves in them as they ought, but are too often drawn in, even beyond their Design, to exceed either in Time or in Words: Hence Disputes arise, and such peevish Debates, that tho' they come not to a Breach of Charity, yet they are very unbecoming the Sanctity of the Day, give Offence to others, and by this ill Example encourage Servants, &c. to the like Diversions, who not having the true Government either of their Tongues or their Passions, hence fall by Degrees into most scandalous Extravagancies, such as they must ceartainly answer for, who, instead of preventing, gave Encouragement to these vicious Liberties.

Neither can they truly justify themselves, who find none of these Inconveniencies either in themselves or others; because those Diversi-

ons

ons have still a kind of essential Profaneness in them, which infects the Mind, takes it so much off from God and all that is Good, that they ought, were it for this Reason only, to be banished from Days sacred to God's Worship, and the Improvement of the Soul. And this Mark the Catechism of the Council of *Trent* has set on them, as being the *Occasions of neglecting the Sabbath*; and therefore it observes, that this Commandment is ushered in with a *Remember*, on Design to make Christians mindful, that they are like to meet with many Occasions and ill Examples, which will draw them off from the due Observance of this Day, particularly mentioning Games and Shews, and those that follow them, as being the too frequent Occasions of Christians contemning and profaning the Sabbath, and neglecting the Duty of it. And 'tis not to be doubted, but by these Entertainments, People are diverted, even beyond Design, from Praying and Reading, and their Minds, instead of being purified something from the World, and raised towards God by holy Exercises, are rendered even more corrupt and worldly than they were before. And what then is become of the *Sunday*, and where are the Effects of it, which being purposely designed for the withdrawing the Soul from the World, giving it leave to breathe a little spiritual Air, and be refreshed with the Taste of heavenly Sweetness, is so abused, if not by vicious, at least by these worldly and danger-

ous

ous Entertainments, that it ferves to clog the Soul ftill more, and inftead of drawing it nearer to God, fets it at much greater Dif-, tance from him by thefe Diverfions, than it was all the Week by working.

And it is on this Head all Sorts of *Gaming, Drinking, Shews,* &c. feem to be cenfured, as not allowable on *Sundays*; not becaufe they are abfolutely finful or vicious, for when they come to this, they are unlawful all the Days of the Week; but becaufe they generally fo engage and diftraft the Mind, that they take it off from God, and hinder it from performing thofe Exercifes of Piety, which are the Duty of the Day. And therefore as the *Trent* Catechifm obferves, as fervile Works are not forbidden on *Sundays*, becaufe of their own Nature they are finful and unbecoming, but becaufe they draw away our Minds from the Worfhip of God, which is the End of this Precept: *Quoniam mentem noftram a Divino Cultu, qui Finis Præcepti eft, abftrahit. Par.* 31. So certainly on this Score are thofe Diverfions to be rejected; for tho' they were as harmlefs in themfelves as working, yet inafmuch as they are no lefs a Diftraction to the Mind, and a Hindrance to the divine Worfhip, than fervile Work will be, how can thefe Diverfions be allowed? Efpecially too, being thus exprefsly informed by this Catechifm, that though fervile Work only be exprefsly forbidden by this Precept, yet under this is comprehended *whatever is a Hindrance*

to

to the Worſhip of God; and that whatever this may be, it is upon this Score to be a-voided. *Quibus Verbis* (viz. Non facies omne Opus in eo) *ad id primum inſtituimur, ut quæcumque Divinum cultum impedire poſſunt, omnino vitemus.* Parag. 31. And ſince common Experience will not allow this to be denied of theſe Entertainments; nay, ſince they are in particular here ſet down as the too frequent Occaſions of withdrawing People from the holy Obſervance of this Day, *Parag.* 14. it muſt be acknowledged they are not ſuitable to the Deſign of this Precept.

And hence you may perceive the true Grounds, why ſpending a conſiderable Part of the *Sunday* in *Viſits, Walking, Converſing,* &c. is blamable, 1. Becauſe however harmleſs all this may be in itſelf, yet inaſmuch as theſe ſo take up the Time, that they are a Hindrance from employing the Day in holy Exerciſes, they are ſo far certainly to be diſapproved and avoided; as alſo every Thing elſe that is a like Hindrance with them; as reading Plays, Romances, Hiſtory, and all ſuch Books as are not for the Improvement of the Soul, Singing, Dancing, Muſick, Diſcourſing of Neighbours, Sleeping, Dreſſing, &c. So that whatever it be, that takes off *Chriſtians* from employing the *Sunday*, ſo to the Honour of God, and the Benefit of their Souls, as God and his Church directs, it is all, you ſee here, by the Rule of this Catechiſm, forbidden in this Commandment.   Q. *Is*

Q. Is there no Diverſion then to be allowed on Sundays ? *Nothing to poor Servants who toil all the Week, and have no Leiſure, but on theſe Days ? Nothing to others of a more liberal Education, who muſt certainly look on* Sundays *as Days of Penance, if they are to be thus rigorouſly obſerved, and nothing to be permitted then of theſe Diverſions ?*

A. I have ſhewn you in what Manner God and the Church requires the *Sunday* to be kept by all the Faithful; that it ought to be principally employed to his Honour, and the Salvation of their Souls; and if you think there is a Rigour in this, pray forget not who it is enjoins it, and who expounds it thus; not any private Hand, but the publick Catechiſm of the Church.

But now, if after this there be many, whoſe Circumſtances require ſome Sort of Relaxation on the *Sunday,* there's no Queſtion there are Caſes in which this muſt be allowed; but then it ought to be done with the Conditions of the Apoſtle, *ſoberly, juſtly,* and *piouſly,* not falling into the common Abuſes, by making the Releaſe of their Minds the Buſineſs of the Day; but employing the Day in the Duties preſcribed, and only taking ſuch a Portion of Time, as both to God and their Neighbour may appear to be nothing but a neceſſary Condeſcendence to human Weakneſs, and a juſt Relief of their Minds: And this in ſuch a Way, as is becoming the Sanctity of the Day, and cannot reaſonably give Offence to the Weakeſt.   But

But however, as to this Particular, I make ſome Exceptions againſt the two Sorts of Perſons mentioned in your laſt Queſtion, for whom you ſeem to plead.

And firſt as to *Servants*. Since God has given to Maſters of Families ſix Days, wherein Servants are to be employed in their Work, and has reſerved only one, wherein they are to ſerve him, and prepare for Eternity ; is it not very unreaſonable that the Diverſion neceſſary for the Relief of Servants ſhould be taken out of that *one Day* ſacred to God and their own Souls, and not rather out of the *ſix*, appointed for the Service of this World? Let Maſters and Servants conſider where the Time can be beſt ſpared; and whether preferring every Thing before God and their own Souls, be what it will at the End turn to the beſt Account. I am certain, if Maſters tie their Servants ſo ſtrictly to their Work all the Week, that they are neceſſitated to ſpend the greateſt Part of the *Sundays* in diverting and breathing themſelves, ſo to prepare for their Work again, ſuch Maſters will have ſomething to anſwer for their Servant's Sins in the Breach of the Sabbath. And if Servants that have an eaſier Life, when the *Sunday* comes take no care to employ it as they ought, but ſpend it in vain Converſation, viſiting and running about, they will certainly be called one Day to an Account for ſo many Neglects of their Duty.

The Reaſon of making this Exception againſt Servants, as likewiſe all others, whoſe
.Life,

Life, like theirs, is a perpetual Toil, will appear more reasonable, if we confider that 'tis almoft impoffible to conceive how they can fave their Souls, if they abufe the *Sundays*, and neglect to employ them for thisEnd, For if we look on them all the Week, they are engaged in a continual Slavery, fuch as hinders them from Praying and Reading ; fo that if they begin and end the Day with a fhort Prayer, 'tis as much as they generally do; and God knows how often, thro' Hurry and Drowfinefs, they omit even this too. Then how are their Minds wholly tied to the World, by the unhappy Circumftances of their Condition! How great does this grow in their Eyes and Heart, by being their whole Concern ! What Variety of hurtful Diftraction! And how often happens it, that loofe Companions undertake to divert them by lewd Songs, idle Difcourfes, and in relating fuch Paffages, which ferve only to inftruct them in Evil! Thus, if we confider them generally, according to the Method of the Week, their Hearts and Souls are fo wholly worldly, if not vicious; fo truly Strangers to Goodnefs and the Bufinefs of Salvation, that they are unfit for dying ; and if they fhould thus enter into Eternity, who would not fear what might be their Lot ?

Now if this be the Condition of their Lives on Week Days, have not they great Reafon, above others, not to neglect the

H

Sunday,

Sunday, but so truly to apply themselves, as far as Circumstances permit, to Devotion and Exercises of Piety, to reading and hearing what is Good; that by these Helps they may strengthen themselves against daily Temptations, purify their Souls from the Filth contracted, and inform themselves of their Duty, and thus learn by Degrees not only to toil for Bread, but to work for Eternity, and be true Servants of their Master in Heaven? And if they omit this, is not their State most miserable? For if they go back all the Week, and make no use of the *Sunday* to recover their lost Ground, but even then go back too, how shall they ever approach to God?

The Case of the other Rank of People you mention, is not very unlike this: For tho' their Education and Quality has placed them in a higher Degree, yet the Method of their Lives is generally so disorderly, that I think they are under a Necessity of carefully observing the *Sunday*; and if they do otherwise, I cannot but apprehend their State to be dangerous.

For consider the Reason you bring in their behalf, for their being dispensed with in the Observance of this Precept: 'Tis because, otherwise, *Sundays will be to them Days of Penance*: Does not this suppose a great Disorder in their Souls; that reading good Things is uneasy to them; that Praying is troublesome; that informing themselves of their
Christian

Christian Duties, is naufeous; that to converfe with God, and labour for their Salvation, is what does not pleafe? Pray reflect ferioufly on this their Condition, and tell me whether 'tis reafonable thefe fhould be exempted from the Duties of the *Sunday*.   You fee they are in an ill Way; their Souls are wholly indif- pofed, if not fick to Death; and is this a Reafon, why they fhould neglect the Means God has appointed for their Cure? Or is it not rather a Reafon why they fhould be ftrictly obliged to make ufe of them? Let thofe that are truly their Friends judge the Cafe.

The Truth of it is this, God has general- ly bleffed this Rank of People with Plenty; and whilft their Condition exempts them from Working, their indulgent Parents take no Care in their Education to make them in Love with any Thing that may be afterwards an Employment to them: Hence being grown up, and relifhing nothing that may be a commendable Entertainment of their Time and their Thoughts, their Life be- comes wholly idle, they feek the Company of others like themfelves, their only Bufi- nefs is to ftudy their Diverfion; and being once entered in, the whole Week and their Life is but a Round; from Mufic to Drink- ing, from Drinking to the Play, from the Play to other Entertainments: Thus by Degrees they grow in Love with thefe Di- verfions and Company, and have no Satis- faction but in this.

H 2

And

And what kind of Habit is contracted hence ? Is it not plain, their Souls become wholly carnal, ſenſual and worldly; they are led along by their Paſſions; Self-love is their Director, and nothing pleaſes that leads them out of this Track: Hence nothing of a ſpiritual Life appears in them, they have no Taſte of Devotion: And whatever Time they are forced to give their Souls, 'tis what ſeems tedious and uneaſy. Hence, to keep the *Sunday* as they ought, is a Penance, becauſe their worldly and ſenſual Habit is ſo ſtrengthened by Cuſtom, that it gives them no Reſt, whenever, aiming at better Things, they weakly endeavour to take another Way. And can you think this their Caſe is ſo ſafe, that they ought to be diſpenſed with in their *Sunday* Duties ? Believe me, I look on them to be in that Danger, that if they uſe not Violence to themſelves, and on *Sundays* apply not their Minds to thoſe Exerciſes of Piety preſcribed, I cannot ſee which Way they are like to be diſengaged from their Snares, but by this Neglect will be linked in faſter, till they become truly the Diſciples of this World, inſtead of God. You know what the Apoſtle ſays: *Amicitia hujus mundi inimica eſt Dei. The Friendſhip of this World is an Enemy to God; whoever therefore will be a Friend of the World makes himſelf the Enemy of God,* James iv. 4. Conſider if this be not ſomething of their Caſe, whether you don't experience in them, that they

ſet

set their Hearts on the World, and are even impatient at every Thing that belongs to God; and what is this, but to love the one, and be averse to the other? And are these to be here dispensed with? What is this but to encourage them in the Evil they have begun, to bid them go on, till they fall into the Abyss of Vice past all Recovery? For you must observe, what I have said hitherto is of such who are not yet engaged in any Thing that is *criminal*, but of those who are willing to think themselves innocent; as being free, as they imagine, from all Vice, and yet are truly guilty of all the Neglects and Disorders above-mentioned, and of the *Omission* of those *great Duties*, which *Charity* and *Justice* oblige them to perform to God, in his Worship, and to their own Souls, in taking that Care of them as is necessary for their Salvation. And this Sort of false and mistaken Innocence is what I fear is too common, especially in the younger People of both Sexes, who letting the World gain Possession of their Hearts, preserve themselves, it may be, from what is scandalous and criminal, but yet at the same Time are guilty of many gross Neglects, such as make them Strangers to Piety; and if not redress-ed, will be the evident Ruin of their Souls.

Wherefore, for the reforming these general Abuses, I cannot but most earnestly recommend to all Christians, the exact Observance of the *Sunday*; making it my serious Request to them, to employ it in the best Manner they

can

can in thofe Exercifes of Virtue, which are moft for God's Honour, and the Benefit of their Souls; thus truly endeavouring to give that Day to God, which he has folemnly challenged for his own, and exprefly commanded to be *kept holy* to him: That fo performing their Duty in Obedience to this Law, they may likewife be fenfible of the great Advantages he has defigned for them; fince it is moft certain, as the Catechifm of *Trent* obferves, the due keeping this Day is the plain and eafy Way that leads to a holy Life, and the moft affured Means of obtaining the Love of God, as the Neglect of it is the Contempt of God and his Law, the Path to Loofenefs and Irreligion, and the Beginning of all Sin; and how highly provoking it is, may be plainly feen in the Severity of thofe Judgments with which God has punifhed the Tranfgreffors of it, *Numb.* xv.

Let none therefore be mifled by ill Example: *Noli æmulari in malignantibus:* But having God's Word to direct us, his exprefs Law to oblige us, the Church to expound his Law to us; let us look for no other Guides, but follow where thefe lead us; that fo giving to God and our Souls what is their Due, we may reap the Fruit of this Juftice in a happy Eternity, and efcape that as lafting Mifery, which will be the Portion not only of thofe who break all, but even *one* of his Commandments.

F I N I S.

A Catalogue of BOOKS *sold* by T. Meighan, *Bookseller, in* Bow-Street, Covent-Garden.

THE Garden of the Soul; or, a Manual of Spiritual Exercises and Instructions for Chriſtians, who living in the World, aſpire to Devotion.   Price 1 *s*. 6 *d*.

The Life of St. *Francis Xavier*, of the *Society of Jeſus*, Apoſtle of the *Indies*. Tranſlated into *Engliſh*, by Mr. *Dryden*. Price 5 *s*.

The Life of St: *John Francis Regis*, of the *Society of Jeſus*.   Written in *French* by F. *W. Daubenton*, of the ſame Society; with a curious Frontiſpiece of the ſaid Saint, done from the *French*.   Price 4 *s*.

The Life of St. *Francis of Sales*, Biſhop and Prince of *Geneva*.   Written in *French* by Monſ. *Marſolier*, a Canon of the Cathedral of *Uſes*, in 3 Vols.   Done from the *French*.   Price 9 *s*.

The Hiſtory of the Life of our Lord Jeſus Chriſt. Faithfully tranſlated from the Fifth Edition of the *French*.   Price 3 *s*.

Inſtructions for Confeſſion, Communion, and Confirmation, by *J. Gother*.   Price 1 *s*.

Seven Sermons upon the Seven Penitential Pſalms.   Compiled at the Requeſt of the Counteſs of *Richmond*, Mother to King *Henry* VII.   By the Right Rev. Father in God, *John Fiſher*, D. D. and Biſhop of *Rocheſter*, who was beheaded in the Reign of King *Henry* VIII.

St